# Midnight Schemers & Daydream Believers

*22 Stories of Mystery & Suspense*

*Edited by*

Judy Penz Sheluk

Superior Shores Press

# Contents

# Featuring

Pam Barnsley
Linda Bennett
Clark Boyd
C.W. Blackwell
Amanda Capper
Susan Daly
James Patrick Focarile
Rand Gaynor
Gina X. Grant
Julie Hastrup
Beth Irish
Charlie Kondek
Edward Lodi
Bethany Maines
Jim McDonald
donalee Moulton
Michael Penncavage
Judy Penz Sheluk
KM Rockwood
Peggy Rothschild
Debra Bliss Saenger
Joseph S. Walker

# Praise for Midnight Schemers & Daydream Believers

"Editor Judy Penz Sheluk has assembled a stellar group of crime fiction authors for this extraordinary collection. Storytelling at its best!" — DAVID BART, SHORT-STORY SPECIALIST, CONTRIBUTOR TO THE ANTHONY AWARD-WINNING MYSTERY WRITERS OF AMERICA ANTHOLOGY "CRIME HITS HOME"

"An engrossing exploration of how far people will go to realize their dreams. A must read!"—DEBRA H. GOLDSTEIN, AWARD-WINNING AUTHOR

"There's not a clunker in the bunch."—JOAN LEOTTA, MULTI-NOMINATED AUTHOR AND STORYTELLER

"Whether it's a down-and-out hopeful seeking a happy ending or an unscrupulous schemer playing the system, the twists and turns in these stories keep the reader guessing."—LESLEY A. DIEHL, AUTHOR OF THE MADDIE SPARKS MYSTERIES

"From thieves in a seedy Detroit bar to a nasty murder in Santa Cruz, *Midnight Schemers & Daydream Believers* reflects the creative knack of editor Judy Penz Sheluk. A fascinating anthology."—WIL A. EMERSON, MULTI-PUBLISHED DERRINGER NOMINEE

# Praise for the Superior Shores Anthologies

**The Best Laid Plans: 21 Stories of Mystery & Suspense**

"Crime doesn't pay, especially for criminals who think they've found a loophole..." —*Long and Short Reviews*

**Heartbreaks & Half-truths: 22 Stories of Mystery & Suspense**

"A memorable collection. Yes, there's heartbreak, but those half-truths will get you every time."—*Crime Fiction Lover*

**Moonlight & Misadventure: 20 Stories of Mystery & Suspense**

"Dialog snaps, characters carom, and plots surprise."—*James Blakey, Derringer award-winning author*

**Larceny & Last Chances: 22 Stories of Mystery & Suspense**

"Sharply written, tightly plotted, and thoughtfully curated"—*Kathleen Marple (Nikki Knight), Derringer and Black Orchid Novella Award Finalist*

Debra Bliss Saenger: Checking Out at the Live Free or Die Motel

Joseph S. Walker: Quincy and Crow

* A Time to Tell originally appeared in *The Algomian: Winter 2025*



Collection compiled by Judy Penz Sheluk www.judypenzsheluk.com

All stories, with the exception of A Foolproof Plan, edited by Judy Penz Sheluk

A Foolproof Plan edited by Ti Locke and Debra Bliss Saenger

Editorial assistance by Amanda Capper, Andrea Adair-Tippins, and Debra Bliss Saenger

Cover Design by Hunter Martin

Published by Superior Shores Press

ISBN Trade Paperback: 978-1-989495-77-3

ISBN E-book: 978-1-989495-78-0

First Edition: June 2025

"But I tried, didn't I? Goddamnit, at least I did that."—
  R.P. McMurphy, "One Flew Over the Cuckoo's Nest"

# Introduction

Two things influenced the theme of this anthology. The first was rewatching, for the umpteenth time, *One Flew Over the Cuckoo's Nest*. If you've never seen it (and you must), Jack Nicholson plays (to perfection) Randle Patrick (R.P.) McMurphy, a convicted criminal who pleads insanity as a means of avoiding manual labor while in prison. Like most schemes, his insanity defense sounds good on the surface, but McMurphy soon learns that the implacably manipulative Nurse Ratched (brilliantly portrayed by Louise Fletcher) rules the psychiatric ward with intimidation and an iron fist.

It's quickly apparent that McMurphy, despite his best efforts, is in a battle of wits that he will never win, no matter how much his fellow patients (and audience) want him to succeed. But here's the thing—he never stops trying. McMurphy, you see, is not just a schemer, he's the ultimate daydream believer. And we root for him because of it.

I was still thinking about *Cuckoo's Nest* when 'Daydream Believer,' released by The Monkees in 1967, and covered by countless bands since, came on my local oldies radio station. That's when it popped into my head. What about Midnight Schemers &

Daydream Believers? I jotted it down (a dull pencil being sharper than the sharpest mind) and went off to walk the dog.

The idea may never have gone beyond that, had not my husband Mike, used to finding (and ignoring) my random scribblings, said, "That sounds like a great theme."

Turned out the short story author community agreed with him, and submissions, capped at seventy-five, closed in under a month. Of those, twenty were selected in a process that included multiple readings on my part, followed by detailed feedback on the long-listed candidates from Andrea Adair-Tippins and Amanda Capper. My appreciation for the efforts of these two individuals, and their belief in me, cannot be overstated.

I was well into the editing process (and still fine-tuning my own story) when *The Algomian*, the magazine of Algoma University, was released. I had a vested interest in it, my own craft article on writing for magazines having made the cut, but upon reading Amanda Capper's 'A Time to Tell,' I knew it was a story that deserved a wider audience. For that reason, and with her permission, I have included it in this anthology of otherwise previously unpublished stories.

A huge debt of gratitude also goes to the talented authors in this collection, with a special nod to Debra Bliss Saenger, who volunteered her editing and English teaching skills to give the stories a final review.

Last, but not least, my sincere thanks to you, the reader. I couldn't do it without you. And I wouldn't want to.

Judy Penz Sheluk
Author/Editor/Publisher
Daydream Believer
June 2025

# Charlie Kondek

**Charlie Kondek** is a marketing professional and short story writer from metro Detroit. His work previously appeared in the Superior Shores anthology *Larceny & Last Chances*, and in such publications as *Black Cat Weekly*, *Dark Yonder*, *Hoosier Noir*, and elsewhere. He is a member of the Short Mystery Fiction Society.

Find him at www.CharlieKondekWrites.com.

# Secretly Keith

## Charlie Kondek

"Big" John Warmer was not a big man, unless you counted his stomach, a characteristic he not only failed to conceal but to which he drew attention by wearing t-shirts a size too small. Equally mismanaged was his hair, bald except for the ring below his crown, which he kept long in a so-called "skullet." A ridiculous dark mustache complemented this and, with Big John's propensity for wearing Levis and cowboy boots, sleeveless flannel shirts and trucker hats, he looked like he'd stepped right out of *The Dukes of Hazzard.* "Warner?" someone would ask, meeting him for the first time. "Your name's Big John Warner?"

"Warmer," he would correct. "As in, 'you're getting warmer.'" He was the local bookie at Fleet's, a working man's bar in Westland.

Big John was not mobbed up but operated independently, albeit with the tacit permission of the bar's owner, Tim Fleet. One had to assume he kicked a percentage of his book to Tim also, a quiet, amiable, but serious and enterprising man that often emerged from his office to stand behind the bar and chat with customers. Still, as small as Big John's operation was, he probably took in a few thousand dollars a month from the bar's regulars and those in its wider orbit betting on professional, college, and even some high school games. Nick Papke, setting up his guitar and amplifier on Fleet's small stage that Friday, tried to remember when he and Rex first got the notion to rob Big John, or if it was simply another in the long chain of questionable ideas and worse decisions that comprised his life's sequences.

Nick, balding, bearded, eyes perpetually offended, had little to show for his forty-eight years on earth. Somehow he'd never been able to run the course laid out for him by his middle-class parents, the schools, the internships. Nor had he ever made it in a trade—that would have required some kind of initiative. And so he was stuck in a dead-end manufacturing job paying rent to his roommate and best friend Rex Haag, who owned a tiny house in Garden City. Nick was divorced. He had a daughter that wanted little to do with him. He had hoped when she turned twenty-one that she'd turn up at Fleet's to hear him play, but she never did, despite his invitations. Which was a shame, because playing guitar and singing in a rinky-dink cover band was all he was really good at. Tim Fleet let Nick and the band play classic rock and country tunes on Friday nights, for an amount that almost covered their tab.

The thing about robbing Big John was, they thought they could get away with it without him ever knowing it was them. See, John, like many of his customers, could barely work his mobile phone much less a banking app, so he only ever took bets in cash. And especially on a heavy betting weekend like this one, heading into the NFL play-offs and college bowl games, that was a lot of money on hand. Whenever Big John accepted a large amount, or if he had to pay some out, he'd go out to his car, always backed into the same corner of Fleet's lot with its rear to a fence, visible under the lights. Naturally, Big John had a ridiculous car, a long, champagne-colored 2006 Lincoln Town Car Classic Edition. When he needed to deal with money, he'd get behind it and open the enormous trunk and do something no one was allowed to see.

"Even if somebody goes out there with him," Rex explained to Nick on one of those nights they were dreaming up the job, "like to get a pay out? John will make him stand in front of the car. He'll say something like, 'Please don't come behind the vehicle.' And he'll look around and make sure no one's watching, and open that big trunk, and fiddle around and come out with the cash. So, what do you think he's got back there? In the trunk of that big old boat?"

"A safe," Nick concluded.

"That's what I think, too. And a couple guns, I bet, in case he ever gets jumped. I don't think he's just keeping his cash in a paper bag."

Among themselves, they referred to Big John's car as his "bank." Thus, steal the car, rob the bank. They never, Nick reckoned, would have robbed Big John himself. Big John, Budweiser in hand, clowning, circulating the bar and the pool tables in a too-tight t-shirt that read FREE MUSTACHE RIDES and belting out Bob Seger tunes, was their friend. He was everyone's friend. But his car? That was like finding money in the street.

And what was a friend, anyway, in a place like Fleet's, and to people like Nick and Rex?

The other guys in the band were starting to join Nick on stage. Bob, the drummer, was an accountant. Ian, the bassist, was a plant rat like Nick. Nick was starting to get nervous because he didn't see Dave Schweitzer, who could play rhythm guitar, keyboards, and sing. Dave was in a couple other bands and didn't show up to rehearse or play with Nick's half the time. But tonight of all nights, they needed him.

That's because, as silly as it sounded, the robbery depended on the band's performance of *Sweet Home Alabama*. It was Big John's favorite song, one that always got him singing along, especially if, as Nick usually did, he changed the chorus to "Sweet Home Ypsilanti," which is where John was from. Rex, a natural and incessant mastermind, worked for Wayne County public works and always had his hand in a half dozen plots. It was no problem for him to hire a car thief that could boost the bank and drive it off the lot. Rex also had a friend out in Waterford named Coop that ran a small repair and welding shop out of his pole barn where, once they got the car there, the safe in the trunk, if it existed, could be cut open with an acetylene torch. But at Fleet's, there were a couple cameras aimed at the parking lot, their monitors hanging behind the bar for everyone to see, and Big John used these rather carefully amidst his glad-handing and carousing to keep an eye on his car. If their plan was going to work, Big John needed to be distracted for the few minutes it would take the car thief to do his part.

"Hey," Bob said, settling behind the drums. "Got a name for the band. Nicky Paprika and the Deviled Eggs."

This was a running joke; the band had never had a name. Nick glanced at his mobile phone to see that Dave had still not texted him back while Ian said, "Bob, that's awful." Dammit, they really needed Dave to play *Sweet Home Alabama*, because Dave could play the keyboards and join in on the choruses while Nick handled the main guitar riff part and sang lead. Tonight, of all nights, he lamented again. Nick glanced at Rex, pig nose, carp mouth, alligator teeth, sitting with some guys at a table near the back where he could watch everything in the bar, and at the clock with the Schlitz logo on it. Nine o'clock. If they were going to keep to their timetable, they had to go on.

"Hell with it," Nick muttered, slipping the guitar strap over his shoulder and turning to his band mates. "All right, boys, *Just What I Needed* one, two, three, four..." Ian throbbed out the notes opening the Cars' song while Nick crunched the guitar parts and Bob started tapping the drums.

Whenever he performed, there was always a moment when Nick wasn't sure if he was going to sing competently or well. Maybe it was the urgency or the fear, the abundant nervousness, but tonight when he opened his mouth to sing about how maybe his girlfriend, her perfume and ribbons, was just what he needed, the voice that poured out was *good*. And as he swerved into the chorus with Ian singing counter, he thought that not only did he sound good, but the band was clicking tonight. The audience, scattered among a dozen tables and the bar, going about their business of chatting and joking and drinking, seemed to feel it, too, because their heads turned toward the band and nodded in time as their toes started tapping or their fingers started drumming. Big John, among them, let out an appreciative yee-haw, and glanced at the monitors behind the bar.

It would have sounded better with Dave's keyboard, but by the time they finished the number, they knew they were in the zone. Nick could see Rex smiling and nodding appreciatively. Nick leaned into the microphone and called, "What's up, Fleet's? Welcome to Friday night."

Their cheers let the band know they had them. Somebody yelled out, "Hey what's the band called this time?"

Laughter among the regulars and the curious. "What'd we say, Bob?" Nick asked into the mic. "Nicky Paprika and the Deviled Eggs?" That got a laugh. "Anyway, thanks for letting us play. We hope you all have a good time." He and the band launched into .38 Special's *Caught Up in You*, a song which would have sounded even better with Dave's extra guitar but still very much on point and Nick's voice never finer.

Was there anything better, Nick wondered, in some part of his brain not occupied by performing, than a laid-back bar in metro Detroit on a Friday night? Happy, friendly people with a few drinks in them celebrating the end of the working week, ignoring the garbage weather or the possibility of overtime, getting ready for some football and banging through the classic rock catalogue? Nobody walking in off the street for the first time would have listened to the band and thought, that's them, that's the next Led Zeppelin, sign them at once. But they couldn't deny that at that time, in that place, this band was a perfect fit for the space it occupied, and it all seemed to depend on the front man.

Beneath all the layers of his life's crap, Nick had this fantasy. He was a huge Keith Richards fan, loved Keith for his ability to put together a simple, punchy riff and bring a gritty, sleazy humor to a song. But if the Stones had not taken off the way they did, Keef would have been a guy just like Nick. Just a blue-collar nobody playing the local watering hole on Friday nights. In his fantasy, Nick was secretly Keith Richards, an alternative timeline version of Keith if he'd been born in Detroit and forced to live undiscovered. Maybe, Nick considered when he indulged in this daydream, that's why he had never been able to make anything in his life work. Because he'd been meant for other things, a troubadour's life on fortune's road, a Keith-shaped peg in a Nick-shaped hole.

Which brought him back to his present situation. The Schlitz clock said it was time to make their play. Face it, Dave wasn't coming. And then Secretly Keith had an inspiration. He played the opening notes of *Sweet Home Alabama*, which prompted raucous cat calls from the crowd, but then stopped. "Hey, Fleet's," he said into the mic. "I got a problem."

Somebody yelled, "What's the problem?"

"Well, it's a tradition here at Fleet's to play *Sweet Home Alabama*. Except here we call it *Sweet Home Ypsilanti* in honor of our good buddy, Big John Warmer." Screeches and whoops from the audience. Big John removed his hat and waved it in circles over his bald head.

"Only problem is," Nick continued, "our other guitarist and keyboardist didn't show up. Now we can probably bang it out but it ain't gonna sound as good as it normally does unless... unless we get some help." He played those opening notes again as he asked, "So why don't we ask Big John his self to come up here and sing it? Tell us about where he's from. Come on, John, whattaya say?"

Nick kept up the riff, and Ian's bass joined in, as Big John waved his hands and shook his head no. But the enthusiasm of the crowd, many hands slapping John's back and many voices urging, "Come on, John, get up there" propelled him to the stage.

"Ladies and gentlemen," Nick crowed, "put your hands together and give a warm Fleet's welcome to Fleet's own—Big John Warmer!"

The drums joined in. Nick kept playing but moved over to Ian's mic. Big John, protesting, nonetheless took the mic, said, "I'm gonna get you guys for this," and then sang about going home to see his kin.

He was mostly off key and forgot a few words, but Nick and Ian joined in on the chorus, and the place went nuts. Tim Fleet came out from his office to stand behind the bar with folded arms and grin. By the time they got to the final bridge, everyone was in a frenzy, and on the last note, they exploded. Everyone was cheering and ordering more drinks and clapping Big John on the shoulder.

Nick risked a glance at the monitors behind the bar. Big John's bank was gone.

It was after midnight. It was cold in Coop's unheated pole barn, even with the acetylene torch flaring, and everyone except Coop, in thermal coveralls, wore their coats and hats. Nick took off his protective goggles to step away from where Coop was working and gaze out the open doorway, onto Coop's property, unlit. The house and garage were set far back from the road, and Nick could see large puddles of frozen water on the long stretch of grass between where he stood and the surrounding tree line, dark against a winter night's sky.

Nick hadn't gotten a good look at the car thief when he and Rex met him in the parking lot of a Target off 275. He kept his hood up while he handed Rex the keys and said, "I checked the trunk. Looks like what you were expecting is in there, plus a little GPS tracker. I threw that in the street." Then the car thief, whom they'd already paid $500, walked away under the parking lot's bright lights to where another car was waiting, and Nick was behind the wheel of Rex's truck following the Lincoln onto the freeway, then up Telegraph, then along streets that wormed around the dozen lakes in Waterford to Coop's neighborhood of isolated houses. Coop, who ran a side business doing agricultural and nautical repairs—and the occasional chop job—out of his well-equipped garage, opened the trunk when they had settled the Lincoln. Removing an old Army blanket revealed a loaded shotgun and the safe, a plain, long black metal box, bolted to the frame of the trunk.

Shouldn't be long now, Nick thought, watching Rex stand behind Coop and listening to the torch's hiss. Nick was thinking about Big John's reaction to learning his bank had been boosted. He and Rex confirmed their observations afterward. John was making his way through the crowd to the bar to accept an offered beer, gazed up at the monitors behind the bar, stopped talking, stopped smiling quite so widely, and walked calmly into Tim Fleet's office.

They weren't sure what to make of that, and Nick was disturbed by it, honestly, but he pushed it now from his thoughts as the torch stopped and Coop announced, "We gotta let that cool for a few minutes." Rex pulled on a pair of thick work gloves.

The safe, maybe six inches deep, not much more than eighteen inches wide, and about two feet long, lay on a scarred and scorched workbench in the middle of the garage while the Lincoln from which it came rested a few feet away, shedding melted ice water from its undercarriage and wheel wells. Now that Coop had done his work, a jagged but precise seam ran all the way around the top of the rectangular box, and after they waited for it to cool down, Rex and Coop, both wearing work gloves, grasped the top by the corners and lifted. It came off, separating from the safe effortlessly, and they set it lightly next to the box on the bench. Now all three of them could see inside.

It was empty.

Coop didn't speak. He already had $200 from Rex and Nick, but Nick cursed. "How the hell can it be empty?" he asked. "You were watching him, right? You saw him take bets?"

"Yes, dammit," Rex muttered tightly, eyes on the empty box under the halogen lights, gloved fingers probing it. "I watched him take action all night. I saw him go out to his bank a few times. Shit." He was calculating, reorganizing his thoughts, then, "There's no way he knew what we were planning. His whole act's a ruse. Big John lets everybody *think* he keeps money in his car to keep people from realizing he's got it on him. Dammit!"

"You figured it out," a new voice said.

Big John's.

All heads turned in the direction of the open doorway. There, in silhouette, stood two figures, one round, the other thin, both with long guns. "Put 'em up," Tim Fleet said. They must have parked a vehicle somewhere along the road and hid in the tree line, the occupants of the garage too distracted by opening the safe to hear the intruders coming across the icy grass.

Nick, like Rex and Coop, put his hands up.

Big John and Tim Fleet stepped into the light, shotguns raised, covering the thieves. "Well, I gotta say this is disappointing," John said. "But I guess I shouldn't be surprised. It worked pretty much the way you figured it, Tim. If anybody was gonna rip me off, let 'em rip off an empty car."

"How'd you know where to find us?" Rex asked, then turned to his friend. "I'm gonna kill you for this, Coop."

Big John shook his head. "It ain't your buddy—Coop, was it? It ain't Coop. We just followed the GPS tracker in the car."

"We ditched the tracker."

"You ditched the first tracker," John said. "The one we let you find." To Coop: "Hey, fat boy. Put the busted safe back in my car. Now, who's got my keys?"

"In the ignition," Coop said, bending to the work bench to follow Big John's instructions.

"Leave 'em there," John said. "And don't think about grabbing that shotgun in the trunk or we'll blow you up."

Nick was strangely calm. Maybe he was still riding the energy of the night. Maybe he was just exhausted. He said, "We're sorry, Big John."

"Not as sorry as you're gonna be," John said. "Look, I may have been born yesterday, but I stayed up all night. Besides, I got Tim advising me, and we got a business to run that depends on its reputation. Now we ain't gonna kill you unless we have to, but we gotta make an example out of you. Might as well start with you, guitar player. Put your hand on the table."

Suddenly, Nick was afraid. "What?"

"I said put your hand on the table there." Big John had edged over to another work bench, where, taking one hand off the shotgun, he picked up a five-pound sledgehammer.

Nick eyed the door. The mouth of the shotgun Tim Fleet held returned his gaze. He'd never make it. "Please, John," Nick said. "Not my hand."

"Hands. Plural," John said, taking a few swings with the hammer. "Get 'em up there, boy. Or we can just shoot you in the hands. Your choice."

Rex and Coop took a few steps away from Nick. All Nick could think to say was, "Please, John. Not that. I'd rather die."

"Don't be like that, son. Coop, Rex, you might have to hold him down. Now listen, you can't make a fool out of old Big John Warmer and expect to get away with it." Shotgun in one hand, hammer in the other, Big John stepped closer to the table while Tim prodded Coop and Rex, who tentatively reached for Nick. "But look on the bright side. Least you can still sing."

# Susan Daly

**Susan Daly** writes short crime fiction in hopes of righting the world's wrongs. Her stories are found in many anthologies, including all five from Superior Shores Press. Her take on the murder of Mr. Collins, *A Death at the Parsonage*, won the Arthur Ellis Award for best short story from the Crime Writers of Canada.

She lives in Toronto, where she is known to consort with criminal types like Sisters in Crime and Crime Writers of Canada.

Find her at www.susandaly.com.

# A Talent for Fame

## Susan Daly

"**W**ait...*what?*"

Kate stared at me, her glass of Northern Spirit Rye paused halfway to her lips.

"You heard me," I said.

"I heard you say you're writing Sylvia Starr's memoir." My big sister took a swig of her drink. "Seriously? That pseudo celebrity."

"It's what I do." I eased back in my chair and took comfort in my own glass of rye.

"And you do it brilliantly, Hallie. Considering all the impressive lives you've brought to the public eye... men and women of unquestioned integrity—"

"Most of them, yes." There *was* that bank robber.

She waved a hand towards the bookshelf near the fireplace. "A Supreme Court Chief Justice, a hockey legend, two Prime Ministers—"

"Of opposing camps."

"—the Arctic explorer, Canada's most revered folk singer..."

She drained her glass and shook her head.

"You have your pick of heroes. Why this rock star/fashion model/trophy wife and merry widow?"

"Don't forget, Sylvia and I go way back."

"As if I could." She got up and refilled both our glasses. "The times you barged into my room and flung yourself on my bed, howling over what your so-called friend had done this time. The boyfriend she stole, the dress she borrowed and ruined, the time she—"

"I know, I know." Nearly twenty years, and Kate had not forgotten.

"So, what's the appeal?"

"Besides being a guaranteed bestseller? It should be a piece of cake for me. I know her from way back, and all these years we've stayed friends." Of sorts.

"Have you? I know she always called on you whenever she needed a favor, or an introduction, or a shoulder to cry on."

Or, I recalled, a place to crash.

"She still does. And believe me, I know the intimate details behind all those shoulder-crying episodes. So, when my agent found out she and Pargeter Press were toying with this memoir idea in the wake of Christopher's death last year, it all came together."

"So once again, you'll do all the work and get none of the glory."

I shrugged. "The lot of a ghostwriter."

Sylvia and I were comfortably settled on the shady deck that looked out over Lake Mistawis, cold drinks at hand (provided by Mrs. Carmichael, Christopher's long-time housekeeper). Lunch was scheduled to appear soon.

This was one of the perks of the project. Spending part of the summer at the beautiful old Corbett summer home in the Muskoka region north of Toronto, not far from our old stomping grounds of November Falls.

Even better, it came with a tiny perfect cottage on the grounds where I could retreat with my laptop when not dragging the intimate details of Sylvia's life history out of her often indolent memory.

I was reviewing some of the notes I'd collected from our initial sessions over the past week, explaining how I saw the shape of the memoir.

But Sylvia's interest wasn't there. She shrugged and leaned back in her deck chair. "Oh, just shape it any way you like, Hallie. You're the writer, after all."

Just like old times. Only new.

I found myself flashing back to our last year at Riverside Collegiate. Sylvia had inveigled me into "helping" her write her final essay on *Middlemarch,* which—no surprise—she hadn't read.

She lay back on the lounge chair, eyes closed, arms draped beside her still slim body, as though the morning session of remembering the past had taxed all her energy. I compared this woman of thirty-plus to the delicate, almost ethereal girl she'd been then.

She still had a look of youthful innocence and helplessness. Her hidden strength all those years ago.

We'd both had big dreams back then. Dreams of leaving November Falls. Of being rich and famous.

"I'm going to be a famous writer," I'd declared. In my secret heart I wasn't sure about the "rich" part, unless you were Nora Roberts or Dan Brown. Literary novels just didn't bring in the money. I might have to settle for fame without the fortune.

"I'm going to be famous too," Sylvia had announced. "*And* rich."

"As what?" I couldn't think of anything she excelled in, that she could even earn a living at, let alone—

"I haven't decided yet. Maybe an actress. No...all those lines to memorize. I know!—a supermodel. Like Natasha Poly. Or Supernova. Or a rock star."

"That sounds exciting." Well, I had to say something encouraging.

She hadn't finished. "Or even a fashion designer. You know how I love clothes."

She seemed to sparkle at this thought, so I hadn't the heart to point out she could neither draw nor sew.

"Or maybe..." she leaned back onto the deck chair on her parents' patio, and gazed up into the trees, "...maybe I'll just marry a rich and famous man."

Damned if she hadn't made every one of those dreams a reality.

My own road to success, I discovered, lay in a surprisingly marketable ability to tell other people's stories. Instead of fame without fortune, I have achieved fortune without the fame. This suits me fine.

Sylvia's varied paths to realizing her dreams culminated in her marriage, six years ago, to Christopher Corbett.

Christopher had been attracting adoration a full generation before ours. Born into a wealthy brewing dynasty, he had nonetheless made his own way. First, as a trailblazing star on the ski slopes, capturing gold all through the 1980s. Then on to a career in the diplomatic corps, culminating in being in the right place and time to stickhandle a delicate mission that earned him the Nobel Peace Prize. After his retirement from world affairs, he became a popular political pundit, shooting from the hip on news programs, podcasts, and interview shows.

Upon the death of his wife Alison, the mother of his two children, he re-entered the social side of life. At a glitzy upscale party in Toronto, he met sometime fashion designer and former rock singer Sylvia Starr.

Two months later, they were married. He was fifty-one; she was twenty-eight.

Five years after that, this globe-trotting diplomat and devil-may-care athlete met a sudden death, falling from a ladder while pruning a pear tree in his own backyard.

My usual interviewing practice soon palled on Sylvia, so we developed a more workable process. I'd nudge her with an event or name from her past, and then she was happy just to lie back and chatter on and on about various memories, chasing ideas around, flitting from one thought to another. She was good with this, as long as I didn't interrupt her to press a point or wander deeper down some path she clearly didn't want to travel.

There was no chronology involved here at all. She might drift away from her stint as a fashion designer to a deep dive into her years on the road with rock star Ptommy Ptomaine.

When she was in the mood, memories would just flow out of her. Other days it was a slog. Sometimes she just shut down.

Especially when I asked about the immediate post-high school years. We'd left November Falls and lost touch with each other. Me to university in British Columbia, her to Toronto for a taste of life in the big city.

Sylvia was reticent. "Oh, you know... pathetically trying to find myself, dead-end job at an insurance company, living in a crappy little apartment. I don't even want to *think* about it. Who'd ever want to *read* about it?

That was a door slammed. Did it matter? Sometimes memoirs are like that. Skip the parts nobody wants to read.

As it turned out, the missing years weren't so boring.

One afternoon when Sylvia was out with friends and I sat on the shady deck, trying to make sense of yesterday's notes, a man came round the side of the house. He stopped when he saw me.

"Uh hi...I was, uh, looking for Sylvia? I knocked, but..."

He seemed an ordinary, nondescript sort of guy about my own age, casually dressed. And...was he faintly familiar?

I got up to meet him halfway and introduced myself. "I'm a friend of Sylvia's. She's out right now, but—"

"Hey..." He suddenly took on new energy. "Hallie Paxton? From Riverside?"

It clicked. Sort of. "Of course. You're Ted, right? Ted...Walker?"

"Ted Walters, yeah."

I invited him to sit, and for a few minutes we did the usual chat based on a shared past—though barely. Some memorable teachers, a school trip. I was racking my brain for something else to ask when he cleared his throat and got to the point.

"I heard Sylvia's writing a memoir?"

Okay, it had been announced in the usual places, so not a secret.

"That's right. She's had a pretty varied life."

He nodded. "So, what, are you helping her with it?"

"Yes. She asked me to help with the spelling and punctuation." It was our agreed upon cover story. "And typing."

"I get it. Like a secretary. You always were really smart, Hallie."

Maybe in Ted's world a secretary was the pinnacle of a smart woman's ambition.

"So, uh, what's she said about me?"

"You?" This was a puzzler. "Well, nothing." I bit off adding *why would she?*

"Nothing?" He seemed surprised. Was he hurt? Or relieved?

I waited.

"That's *good*. I mean, it's really Beth-Ann, you know. She doesn't want anyone finding out."

"Beth-Ann?"

"My wife. Well, my second wife."

"Wait. So you had a first wife? And that would be...?

"Sylvia." He looked puzzled. "Didn't you know? Like, you being old friends and all?"

Before I could gather up the reactions and clues ricocheting around my brain, we were joined by Beth-Ann herself. She must have been waiting in the car. She was only slightly less nondescript than Ted, pale thin face, pale wispy hair, pale pinkish top over a gray skirt.

"Ted? What does she say?" She indicated me, no doubt assuming I was the woman calling the shots.

We both stood up and Ted introduced us, explaining my secretarial status.

"Hallie says Sylvia's never even mentioned me. She isn't including me in her memoir."

"Really?" She looked at me with a dose of suspicion, and I could hardly blame her.

"Sorry, Beth-Ann, I don't know her intentions. I only know she's kept quiet about that time in her life. Never a word about the years right after high school. I never realized she and Ted were even—even knew each other all that well."

Beth-Ann looked from Ted to me and back, and then said, "Ted, can I talk to Hallie alone?"

Ted took this edict mildly. "Sure honey. You can explain it better than me." And he was gone.

I let Beth-Ann take the lead. She got all confidential.

"It's like this. I had no idea Ted had been married before. When he heard about this book she's writing, that's when he told me. I mean, if I'd ever thought..." she glanced off to where he'd disappeared around to the front of the house, "...well, I guess I might not have married him."

"Oh?" One of my favorite prompts.

"Not that I don't love him. I *do*. But, well, it's my Church."

She went on to explain, as tears threatened to spill. She belonged to some denomination I'd never heard of, some hard-nosed evangelical group where, it seemed, the pastor held sway with his personal beliefs about Sin, Marriage, and the Big D. Divorce. Marriage was for life, and so on.

"You mean," I wanted to tread warily, "they'll kick you out of the church?"

She shook her head, and the dislodged tears flowed down her

cheeks. "They'll forgive me, maybe, but they won't let me be in the Ladies' Guild or run the Nursery Classes anymore." The distress seemed to crush her. "And they won't allow me to sing the solo at Fellowship Hour."

I refrained from suggesting she was probably well out of such a judgy congregation and told her I'd make sure Sylvia kept their names out of it.

Her gratitude humbled me.

I waited until Sylvia and I were settled in the sunroom with our pre-dinner drinks. Then I let her have it point blank.

"Why didn't you tell me you were once married to Ted Walters?"

She went dead white. Like a medieval princess on the receiving end of some ancient curse. She said nothing.

"Ted was here this afternoon with his wife. Was he making it up? Because believe me, they are very, very concerned that no one ever find out about it."

She seemed to find her breathing muscles again and blinked once or twice.

"Oh? They don't want it known?"

"Absolutely they don't. Any more than you do, apparently, with all that bull about how boring your post-graduation years were."

She pulled a petulant look and took refuge behind her gin and tonic.

"Well, it's true. Nothing's more boring than a stupid, *pointless* marriage that didn't even last six months. I just wanted to forget all about it."

"Sure. But listen, Sylvia, I'm not exactly thrilled to hear this."

"What does it matter to you?"

"I'm the one who's writing these memoirs, remember? I don't want to find out, after they're published, about crucial events I never suspected, that *should* have been in there."

Another stubborn look. "It's my life, and I want it left out."

"Okay. We'll leave it out. But I'm not going to lie about it. If I know about it, we can work around the time where 'nothing' happened and make it credible. But if we just leap over it, readers will notice the gap. And they'll wonder."

She was silent for a few moments, then said, "Are you sure Ted and...?"

"Beth-Ann."

"...that they want it kept quiet?"

"Absolutely." I explained the relentless, unforgiving nature of Beth-Ann's church. "She's terrified of the consequences if anyone finds out she married a divorced man."

Sylvia was silent, thoughtful.

"In fact," I went on, "I pretty much promised her."

Sylvia sighed. "Okay, you win. From now on, I'll tell you everything. Every teensy *boring* detail."

I decided to believe her.

The project continued on course. By the end of the initial three weeks, as planned, I had collected enough for a detailed outline on how the book would go. Though I still wondered what else she might be keeping from me.

Now I was able to divide my time between my writing retreat on the grounds, and trips back and forth to Toronto for other aspects of my life.

Beth-Ann's concerns were still on my mind, so I figured, since Sylvia was in agreement, I should deliver the good news she could still sing at the Fellowship Hour and pour coffee for the congregation.

They lived on a quiet street in November Falls. I found them both at home on a Saturday morning. Beth-Ann seemed apprehensive at my arrival, but I put her and Ted at ease over coffee in the kitchen.

"I just want to assure you, Beth-Ann, that Sylvia is entirely on board with keeping her marriage to Ted out of the book." I looked over at Ted, who was gazing into his mug. "We talked it over. It's a part of her life she wants to forget as much as you do."

He nodded. "Yeah, I guess I can get that. I mean, her husband probably wouldn't like to have a big deal made of it either."

"Well, her husband died about a year ago, but yeah, it's all water under the bridge."

"So..." he looked up from his mug with a smile, "we're all good with that."

Yes, we were.

Until two months later, when Ted, driving home from some guy thing late one rainy night, somehow missed a turn, and drove into the November River.

And drowned.

I felt terrible for Ted, worse for Beth-Ann, and even a little bad for Sylvia. After all...

"You were married to him once," I blurted out, one afternoon at her place, after we'd spent hours reviewing the latest arrangements of her life story, which was falling nicely into place. We even had a title. *Dream Big, Dream True.* "Don't you feel, well, some sense of loss?"

Sylvia glanced up from the page she was more or less perusing. "It's sad, of course. Sad for his wife, his friends. But since I'm neither of those, can we just drop it?"

We dropped it.

It didn't stay dropped.

Ted had lots of friends in November Falls. Old school buddies, hockey buddies. Inevitably when they sat around the bar and talked about good times with Ted, stories from the past came up.

Someone remembered that Ted had gone to Toronto just after high school. Wasn't there something about him meeting up with Sylvia Starr then? More than that. Didn't they, like, live together? Get married? No way. Oh wait, yeah, they did.

Beth-Ann, of course, was hit hard. Again.

I'd seen her after Ted's death, before this latest truthiness had come to light. Now she came to see me at my writing retreat, in a state of crashing and burning.

"They're after me," she said, twisting her hands in anguish.

"Who are?" But I could guess. The Ladies' Guild out for her blood, with Pastor McNasty at the fore.

Bit by bit, the story came out. It was worse than I imagined.

The pastor and the elders (yes, they had men of that ilk calling the shots) conceded they *might* forgive her for marrying a man who had already pledged his troth to another woman, and even—grudgingly—for her perfidy in keeping this transgression from them. *But—* first they demanded evidence of her innocence, in the form of Ted's divorce papers and her own marriage certificate. Only then could they see their way clear to admitting her back into the fold.

I held my tongue until I could speak without expressing an opinion.

"I'm so sorry, Beth-Ann. Is there anything I can do to help?"

She nodded. "Can you get the divorce papers from Sylvia?"

Really?

"Sure, I can ask her. But didn't Ted—?"

This brought on fresh anguish.

"I can't *find* them. I've looked everywhere, through all the papers in the house. They're just not *there.*"

I went into pacification mode.

"It's okay, Beth-Ann. It's all right. Sylvia will have them for sure."

It should have been that simple.

Sylvia's reaction to my request was not what I'd expected. She looked up from the latest issue of *Marie Claire*.

"Divorce certificate?" she echoed, with that remote gaze she's so good at.

"Yours and Ted's." I explained Beth-Ann's dilemma, toning down the extremist zeal.

"Well, I'm not going to go digging around for it. If Ted lost his copy, she can just tell them to take her word for it." She returned to her magazine. "Or find a new religion."

That was pretty much my view, but still...

"It's got to be among your files and documents somewhere, Sylvia, and since you've already given me access to everything, I don't mind looking for it."

"Oh, for heaven's sake." She tossed aside the magazine and gave me a look of resigned patience. "Fine. You're welcome to look. I haven't seen it in years."

I'd already researched my way through mountains of papers. Letters, programs, photos, invitations, contracts, fashion designs, and so on. There was little order to her cartons of paraphernalia, except what I'd managed to impose along the way.

"Though now that I think about it," Sylvia said, "it was probably in the file boxes that got destroyed in that apartment fire."

Great. I lost all heart at the prospect of searching the chaos for a potentially nonexistent document. The obvious step, I figured, was for Beth-Ann to apply to the provincial records office for a copy.

I returned to Toronto to work on the final draft. It was a relief to be in my own home, with Sylvia at a distance.

As *Dream Big, Dream True* was working its way towards a polished manuscript, I gradually admitted I'd been dreaming myself, believing that by knowing Sylvia so intimately, the work was half done.

Not even close. I hadn't reckoned with the blinders that shaded the real Sylvia. There was no excuse for not seeing it up front. The girl I thought I knew and the woman she'd become were worlds apart.

Over the course of this project, it had become clear that—like the essays I wrote for her in school—as with virtually everything else in her life, she'd been faking it.

With each episode, I found the truth slipping out, shifting the legend. And every time, she would blow that truth off as something that didn't need to be included in her memoir.

Each time that happened, my desire to care about it diminished.

Sylvia's life was one big fairy tale. A series of dreams and illusions. A million lies.

Her glorious career as a fashion designer. For a time, she even had her own label and modeled her own brilliant creations. She was flying high. Until the struggling fashion students she paid to design them finally rebelled and went out on their own. It didn't end well.

The singing career with Ptommy Ptomaine's band. Her one hit, "Shining Through the Glitter," that she'd composed herself. Well, sort of. She wrote the lyrics, which consisted mostly of repeating the title. It was the music—by Ptommy himself—that made the song so huge. After that hit single, she never had another. Ptommy dumped her from the band. And his bed.

That final ambition, however.... Marry a rich and famous man. Well, that's when she at last made it real. Marrying Christopher Corbett was the one thing in her life she'd achieved honestly.

But I no longer cared.

I gathered together the printout of the third draft and shoved it into my case with a sigh. Back to November Falls.

October was coming to an end. The colors of the season were muting to browns and dull yellows as I drove the last stretch between the town of November Falls and the Corbett house on the lake.

Fuming.

Sylvia was ready to have the place closed up and relocate to Key West or St. Moritz or one of Christopher's other glamorous retreats.

She seemed delighted to see me again, and more than ready to see the final draft. We sat in the lounge by a generous fire in the old stone fireplace while Mrs. Carmichael brought us red wine and a tray of cheese and crackers.

We settled back in the deep couches. I fortified myself with a generous swallow of cabernet and plunged in.

"I stopped off on the way to see Beth-Ann," I said.

"Who? Oh, right."

"Aren't you going to ask if she ever found the divorce certificate?"

"Okay...did she?"

"You know she didn't." I let the words hang there.

"How would I know that?"

"Because there isn't one."

"Of course there is. Or there was. I told you, mine was probably lost in that apartment fire—"

"That apartment fire was ten years ago, Sylvia. You married Christopher six years ago. How could you have done that without proof of divorce? Or did you just forget to tell him you'd been married before? Like Ted forgot to tell Beth-Ann?"

"That's crazy," she informed me.

"Yeah, it is, isn't it? How come you didn't just file for divorce back then?"

"We *are* divorced. We were separated for over a year and then Ted took care of it."

"Did he? Then how come there's no record of a divorce in the provincial records office?"

"Says who? Beth-Ann? I'm sure she hasn't a clue how to—"

"She had her uncle the lawyer do it. There's nothing. Marriage certificate, yes. Divorce certificate, no."

She just looked at me. Admitting nothing. Showing no emotion.

"Come on, Sylvia. You must have known your marriage to Christopher wasn't legal."

She gave a half shrug. "Well, no one cares about that anymore, do they?"

"They care quick enough if there's no will. Did he make a will leaving everything to you? To his wife? Or—"

"Stop that!" She slammed down her glass, splashing red wine all around.

"Are you even entitled to this?" I waved my hand vaguely. By now, I had lost all concern for her feelings. "Any of this? The Key West condo? Life in the luxury lane? Did *he* know you weren't legally married?"

"We *were* married. Just because that idiot Ted forgot—*forgot*—to file for divorce doesn't make any difference."

She jumped up and began a frantic sort of pacing the room, as though looking for something to give her strength.

"He was supposed to take care of it. I should have known he'd screw it up."

I gazed at her, fascinated. It flitted through my writer's mind that this would make great copy in her memoir, but the chances of publication were rapidly diminishing.

Still, I couldn't help continuing in interview mode.

"So, when did you find out there was no divorce? Before you married Christopher? After he died?"

"Oh, what does it matter?" She seemed to calm down a little. "Just a few months ago. It was after he and Beth-Ann first showed up. He came over one day and confessed he'd never initiated the divorce. He claimed I was supposed to do it."

She shook her head and gazed down at the red wine stains on her lounging outfit.

"This will never come out."

She didn't mean the wine.

"It's already come out, Sylvia."

She shook her head. "Ted and I were the only ones who knew. About still being married, I mean."

Really? Wasn't she doing the math? I stood up to look at her squarely.

"Sylvia, what else did Ted say when he told you about the non-divorce?"

"What do you mean?"

"He didn't try to blackmail you, did he?"

At her look of contempt and disbelief, I expanded on my thoughts.

"Because he might have thought you'd pay big to forget all about it. And now he's, well, dead."

She didn't get mad or defensive. She just laughed. Bitterly.

"Hallie, *listen* to yourself. You think I somehow found a way to, what? Disable his brakes? Get him to go out alone on a rainy night, along the river road? Seriously?"

Okay, it *was* a bit nuts.

"No, of course not. Stupid of me. I'm sorry."

We stood looking at each other for I don't know how long. Then Sylvia, slowly, deliberately, picked up the manuscript from the coffee table and walked over to the fireplace. She shoved it into the flames, then picked up the poker and ensured my words were well on their way to hell.

Without looking away from the burning pages, she said, "My publisher will be in touch with your agent."

"Works for me." I gathered up my things and headed towards the hallway. Before leaving, I had one thing to add. Just in case.

"Oh, don't forget, Sylvia. It's *not* just you and me who know. There's also Beth-Ann and her uncle the lawyer."

She shrugged.

"And the pastor. And the elders. And the entire Ladies' Guild."

"Get out."

I got out.

"All that work, all those months. For nothing?" Kate shook her head in disbelief and sipped on her Northern Spirit Rye.

We were back in my cozy living room in the city, by a friendlier fire, as I recounted the complicated tale for my sister. It felt good to let it unroll.

"That was a shocker when it hit the news," she said. "Christopher Corbett's non-wife left out in the cold, without a penny."

Because he hadn't made a will prior to his unexpected death.

"It wasn't quite as bad as that. His kids—they're our age—gave her a settlement, including the Ottawa condo. Not bad, but nothing like what she once had. I mean, the son and daughter already had their initial portion of the estate, but now they get it all. And all the properties."

"Should I feel sorry for her?"

"No." Though sometimes I did.

"And that other woman? Did they kick her out of the church?"

I enjoyed filling her in on Beth-Ann's fate. As it turned out, the pastor and the elders had tried to do her the dirty, but to everyone's surprise, the Ladies' Guild had rallied to the defense of their friend. They made it crystal clear that any reasonable person could see she was innocent of wrongdoing, and the men had better stop acting like a bunch of Pharisees, or they'd be running their own nurseries and making their own coffee.

"Here's to the Sisterhood." Kate raised her glass.

She refilled our glasses and asked again about the cancelled project.

"You don't seem too downhearted at the loss of Sylvia's life story. Have you got something else in the works?"

I couldn't resist grinning. "Well, it turned out, Christopher's kids have been thinking about a biography. But Sylvia wouldn't give them access to his private diaries. Now they've got them back, and they want *me* to write it."

"That's great. You mean as a ghostwriter?"

"No. As his authorized biographer. Under my own name."

"Well, here's to you too, then. To your name on the cover."

I raised my glass. "To fortune *and* fame.

*Epilogue–after another shot of rye*

"Did you mean it, Hallie, when you sort of accused Sylvia of killing Ted?

"Well, maybe I let my imagination run away with me. But damn it, it seemed like a perfect setup for blackmail. And then his sudden death—his accident—was so convenient. For Sylvia, I mean. She was on the verge of losing everything.

"But the dominoes toppled over after all. His friends reminisced about his past. They eventually remembered the rumors about them getting married. Beth-Ann's church went into self-righteous mode. No one could find the divorce certificate..."

"It was a bit farfetched," Kate mused. "I mean, the brakes failed, he lost control on a rain-soaked road at night... There's no way she could have done any of that."

"Of course not—"

Oh shit.

All the warmth of the rye and the fire drained out of me.

Sylvia's lifelong superpower.

Finding someone else to do the things she couldn't do herself.

# Pam Barnsley

**Pam Barnsley** is a former journalist whose stories have appeared in *Ellery Queen Mystery Magazine*, *Storyteller Canada*, and several anthologies. Her novel, *The River Cage*, was shortlisted for the Crime Writers of Canada Best Unpublished Novel Award in 2020. She is a member of Crime Writers of Canada and Sisters in Crime. Pam is also a former snowboard instructor, award-winning poet, and from her father she learned the ancient art of training a cat to jump over a stick.

Find her at www.pambarnsley.com.

# The Underground

## Pam Barnsley

With only a slight tremor in his hands, Chaucer turned the last card over. The small crowd gasped, then laughed at their own gullibility. A few coins clinked into the old man's hat, not enough for a sandwich, but possibly a coffee and day-old donut.

He gathered the deck of cards and slid them into the sagging pocket of his jacket. He wondered where to put the coins this time. Nowhere was safe from Bodie and his crew. Eventually Chaucer fed them through a gap in the hem of his threadbare gray suit jacket, where they settled in a low part at the back.

He shuffled slowly back through the dwindling pedestrians as the gray daylight succumbed to the city night. Should he spend the money now, or risk trying to save it for a morning meal? He calculated the odds were probably forty-sixty, not in his favor.

Chaucer lived in the underground tunnels beneath the city, and a morning donut and coffee wasn't just sustenance. It was being allowed inside a warm café, instead of being told to move along. It was hot liquid reviving his aching body after a night in the bone-chilling cold. It was security from Bodie and his gang.

Life was full of chances. All his life Chaucer had lost most of them, and the past two months had been the worst. Now the stiffness in his neck prevented the old man from seeing Bodie until it was too late.

"Whoa there, Chaucer. What's the hurry?"

Bodie was skinny and short, but made up for it with meanness. He had a tattoo of a flaming tiger the size of a man's hand that ran up the left side of his neck and over his jaw. Chaucer thought it looked more like a weasel that someone had lit on fire as a cruel trick.

Bodie's two sidekicks, Curtis and Jimmy, appeared on either side of Chaucer. The palsy in his limbs increased.

"S-s-s-strutting your s-s-stuff for the old b-b-biddies?" Bodie taunted.

The three young men laughed. Chaucer barely felt their hands, slick as letter-openers, as they lifted the deck of cards from his pocket.

"This all you got?" Curtis was the biggest of the three, but he had the smallest eyes.

Chaucer lifted his hand. "It's my last deck. Please."

Curtis flexed the deck between his meaty thumb and fingers, let the cards fly into the street. As Chaucer stepped down off the sidewalk, his left hip ached in protest. In this part of town there were few cars, and certainly no one foolish enough to interfere. He gathered the cards up one by one, wiping the mud off against his jacket. As he moved, the coins confessed their small silveriness against one another.

Rough hands hauled Chaucer around, and cold eyes stared into his.

"You holding out?"

The hands snaked into his jacket.

"What's this?" Bodie felt the coins, and with a fierce yank ripped the hem of Chaucer's jacket. The coins spilled onto the ground.

"That's it?" Jimmy kicked at the coins with a disdainful army boot.

"I ain't had no luck lately," Chaucer said. The last time he'd had more than a few dollars was over a month ago. These three had relieved him of his windfall then too.

"How come you never got any bigger stuff anymore? Where's all your dumpster treasure?"

Chaucer's head bobbed on his neck, but he said nothing. He was getting too old to walk uptown to where the good garbage could be mined.

Curtis stuck his chin out at Chaucer. "He's probably got a whole stash of loot underground. I heard there was a guy living under cardboard, had a couple lottery tickets worth millions. Too crazy to cash 'em in."

"Yeah," Jimmy said. "Looney Bin Lou that runs the Laundromat has jewelry you wouldn't believe. She could cash that in and go live on easy street."

Curtis nodded. "People like that don't deserve to have it, if they don't know what to do with it."

Bodie looked down at Chaucer's scrawny figure shaking in the street. "Being old sucks," he said, and spat.

Chaucer made his way back underground. Underground was cold and dark, but it was safer than the street. Those who lived here were running from many of the same things, and mostly they left one another alone. Occasionally someone would steal from another undergrounder's stash of blankets, coats, and scavenged odds and ends, but not often. Undergrounders hoarded their goods fiercely, and no one knew who was desperate enough to stick someone with a knife if they touched their collection of broken umbrellas.

Chaucer limped into the darkened nook that held his own nest of castoffs. It looked like a pile of rubble and discarded garbage, both because that was what it was, and because that was how the undergrounders designed their nests for camouflage.

When Municipal workers came through the tunnels, with their

mandate to clean out the indigents, they could be as ruthless as any thief. But the undergrounders knew when the work crews were coming and were able to keep out of sight. Last week, after a year of construction, workers had come down to post warnings signs on the new sewer line. Chaucer moved his possessions in the middle of the night, the way a mother cat desperately moves her kittens to a safe haven.

Chaucer wondered how much longer he could survive the gauntlet of Bodie, Curtis and Jimmy. He looked around at all his dumpster treasure and wondered if there was something he could use to buy them off. He cracked his tattered deck in half and the Joker grinned up at him. Maybe there was another way to even the odds. But could he pull it off?

Three days later, Chaucer was finally ready. He waited in the street until it was time. Bodie stuck his tattooed neck out of the doorway where he'd been lurking, and Chaucer shuffled towards him. Chaucer sucked in his breath. He had only one chance to get everything right.

"What's happening, geezer?" Bodie said.

Chaucer flinched as the sidekicks' hands darted through his clothes. He looked back down the street and started to shake.

"I have to go."

Bodie, Curtis, and Jimmy laughed.

"He has to go," Bodie said. "Very important meeting."

"What's he hiding?" Curtis asked. "He's hiding something."

"No." Chaucer's voice quavered, and the whites of his eyes rolled. Careful not to overdo it. "No, I'm not."

Curtis ran his hands roughly through the old man's clothes again and came up with nothing more than the deck of cards. This time he didn't even bother to fan it before he dropped it onto the street. Chaucer made no protest.

"Can I go now?" he asked.

Bodie narrowed his eyes. "Why you in such a hurry? You aren't even worried about your precious deck of cards."

Curtis stepped back. "I checked him, he ain't got nothing."

"Check him again. Something's up."

Curtis ran through Chaucer's clothes again. Chaucer struggled for somewhere to look and tried to move away.

Jimmy got in on the action, grabbing Chaucer by the collar. "Give it up."

"I haven't got anything. I—" Chaucer said, but Curtis was looking down at Chaucer's feet.

The toes of Chaucer's shoes were curled because they were too big for him. Chaucer slid his right foot slightly back.

"Take 'em off."

"No. Please."

Curtis reached down and yanked off one of the shoes. Chaucer's socks were full of holes. Curtis held the shoe up and peered in. He threw it down and held out his hand for the other. Carefully Chaucer eased off the second shoe. Curtis reached down and snatched it up. He shook the shoe, and a small piece of folded paper fell out.

"What's this?" Bodie asked.

Chaucer looked away. "Nothing."

Bodie unfolded the paper and studied it. He looked at Chaucer.

"What's the deal?" he said.

Chaucer shook his head. Softly, softly, reel them in.

"Spit it out or you won't have nothing left to spit with."

"No," Chaucer said, and his head bobbed.

Bodie laughed. He twisted Chaucer's arm. The old man stayed silent. He twisted it again, harder.

Chaucer didn't even see Bodie give Curtis the sign. The pain from Curtis' fist in his stomach was so fierce, Chaucer doubled over and retched. He tried to suck in air, but his lungs wouldn't work. He wondered if he would die right here of a heart attack, his whole plan come to nothing.

"You know you're gonna give it up anyway," Bodie said, "so let's hear it."

"It's just a map," Chaucer wheezed. "Doesn't mean nothing."

"Like hell. This is a map of the underground." Bodie waved the piece of paper in front of Chaucer's face. "And I want to know what you got stashed where these little X marks are."

Chaucer shook his head, though it took everything he had. The second blow was even worse, and he crumpled to the ground. "Alright," he said. "I'll show you."

Bodie, Curtis and Jimmy were not so cocky in the catacombs. They walked behind Chaucer as he shuffled along the maze of tunnels as they wound their way deeper through the underground. They ducked beneath rusty pipes and waded through murky puddles.

"This better be good or you're a dead man," Jimmy said, as he tiptoed his fancy trainers through a deep puddle.

Chaucer limped, and the pain in his gut made him hunch over more than usual.

"Get a move on, old-timer," Bodie growled. "I want to get out of this stinking hole."

"You and me both," Curtis said. "You gotta be crazy to live down here."

At last they came to a heavy steel hatch in the wall of the tunnel. Chaucer pointed. "It's in there."

"How do we open it?" Bodie asked.

Chaucer's watery eyes were full of fear. "I have a bar hidden, there." He gestured to a pile of garbage further along the wall.

"Get it," Bodie said.

Chaucer shuffled over and brought the bar back. Curtis grabbed it from his hands. It was a large bar, t-shaped like a giant tire iron, with a special hex-key head for opening and closing the hatches.

Chaucer had added it to his cache when a municipal worker had left it behind.

Curtis worked the fastenings loose with the bar. He dropped the bar, then pulled the round door open and looked in. The other two crowded beside him and peered into the darkness.

Bodie turned back to Chaucer. "How far inside?"

Chaucer tried to shrug, but his shoulders just shook harder. "A little ways."

"In you go."

Chaucer opened and closed his mouth like a fish. This wasn't part of his plan.

"I can't," he said.

"Get moving."

Chaucer struggled through the hatch and took hold of the steel ladder that led down the side of the huge pipe they were entering. It was only ten rungs down to the floor, but it seemed to take him forever. Above him the young punks cursed and threatened, irate at Chaucer's snail-like progress. Chaucer looked up and saw them hunched above him like vultures.

When at last they were all in the pipe, Chaucer moved along the wall. It was the new tunnel, free of the filth that coated the older ones. Bodie's flashlight carved a shifting channel of light, the shadows lunging like ghosts.

Chaucer fell twice and had to be dragged most of the way.

"This is the first one," he said, stopping at a small pile of bricks. It had nearly killed him climbing down the ladder with them one by one, making this little cache the last two days.

Curtis tore the bricks aside and found the stack of papers. Bodie shone the flashlight as they all leaned in closer.

"Bearer Bonds," Bodie read. "Five thousand dollars."

He rifled through the stack of certificates. "Five thousand, five thousand, five thousand. I had an uncle had one of these. Bank lets you cash them in, legit."

The three punks looked at one another. In the harsh light their eyes glittered like glass. Bodie laughed and the other two laughed with him.

"We're on easy street now, boys. There must be fifty grand here."

Chaucer lay like a discarded coat on the cold floor. Bodie prodded him with his boot. "Let's get the rest of it, old man."

Chaucer did not move. Bodie grabbed him by the arm and hauled him up. He looked half-dead.

"How much farther is the next one?" Bodie asked.

"Half a block," Chaucer whispered.

"Same thing as this? A stack of bricks?"

"Same."

Bodie let go and Chaucer crumpled back onto the hard cement floor.

Bodie started in the direction Chaucer had indicated. "We don't need him. He's just slowing us down."

Chaucer listened as their hard footsteps faded. The flashlight's arc grew dimmer. Chaucer got to his feet and struggled back through the dark toward the hatch, his hands sliding along the wall. His chances weren't good. He was too slow. Too late. At best he'd give himself a fifty-fifty chance.

And then he saw the murky light from the open hatch. The ladder stretching upwards. Not impossible. One hand. One foot. One hand. One foot. Halfway up he stopped and closed his eyes. He hadn't worn a watch for the past thirty years, but he knew it was almost midnight. He'd cut it too fine. He opened his eyes and looked up at the four rungs above him. Maybe he could beat the odds just this once. One hand. One foot.

He clawed his way out, leaning against the hatch to close it. His hands shook as he closed the hatch fasteners with the special bar. It wasn't as tight as the way the municipal workers left it, but it would have to do.

The noise was as faint as a hearing aid hiss. Was it his imagination? Chaucer cocked his head, but he could make out nothing else.

He turned and limped back to his cardboard nest, his breathing ragged.

Among his life's possessions Chaucer found the piece of paper he wanted, more valuable than all the empty promises Bodie and his sidekicks now held in their hands. Bodie had called them bearer bonds. Chaucer had once believed they were his ticket to freedom too. His way out of the cold underground to his own apartment, and at least one hot meal a day. He had taken those pieces of paper to a bank, but the manager hadn't even looked at them, just shooed Chaucer away. Those papers had fooled Chaucer once, and now they had fooled Bodie, Curtis, and Jimmy.

Back at the hatch, Chaucer smoothed the piece of paper against the wall, pressing the adhesive tape back down to hold the notice in place. The noise was louder now, more like a swarm of angry bees than a faulty hearing aid. He looked at the warning notice posted by the municipal workers the week before. Like some of the other underground dwellers, Chaucer could not read, but they all knew what this paper meant. The numbers that warned of midnight.

The roaring was enough to give the underground a tremor like his own now, a noise of the hounds of hell being swallowed alive. Chaucer listened as the new sewer line reached full capacity, then turned and made his way slowly back to the light.

# Rand Gaynor

After a decades-long career in publications and book design, **Rand Gaynor** has turned his attention to his own writing, publishing an illustrated children's book, and a collection of LGBTQ+ short stories. A member of the Writers' Federation of Nova Scotia and a judge in recent Crime Writers of Canada Short Story and Novella Competitions, his first mystery short story appears in *Crimeucopia* from Murderous Ink Press.

Find him at http://www.amazon.ca/stores/author/B07Z7984L5.

# Julia's Garage

## Rand Gaynor

A bumblebee, held down by a set of calipers, struggles against having its stinger pulled out by a small pair of tweezers. Several wide-mouthed bottles are lined up on the freshly painted blue windowsill, buzzing with many more bees awaiting their own procedures.

Ten-year-old twin sisters, the Twinnys, focus intently as they perform the operation. One six inches taller than the other, they still wear matching outfits—colorful pinafores, bright yellow, splashed with juicy red strawberries. Eventually Short Twinny will grow into Tall Twinny's hand-me-downs—identical, larger sizes of the clothes she had just grown out of.

"There, that one's done," Short Twinny says, wiping a bit of bee goo off the tweezers.

"Can I pick him up now?" Tall Twinny is always anxious to hold them, let them crawl around on her hand.

"Maybe wait a minute," Short Twinny says, "he's probably sore."

She drops the stingerless bee into an empty bottle. Its legs flail in an attempt to turn itself over. Then it stops.

"He died before I had a chance to play with him," Tall Twinny says.

Short Twinny inspects the bee, poking it with a straw from an old broom.

"Yep, dead," she says, drops it into a small matchbox. Later, they'll bury it in their bee garden outside, with the others.

"Why not make a sign for the bee hospital?" Short Twinny suggests. "There was some blue paint left after you finished the windowsill."

Reaching for the paint can, Tall Twinny clumsily knocks over a bee-filled bottle that shatters on the workbench. The sisters scream, frantically swatting at the swarm, breaking more bottles, releasing even more bees.

"I'm getting stung everywhere!" one of them cries, sweeping bees off her pinafore with bee-covered hands.

"I...I...can't...breathe..." the other gasps, clutching her throat as they both slump to the floor.

The blue windowsill is empty. Broken bottles litter the workbench and the floor where the Twinnys lay. The buzzing of bees continues for a few minutes, then gradually fades out.

Afternoon sunlight streams into the meditation hall at the Mountain Retreat Centre. Floor-to-ceiling windows on every wall present a ground-to-sky view of the rock gardens outside, the wildflower meadows beyond, and snow-capped mountains in the distance. Julia and her friend, Tara, are among dozens of others sitting on meditation cushions arranged in orderly rows.

Their teacher, Baba Ganouj, enters the hall and sits on the Asian-styled black lacquered chair facing the participants.

"Most of you have traveled great distances to attend these seminars, many have been doing this for several years," he begins. "All of you have a deep understanding of our mindfulness practices and could now make them available in your local areas."

"That is very inspiring," a participant says. "How would we do that?"

"When you return home," Baba says, "you could start a group like this one."

Julia appreciates how this simple practice has been beneficial to her, and there are several people she knows, and thousands she doesn't, who might benefit as well.

Returning home to Long Beach, a seaside village on the Bay of Fundy, Julia and Tara look for a place to rent for their nonexistent group. An abandoned, two-storey garage on Main Street is in pretty good shape having survived a hundred years of pleasant summers and brutal winters. A double-width garage door with stacked horizontal windows opens directly onto the Main Street sidewalk, though with a raised curb in front of the building, it doesn't appear to have ever been used as a garage. A power wash and several gallons of paint would restore its humble elegance.

"There's a For Sale sign in that window," Julia points out, "but it's so faded you can hardly read the phone number."

"Try it anyway," Tara says. "You never know."

Surprisingly, a real estate agent answers. Twenty minutes later, they are standing inside the garage.

The agent glances around. "It's definitely a fixer upper. Originally it was a general store, and then a carpenter's workshop. After his death thirty years ago, the place was abandoned."

The original oak plank floor is in excellent condition, with areas that have been painted in odd patches of random colors. But with sanding and refinishing, it will glow in the diffused light from the garage door windows. The large space would be ideal for meditation and yoga groups, and with a few partitions a reception area could be created.

"Neighbors say they've seen people who have broken in here occasionally," the agent says. "It's dark inside with the power off. No one has been able to identify them."

A kitchen area and bathroom occupy the back half of the second floor, the front half an undefined open area with two small, arched windows that overlook the street, all of it easily upgraded with a few, probably several more, gallons of paint. Julia turns to the real estate agent.

"I'll take it," she says.

A bumblebee buzzes and bangs itself repeatedly against a windowpane. Julia will have to see if she can reopen the window, sealed shut by decades of repainting. The buzzing sound amplifies as if a thousand bees have joined in. She rescues the hapless bee trapped on the window using a Mason jar and a piece of paper and goes outside to release it. She checks under the windowsills and eaves where hornets' nests are often found, and finds nothing, except some decayed wood that seems to have once framed a small flower bed. The buzzing sound fades away. There is dead silence.

Back inside the garage she finds the whole interior has changed, as if she has walked into a movie set of an old workshop where everything has been painted gray. Many items, not here when she went out outside, have somehow appeared—a gray sawhorse, a gray table saw and planer, various gray hand tools and several empty bottles on a gray workbench, and, amid it all, a young girl, just standing there. Her complexion is ashen, her face and arms matching her colorless pinafore with its gray strawberries.

"Hello," Julia says. "Who are you?"

"Everyone calls me Short Twinny. My twin sister is taller than me. She's Tall Twinny."

"Where is she?"

Short Twinny points toward the window.

"She's right there."

Tall Twinny sits on the workbench painting the windowsill.

"Who are you?" she asks Julia.

"I'm Julia. I just bought this old garage."

"This is a workshop." Tall Twinny corrects her.

"Well, it used to be a workshop, but I plan to make it something else. Why did you girls come in here?"

"To work in the bee hospital," Short Twinny says.

Julia hears that buzzing sound again, quickly getting louder. Tall Twinny becomes agitated, frantically waving her arms as the buzzing volume increases.

"Twinny!" Short Twinny screams. "We have to go!"

Julia turns toward Short Twinny, who is no longer there. She turns back toward Tall Twinny who also is no longer there. The buzzing sound fades out. The sawhorses and tools and empty bottles seem to evaporate as the gray workshop gradually shifts back into Julia's full color garage. The windowsill has been freshly painted blue.

Unnerved by the Twinnys, Julia texts Tara to come right over. Julia hears her come in, her several layers of jewelry jingling, always prepared with her protective Middle Eastern evil-eye pendant and small leather pouch stuffed with powerful gemstones and other trinkets covering all her cosmic bases.

"I've brought my smudging kit," she says, "some powdered juniper and a piece of charcoal."

"I thought you used white sage to smudge," Julia says.

"You can," Tara says, "but I prefer juniper, I hate the smell of sage. I'm not surprised it drives out negative energies, they probably can't stand it either."

She places the charcoal in a small bowl, lights and fans it until it glows. A few pinches of juniper sprinkled on the hot coal releases a burst of smoke, its ethereal, woody fragrance invoking images of mystical mountain kingdoms.

"You have to get it in all the corners," she says, carrying the bowl around the room. "It's like turning on a light in the dark."

Finally, she places the still-smoldering bowl on the freshly painted windowsill, to let the charcoal burn out. Infused with the fragrance of burning Christmas trees, the space in the garage does seem clearer, brighter, somehow.

Tara pitches in to help Julia clean out the junk that has been left behind by who-knows-who. There are a few empty wooden crates, their contents pilfered while the garage had been abandoned for all those years, and a workbench covered with random cuts and gouges, evidence that it had been well used. An old freezer lying on its side, its door flung drunkenly open, partly covers a mottled, reddish-brown stain.

"I wonder what happened here," Julia says, pondering possibilities.

Tara relaxes her extrasensory perception.

"I don't think I want to know," she says.

A voice comes from behind them, seemingly out of nowhere.

"That's sponge painting."

Julia and Tara look up from the stain. An elderly woman stands there, her skin ashen, matching the gray cardigan she wears over her gray housedress.

"I did it myself, the whole floor. Dabbed it with paint on a sponge. That patch is all that's left."

"Looks like that was quite a project," Julia says, acknowledging her effort. "My name is Julia, this is my friend, Tara."

"I'm Mrs. Cole," the woman says. "Beatrice."

She stands at a counter in what appears to be a general store, where the display cabinets and shelves and all the products on them are various shades of gray. Gray sleigh bells hanging on the front door jingle. An elegant lady comes in, her grayish complexion matching her long gray coat and boots.

"Hello, Beatrice," she says, "I've just come in to pick up a few things."

Julia and Tara look back toward Beatrice who, along with her store, has disappeared.

Taking sledgehammers to the walls and ripping out old insulation gives Julia and Tara a sense of accomplishment, adding to the pile of demolished wallboard and dried seaweed, often used for insulation in these old, coastal buildings. All this destruction has exposed a rusty old hammer and a bunch of newspapers used to supplement the seaweed. Tara sets them aside in a wooden box, a kind of time capsule.

Opening the walls exposes the toll that winter storms have taken on the structure, with dry rot damaging many of the studs. Dangerous wiring needs to be replaced, as does someone's do-it-yourself plumbing and the single-pane windows and misaligned doors that probably let in snow on blustery winter days.

"I wasn't planning on all of this," Julia says. She appreciates Tara's offer to do tarot readings and gemstone workshops that might help raise some funds, but still. "I was thinking we'd just have to do some painting and refinish the floor. But now we need carpenters, electricians, plumbers and—"

"Look at this," Tara says, interrupting her. "There's something written in pencil on this stud. 'December 14 first big snow'...on this one it says...'bee balm in bloom.'"

"Here's another one," Julia says, reading from another stud.

"What's it say?" Tara asks.

Julia shivers. "You'll take this to your grave."

Beatrice Cole stands motionless in her ransacked store silently biting her nails, watching as the diminutive Mr. Cole stomps around, grumbling and cursing, his irascible nature appropriate for his rat-like appearance, slightly hunched over, with a long, pointy nose and beady black eyes.

"Sons-of-bitches broke in here and trashed the place, probably pissed off because we don't keep any money in the cash register overnight."

Beatrice switches to her other hand, chews off a bit of jagged fingernail that keeps catching on things.

"Clean up that broken glass over by the window," Mr. Cole snarls at her. "I'll have to fix that wall over there, where the bastards ripped off the wall board and pulled out the insulation."

Beatrice doesn't know that he had hidden some newspapers in the seaweed, and that they are missing.

Early in the morning Julia goes to the garage to deal with the debris pile she and Tara had created. She picks up a broom and begins to sweep, creating a cloud of dust. She hears the swishing of another broom, looks up, sees someone, also sweeping the floor. A scruffy-handsome carpenter about her age, thirty-ish, his shirtless skin dusty gray in gray bib overalls, sweeping up broken glass that had shattered on his workshop floor.

"Hello," Julia says.

He acknowledges her with a slight nod but doesn't speak.

"My name is Julia. I just thought I'd clean the place up a bit."

"Thanks," he says.

His smile seems genuine but not without some effort, as if smiling were difficult for him. He continues sweeping the glass, experiencing every sharp-edged, scratching sound as if his own skin is being scratched and cut. He has been amused by this odd synesthesia before, like the time a shiny black crow flew past the window, and he simultaneously tasted licorice. But this time, it is painful.

"I appreciate your help," Julia says, "but...I don't even know your name."

A delivery truck with building supplies pulls up in front of the garage.

"Jackson," he says.

Julia looks back toward the delivery truck, which has already gone. She turns toward Jackson, who is no longer there. Several sheets of new wallboard lean against the old, exposed studs.

The Coles had shifted from merchants to landlords when they closed their store and rented the space to Jackson for his workshop. Mr. Cole never cared much for Jackson, too quiet, mysterious, probably secretly plotting something. He hated the renovations Jackson made to his building, replacing the single-entry door with a large garage-type door. The building would never be a garage, and he thinks the doors just looked goddamned foolish.

Now that the walls have been opened and the old insulation removed, carpenters arrive to frame in partitions for a reception area at the back. The rest of the floor will be good for office space and storage.

Then there is updating the plumbing for the existing upstairs kitchen and bathroom. This should be fairly straightforward, but when the plumbers run a camera through the old, original pipes, they find they are cracked and leaking, and needing to be replaced. This will involve a major excavation since the pipes run under the building.

"This is getting out of hand," Julia says. "My dream didn't

include bankruptcy. I might have to pull the plug on this place, just sell it as is."

A couple guys from down the road with a plumbing business suggest Julia have them seal off the old sewer pipes, leave them there for future archeologists, and install new ones in trenches alongside the building. In small towns it seems everyone knows someone who can do something, even on short notice. A toy-like replica of a full-sized excavator, operated by a rotund, middle-aged man squeezed into it, arrives in the driveway. He begins digging in the area plumbers had outlined with spray paint and pulls out a few rotten boards, suddenly swinging the bucket wildly up and away from the building to avoid hitting two young girls standing there. They are dressed alike, in all-gray pinafores with gray strawberries, and seem to be covered in gray dust.

"Our bee garden's ruined," the shorter one says.

From: Mountain Retreat Centre

Exciting plans for next Spring!

We are pleased and excited to announce our very first Spring Coast-to-Coast Travel Schedule for Baba Ganouj, who will be making stops in various locations to give public presentations. For local groups interested in hosting Baba and his two attendants, please reply. We will be happy to work with you to create a truly auspicious event in your community.

"Have you seen this email?" Tara pushes her phone into Julia's face. "Can we do this?"

"Wow," Julia says, after reading it. "That would be incredible."

Tara rummages through her multicolored jute bag with sequined elephants, trunks up.

"Here it is," she says, breathlessly. "Take a card."

"Take a card? This is how you do a tarot reading?"

"It's my emergency version, remarkably accurate."

Julia smiles, takes a card. "Four of Cups."

"Opportunity," Tara says, "not to be missed!"

With electrical and plumbing and drywall completed, Julia explores her new spaces with understated excitement. She plugs in an electric sander, begins removing decades worth of dirt and discoloration, gradually exposing the beautiful oak floor.

"There goes the last of my sponge painting," Beatrice says, just standing there, no longer in her store, but in Julia's new space, gray hands on her gray house-dressed hips.

Julia stops sanding and lifts her dust mask.

"I just want to expose this beautiful floor," she says.

"I liked the sponge painting better," Beatrice says. "Puts me in mind of better times."

"Better times?"

"Before Jackson went crazy."

"Jackson went crazy?"

"After the Twinnys. Found them right over there under that window. Loved his sister's twins as if they were his own, so sweet, so curious, fascinated by everything. Always helped them with their usually short-lived whims.

"You said he went crazy...?"

"Got all quiet, never talked about it. Started avoiding people, even his friends. Stopped answering the phone, lost his business because of it. Got killed when he accidentally banged his head and bled out, right there." She points at a once gaily colored, painted spot on the floor. "I tried to cover over the stain."

The oak floor, released from decades of suffocation by paint and grime, glows as if illuminated from within. Julia has one last patch to do, the colorful area where Beatrice, who is nowhere to be seen, says Jackson died. Newer, thicker paint clogs the sandpaper. Even Julia's dust mask gets clogged. She tosses it aside.

As she moves the sander slowly over the stain, a rust-colored dust rises from the floor, settles onto the workbench, her clothes, the walls, infusing the air with particles of Jackson's blood, dried and preserved, that Julia inhales, tastes. The sander makes a strange, moaning sound. She pulls the plug, the sound of moaning now mixed with sobbing. Jackson kneels on the floor, stroking his gray arms and chest in a futile attempt to soothe the pain of a punishment he believes he deserves, the unbearable burning sensation of his skin being sanded off.

Just after midnight, a dull thud startles Julia awake. When she opens her eyes, a shadow appears among the partitions, a dark, translucent silhouette of a person, just standing there.

"Tara...is that you?"

The shadowy figure turns and moves away. Julia gets out of bed, slips on her housecoat, and moves toward it. A Jesus nightlight is turned on, but even though his light is getting dimmer, he is still able to illuminate a woman sitting on a chair that she has placed next to the kitchen door.

"Can I help you?" Julia asks.

"Warmer here," the woman says, looking at her ashen hands, folded, resting on her lap.

She looks older than her actual age of mid-thirty something, her lifeless face drawn, expressionless. A gray, calf-length Melton cloth coat meets the tops of her calf-high winter boots.

"Who are you?" Julia asks.

"Beth," she says, then stands and without opening the kitchen door, leaves through it. Julia follows her into the stairwell that connects her apartment to the main floor downstairs. A few steps down, she hears voices in the garage, hesitates, camouflaged by all the construction materials.

"I curse every miserable breath you take!" Beth yells. "It's all your fault!"

The accusation hangs unchallenged for a few moments, until a softer, deeper voice responds. "I know."

Julia peeks into the garage, now looking less like a construction site, more like a workshop. Jackson sweeps up shards of glass, wincing from the very real sensation of his flesh being cut.

Beth, red-faced, breathing rapidly, jabs an index finger into Jackson's chest.

"You killed my daughters," she screams, sobbing uncontrollably, "letting them use your workshop for their bee nonsense."

"I didn't see any harm in it," Jackson says, "how was I to know?"

"Well, you should have known," Beth screams, grabs a hammer from the workbench and pounds it into Jackson's forehead.

Jackson crumples to the floor. Beth stands, legs spread like a western gunfighter, watching the red pool spread silently across the floor, undistracted, until the rat-like Mr. Cole slinks in. Their eyes meet. Beth places the bloody hammer on the workbench, turns, casually walks out the back door.

Mr. Cole picks up the hammer, wipes some blood from it onto a sharp corner of the workbench. And then, as it would be beneficial for Beth and lucrative for him, drops the hammer into an opening where the wallboard doesn't meet the ceiling, hears it drop all the way to the bottom inside the wall. The workshop fades away.

Julia is left standing in her construction site, in the middle of the night, in her housecoat.

Julia texts Tara, "Bring smudging kit." She wonders if the lovely evergreen fragrance is attracting, rather than repelling, these gray people.

Her smudging completed, Tara reaches under the workbench, pulls out the wooden box with the rusty hammer and the newspapers that are in surprisingly good condition. As she flips through a few pages, twenty- and fifty-dollar bills begin falling out.

"This was not insulation," she says. "There are several thousand dollars here. Who puts cash in a bunch of newspapers and buries it in a pile of seaweed?"

Julia glances at the papers. One headline jumps out at her.

## FOUL PLAY RULED OUT IN WOODWORKER DEATH

A public inquest into the circumstances of the death of Long Beach woodworker, Jackson Wolfe, concluded the death was accidental. Mr. Cole, his landlord, described finding Mr. Wolfe on his workshop floor after he had fallen and hit his head on some woodworking equipment.

"Tara," Julia says, "let me see that hammer."

"I don't like touching it," Tara says. "Something creepy about it."

"I think I know why," Julia says, tells her about the horrifying scene she had witnessed, or thought she had witnessed.

But she *had* seen Mr. Cole drop a blood-soaked hammer into the wall.

"We should take this to the police," Tara says.

"And tell them I saw a ghost commit a murder thirty years ago?"

"Then pass me the hammer."

Tara winces when Julia places it in her hand.

"I'll smudge it," she says.

Mr. Cole needs to find the newspapers that are missing, thanks to the bastards who trashed his walls. He had installed that seaweed insulation after Jackson died. He told investigators everything he saw, except one detail deliberately left out, forcing Beth to water his continuously blossoming money tree. At least until her inheritance ran out. Kept her out of federal prison. Win-win.

A package from Mountain Retreat Centre arrives in the mail, full-color glossy posters for the visit of Baba Ganouj, with space at the bottom for individual groups to fill in their times, places and dates. The wooden telephone poles on Main Street have long been used as a kind of community bulletin board, with thousands of staples left there from posters advertising yard sales, political rallies, and lost pets. Julia and Tara remove any shabby, out-of-date posters still hanging on. Their colorful posters, placed at eye level around every pole along Main Street, create the impression that something big is about to happen.

"Who are all these people?" Beatrice wonders.

Her store has been overtaken by several rows of people sitting on matching cushions. Some are wearing loose clothing that is unflattering but looks comfortable from Beatrice's girdled point of view. A few people sit on chairs lined up behind the cushions. Most wear exotic jewelry with beads and trinkets from someplace where even the men wear strings of beads around their wrists. Mr. Cole harrumphs when he sees this, scurries into the kitchen to sniff around the sweet and savory delicacies people have brought for the potluck celebration afterwards.

Tara enters the meditation room carrying a brass bowl with a smoldering mound of powdered juniper. Sunlight pours through the garage door windows, through the evergreen-fragranced smoke, creating an immersive, otherworldly environment. Julia escorts Baba Ganouj into the hall and introduces him. She sees that some of her contractors have shown up, some to support her, some out of curiosity. On the end of the row of chairs, conspicuous by their grayness and the occasional faint buzzing of bees, the Twinnys sit quietly.

Standing in a corner behind the people seated in chairs, his eyes lowered, looking at the floor, Julia is startled to see Jackson. He pays close attention as Baba talks about how we all create our own personal worlds and then believe in them.

"We could be suffocated by the thick dust of false beliefs," Baba says, "or we could see the dust for what it is."

Jackson raises his head. His eyes widen.

"Could someone open that big door?" Baba asks.

One of Julia's contractors activates the garage door. Sunlight streams into the room.

Short Twinny gasps. "Let's go out there," she whispers to Tall Twinny. "We haven't been outside in a while."

As they approach the door, patches of gray dust begin disappearing from their pinafores, their gray strawberries ripening to a vibrant, juicy red on a sunny yellow background. Color returns to their faces and arms, the sound of bees fades away.

"C'mon, Uncle Jax," Tall Twinny calls to him.

"C'mon, Uncle Jax," Short Twinny echoes.

Jackson ignores his tendency to stay in the background, strides toward the door. Gray dust falls from his overalls, from his arms and chest still tanned by sunny summer days, and from his tousled, sandy hair. Approaching the open doorway, he hesitates, turns toward Julia. His smile is genuine and unashamed and beautiful.

# Amanda Capper

**Amanda Capper** is the author of *A Bother of Bodies* (as A. J. Capper) and her short stories can be found in *Every Day Fiction*, *Painted Words*, and *The Algomian*. When she is not reading, writing, or roaming the woods, she volunteers at the Royal Canadian Legion Branch 25 as their treasurer. She is a member of Sisters in Crime and the Short Mystery Fiction Society.

Find her at www.amandacapper.com.

# A Time to Tell

## Amanda Capper

I started collecting secrets when I was six. Not by design. More by the unfortunate circumstance of being a sickly, solitary child, cursed with curiosity. I hovered in doorways, or stared out windows, and was always startled when someone noticed I was in the room. I had, at one time, concluded I was invisible and that was okay. Good even, because I saw things. I knew things.

I know what happened to the cook's cat. I had proof of Father's stolen wallet, and as far as Mother's engagement ring disappearing, I did find a slip of paper that could explain.

Secrets wouldn't be secrets if they were spoken. There wasn't much to tell in my small world, and no one would be interested in listening. There was Cook (too busy), Madeline, the maid, four years my senior (far too superior to chat with a child), a couple kitchen girls whose names I never learn because they don't stay long, and Robert, who lives above the garage. Robert had served under Father during the war and was now our hired hand. Robert reminds me more of a devoted bulldog. Where there is Father, there is Robert.

So, secrets are easy to keep. Until the one that wasn't. But I am writing this out of sequence. Let me begin again.

For my eighth birthday, December 31, 1948, I had asked for, and received, a pair of binoculars. Father wasn't affectionate but he was generous, and being an only child, I was indulged. I also think he was intrigued to see how they worked, but soon lost interest, whereas I never did. For the next four years they were forever around my neck.

It was a relief when Mother broke her neck. There was less shouting. Less demands and criticism. The crystal remained intact. It was an effort to appear grief-stricken when the constable showed up. The servants didn't even bother to try.

Again, I digress. I'm finding it difficult to set this secret free. I'll try again.

From our attic, and with my new present, I could see the world. The church, the graveyard, the school I longed to attend. And the lovely little house where the Barnswolds lived, abutting our estate. Every morning except for Sundays, I would watch as Mr. Barnswold squeezed his large bulk into an old, rusty Ford and leave for the local penitentiary where he worked as a guard. Then I would turn my attention to Mrs. Barnswold.

She would hang her laundry on Tuesdays, tend to her gardens on Wednesdays, do her shopping on Fridays, and entertain her lady friends at teatime on Saturdays. Mondays and Thursdays she entertained my father.

Mother was still alive at this time. I'm not sure how long she knew about her husband and Mrs. Barnswold, but one lovely spring morning, a Thursday, I stood at the bottom of the back stairs and listened as Mother called the penitentiary. She demanded to speak to Mr. Barnswold citing a medical emergency concerning his wife. When the receiver clicked back onto its cradle Mother headed straight for the front parlour where she'd be able to see Mr. Barnswold's car pull into his driveway. She didn't notice me at all.

I was conflicted at the time about what to do as my mother set up my father for what would be, at the very least, a severe beating from an angry husband. But when I saw my mother's face, with its eager delight and slightly malicious smile, the decision came quickly. I hurried to my father's study, spent agonizing minutes finding what I needed, then ran through the back gardens (so Mother wouldn't see me).

Mr. Barnswold's car was already in their driveway. I was too late! I peeked into their kitchen window and saw my father standing rigid, bare-chested and unhurt, against the kitchen wall. I ducked away immediately for fear of being caught but didn't look away for long. Cursed with curiosity.

Mrs. Barnswold stood in a doorway, her long hair loose and untidy and her arms folded across her chest in a defensive-type stance that also helped to keep her dressing gown closed. Mr. Barnswold lounged in a kitchen chair, cigarette in hand, and was obviously the most relaxed of the three. I couldn't hear what was being said but I was poised to act, to barge in and hand my father his gun if there was even a hint he would need it. But the hint never appeared. Mrs. Barnswold turned and left the room, dismissed apparently, by her husband. My father's demeanor then eased. His forehead, previously creased in either concern or confusion, smoothed as he nodded at whatever Mr. Barnswold had to say. And Mr. Barnswold had a lot to say. Eventually the two men sat at the kitchen table and shared from a bottle Mr. Barnswold pulled from his coat pocket.

I walked back home. Wandered between rooms but the house seemed empty. Mother must have sent the servants away. A bad omen. A bad omen, indeed.

I finally found Mother in one of the second-floor guest rooms, standing by the window and thought, very briefly and rather wickedly, about informing her of a better view of the Barnswold's house from the attic.

"Are you all right, Mother?" I asked.

She gasped, turning so swiftly she stumbled. "You. What do you want?"

Not waiting for a response, she spun back to the window.

"Always skulking around, you frightened me. Go to your room, immediately. Your father and I have things to discuss."

We both turned when we heard the front door open. Mother hurried past me, but I stayed where I was, nervous of what would, no doubt, be an ugly scene.

I heard her voice, shrill and harsh, before Father even closed the door.

"He didn't kill you. He didn't even beat you."

My father closed the door. His reply was steady. "It was you, then, that called Henry?"

"Of course it was me, you fool. It was time he knew." I could hear my mother's dress rustle as she moved, probably circling my father like he was prey. "Knew how his cow of a wife was whoring while he worked to support her. I bet he doesn't see a penny of what you give her." The rustling stopped. "How much does it cost you, Michael, to bed the slut?"

"Up until now, not a penny, Andrea."

"It's love then is it, Michael? Oh, give me strength. You're totally incapable of eliciting love. You haven't the passion of a guppy."

I waited for my father to defend himself, but he was silent. Mother, however, was just getting started. "Why? Why are you not hospitalized? Are all men spineless?"

I heard the front door reopen and my father say, "I think it was damn brave of me to stay with you for as long as I have."

My mother screamed incomprehensible words, but I had listened long enough. I left the guest room and headed for my attic sanctuary. From there I heard the sharp, high-heeled steps of my mother as she entered her bedroom and slammed the door. From my window I saw Father leave in his car. I didn't see him return.

I rarely saw my mother and father in the same room after that episode. My father continued his association with Mrs. Barnswold. Mr. Barnswold also kept his regular schedule, though I noticed he was returning later and later Mondays and Thursdays, to the point where he didn't come home at all on those days. Very strange, I thought at the time. Very accommodating.

Mother decided to punish my father with the silent treatment but when it became apparent to her that this was more of a relief to him then a rebuke, she grew increasingly morose. Wore nothing but black. Mourning black, with a veil.

Scared me to bits but didn't seem to bother Father in the least.

This lasted for two weeks when, suddenly, she reversed. One Monday afternoon Mother came out of her room dressed gaily in pinks and yellow, her hair styled, and a smile on her lips. She called for Robert to bring the car around and drove off to no one knew where. When she returned two hours later, she sailed into the house still smiling and even gifted me with a small pat on my shoulder as she passed me on the stairs. I was stunned.

After her fourth trip in two weeks, I decided it was time to investigate. A new secret was obviously in the making.

I entered Mother's room using the spare keys Father kept in his desk and opened the French doors, so I'd hear when the car returned. I expected to find letters from a man stashed away in her writing desk. A lover. It seemed the obvious choice for revenge.

Instead, at the last moment, I found four small boxes of Fowler's Solution, hidden deep in a cedar chest among her winter dresses.

I sat on the chest and thought about my find. Why would Mother be hoarding Fowler's Solution? It had been prescribed to me for my asthma, but I knew the uses of the treatment were many. Mr. Hansen, our very charming and slightly flirtatious pharmacist, had also mentioned it was found to help with Malaria and eczema...and then I remembered.

And then I knew.

I heard the car pull up to the house. Left the boxes in the chest and ran. I went to sit in my father's study to wait for his return.

Father was surprised to find me there. "What are you doing in here, girl? You know this room is off limits." He said this without malice. I even dared think there was a morsel of affection in his words.

But I still hesitated before I spoke my concerns. This was, after all, a strange and momentous occasion. Not only was I about to accuse my mother of contemplating murder, alone an unthinkable act, but I was also, for the first time in my life, about to destroy most of my precious secrets. Once I spoke the words out loud, they would be no more. Worse yet, no one would recognize my sacrifice. My collection of secrets was a secret unto itself.

I started talking for fear of losing my resolve and got right to the point. "Mother is stashing arsenic, Father. Boxes of it. I can't believe it's for anything good."

He sat behind his desk, looking mildly amused, and studied my face. "That's a very serious accusation, Rebecca. How would you even know what arsenic looks like?"

"I don't. But I know it's an ingredient in Fowler's Solution. I take it for my asthma."

Now he looked confused, and I realized, rather unhappily, that he probably had no idea of my illnesses. "The solution contains only a small amount of arsenic," I continued, "but I'm sure Mother could get higher doses if she were to ask..." I paused deliberately, *"Mr. Hansen"* putting emphasis on the name. Then kept my eyes on my father and waited.

He was quiet. Looked at me as if he had only just met me, then asked, "Do you honestly think your mother is capable of what I believe you're trying to tell me?"

I sat down, crossed my ankles and folding my hands on my lap, proceeded to part with my precious secrets. Did he know Mother hated cats? Was he aware how sad it made Cook when the cat, supposedly, ran away? I suggested he look in Mother's bedroom closet for his wallet. It still has ten quid in it. And as for Mother's engagement ring, Father should check the pawn shops, only not the local ones. She went farther afield.

He leaned toward me. "Why should I believe you? A child? With a child's imagination." He stood and coldly dismissed me. "Go to your room. We'll not speak of this again. And you will not discuss these wild accusations with anyone else either. Do you understand me, girl?"

"I do, Father. I only wanted to warn you." I walked to the door, hesitated, and turned back. "I do wish the best for you." He didn't respond.

I ran to my bedroom and daydreamed a world away from this house. A world with giggles, and friends, and no secrets at all. Eventually I fell into a restless sleep and dreamed of boxes and boxes of jars of poison, some full, some empty.

Cook's scream woke me. I waited, clutching my bedsheets, trying to figure out where the scream came from. It wasn't loud and had sounded hollow. Did I imagine it? Then my father's hurried steps passed my door and descended the stairs. I didn't move. Curious, I may be. Stupid, I am not.

Not long after I heard him return and stop at my door. He opened it and stood staring at me. Eventually he told me my mother had fallen down the cellar stairs, and to get dressed. We'd have company soon.

Company consisted of a constable with a few lads and a doctor. I wasn't privy to any of their conversations, but I still heard. Because I was invisible.

Father, his voice low with humiliation, explained to the constable that his wife was fully dressed because she was keeping strange hours the last few days, he believed, with an unknown lover. He had no idea when she arrived home or how. The doctor concluded that Mother had broken her neck after falling down the cellar stairs, and the Constable agreed. Mother's high heels, and the smell of whiskey on her clothes, had obviously contributed to her accident. No one seemed to wonder what Mother was doing anywhere near the cellar, especially after dark. I doubt she even knew we had a cellar. But no questions were asked.

It's been relatively quiet in the four years since. There are less secrets to collect these days. I find myself more of a keeper than a collector. Mrs. Barnswold still lives next door, though Mr. Barnswold, with his brand-new Ford and his brand-new luggage, moved out of town. Father frequently visits Mrs. Barnswold, though I have yet to meet her. I am often alone in the house, except for Cook and Madeline, the maid.

And Robert. Remember Robert? He still drives me about town, but now believes he may, one day, be master of all. I think Father has made him a promise. Or owes him a debt.

So, we'll see. I am neither as meek nor as obedient these days as both Robert and Father seem to think. After all, I am the daughter of a woman who conspired to murder, and a man who brought one about.

I have kept none of my mother's possessions, other than the cedar chest I keep in the attic with all its hidden little boxes. From what I've seen of husbands, I thought it best. Just another secret, only this time, one of my own.

# Linda Bennett

**Linda Bennett** is an author and freelance editor. Having lived in South Africa, New Zealand, and the UK, she brings a global perspective to her writing.

Linda holds an MA in Creative Writing and is a member of Sisters in Crime International and the New Zealand Society of Authors. She has written non-fiction for *Learning Media*, had work published in *Turbine*, and was a contributing writer to the 2014 Kiwi short story collection *Sweet As*. In 2017, Linda was one of two writers awarded NZSA / Hachette Australia mentorships.

Linda, based now in rural Herefordshire, is working on a psychological suspense novel.

Find her at https://finelineeditservices.com/.

# The Artist

## Linda Bennett

Saturday afternoon and Nick tells Michael it's time to take the new guy out with the crew.

Michael shrugs. Sure, he'll do it—Nick's the boss—but Michael's not a fan of the new guy. He thinks Frankie's too cocky, with a mouth on him that's going to get him in trouble one day, and even though he's mid-twenties, he seems like an overgrown kid, all stupid jokes and dumb backwards baseball caps.

But the rest of the crew like him. Even Nick likes him, reckons he's got finger skills second to none. Michael frowns. They'd first spotted Frankie working single-o outside Waterloo, lifting wallets and phones. He'd got himself quite a stash by the time Nick and Michael cornered him behind some rubbish bins.

"This is our territory," Nick had said, giving him a hard stare. "Either shove off and go do your thing somewhere else—or we'll give you a trial, see if you're a good fit for us. But if you muck it up..."

Frankie, who told them he'd been living rough for a couple of months, jumped at the chance. Now he's sleeping on Nick's floor, making himself useful and not complaining about the grub. Nick's a good boss, but they all know he can't even boil water.

Now Michael parks Frankie outside a Costa and tells him to keep his distance. "Circle round and watch. You know who's who?"

Frankie nods. "Tank's the stall, you're the mechanic, Cal's the shade and I'm—"

"The learner." Michael gives him a withering look. "You're not hands on yet. Got it?"

"Got it," Frankie says, grinning and giving Michael a two-finger salute, like they're in the army or something. "You're the boss, boss."

The street is dense and busy, the way Michael likes it. He scans the crowd for a mark, checking and discarding with ease born of long practice.

Old Asian lady? No.

Middle-aged guy in trainers? No.

A couple of young mums with small children—maybe. One of the babies is squirming in a fancy pushchair, red-faced and tearful. Both women are wrangling baby gear and bags and look exhausted.

Perfect.

Michael gives Tank the nod. Tank steps forward and stumbles as he passes the women, bumping the blonde off balance. Tank's a great stall with perfect timing. The blonde tries to catch herself but lurches into her friend with the pushchair. Their bags cascade across the ground and a baby bottle rolls into the gutter.

"Whoops!" Michael is so close behind them that he nearly steps on a Browns Fashion bag. His voice is soft and soothing. "Steady on, ladies. Here, let me help." He hunkers down, easing into position as the women grab at their things. He's super helpful and within seconds, their phones and wallets are in his pocket. He hands the baby's bottle to the blonde.

"That'll need a wash, I reckon."

She nods, hovering between annoyed and grateful. Michael dusts his hands off and keeps walking, checking out of the corner of his eye for Frankie.

The kid's nowhere to be seen.

"So where were you?" Detective Sergeant Leonard has summoned Frankie for an update, wants to know what's happening. It's late, nearly midnight and the feeble light inside the DS's patrol vehicle makes him look old and tired.

"I ducked, dude." Frankie wrinkles his nose. The patrol car smells of sweaty cop and stale cigarette smoke. "Minute I saw those girls, I ducked. I knew them, both of them."

"From where?"

"Around. Clubs and stuff. Whatever, man, it doesn't matter. But if they'd seen me with the crew... Anyway, I nipped off for a bit."

"What did you tell Michael?"

"Aw." Frankie grimaces. "I told him I got bored, and I told him they were doing it wrong." He rolls his shoulders. "And it's the truth. Their techniques—I mean, what are they thinking?"

DS Leonard scowls. "It's not your job to change the way they work."

'I know, but seriously. It's like watching a herd of elephants crashing around."

"OK," the DS says. "But—"

"I don't work like that," Frankie says. "The way I work is art, man. I'm an artist."

"You're a thief." DS Leonard shifts his bulk on the seat. "Don't blow this, okay? You're damn lucky it was me that caught you. Another cop would have thrown your arse in jail."

"I won't. Hey, is this yours?" He holds up an iPhone. DS Leonard reaches into his pocket and rolls his eyes when he finds it empty.

"Give that back and get out of here."

Frankie laughs and hops out the car. "Art, man."

The following Saturday they're back at the pitch. This time, Michael wants him closer to the action, so Frankie pulls his cap down and stays in tight. They pull the wallets off a small group of men in dark jackets, they lift a couple of phones, and it's all going well. Then Frankie sees Michael give Tank the eye. Coming toward them is a woman in sunglasses with a big handbag swinging at her side. Before Frankie can do or say anything, Tank's moving into it, bumping her off balance, setting the con in motion.

But something's wrong. Frankie scans the street and instantly spots two undercovers eyeballing the woman. He looks again—it's the blonde from last weekend.

Aw, crap.

It's a setup. Must be. But it can't be DS Leonard—they're nowhere near ready to go yet.

Michael goes into his kneeling down *let-me-help-you* number, and the woman's phone and wallet disappear inside his jacket. He stands up, dusting his hands, smiling. The undercovers are walking faster now.

Frankie stops thinking and starts moving. He slides past Michael, his hands drifting like birds, and then he's got the wallet and the phone, safe and sound. He keeps walking, doesn't look back, doesn't turn around, not even when a commotion erupts behind him and the two undercovers whip past at top speed.

A block away, he spots a boy, early teens, the kind who'd be keen to earn a few pounds. He makes the deal, sends the boy back to where Michael is still protesting his innocence while the woman yells and points.

Michael is livid. Not only did he have to deal with the cops trying to bust him, but to make it worse, the new guy—the damn kid!—is the one who saved him. When the cops made him turn out his pockets, he was shocked to find them empty. He hadn't felt Frankie make the lift, hadn't even seen him go by. And then a young boy runs up, holding the stuff—his lift!—saying he'd found these on the pavement, were they hers?

Now Nick has them both on the carpet. Michael clenches his fists. He'd like to smash something, or someone, very soon.

"Frankie," Nick says, narrowing his eyes. "How did you know it was a setup?"

The kid is leaning back, hands behind his head, legs splayed. Like he owns the place.

"I recognized her," he says. "She was dressed different, but she was one of the hits from last Saturday. When I saw her back again—man, it just smelled wrong."

Michael says nothing. The woman hadn't looked even vaguely familiar to him. His heart sinks. He knows Nick, knows his style. Nick likes people who are quick and on their game. Until the damn kid showed up, that was Michael. But now maybe it's not.

Nick tells them there'll be a showdown. Michael versus Frankie. Winner will be mechanic going forward.

"No."

Michael looks up. What? What is the kid saying?

"No," Frankie says again. "I don't want to go up against Michael. I've shown you what I can do against him—he didn't even feel my lift." Everyone is looking at him now. "I want to go up against *you.*" And he nods at Nick.

Three days later and the crew is on the street again, but this time it's the Nick and Frankie show. The guys have bets riding on the outcome. Nick picks first and sends Frankie to a girl sitting on her own outside a café.

"Watch and phone," he says. Some of the guys smirk. The girl's in a sleeveless sundress with a thin gold watch on her left wrist. There's a bag at her feet and she's reading a book. No phone in sight.

"No problem," Frankie says. He can do this in his sleep but today it doesn't really matter how well or badly he works. His lift is not the one that matters—it's the lift he's going to get Nick to make that really counts.

Just you wait, mate. Just you wait...

He holds back until there's a crowd pushing by, then moves in. He uses the did-you-see-that-guy technique and within moments, the girl's bag is up on the table and she's scrabbling through it. Everything's there, she says, relieved. He smiles, helps her put the bag back down at her feet. With her phone in his pocket, he goes for the watch.

"Thank you so much," she says, accepting his handshake. "That was so kind of you. You can't trust anyone these days."

Doesn't he just know it? Her skin is cool beneath his fingers and the clasp slides apart easily. He gives her a flirty smile and then he's gone.

The guys give him a slow clap when he shows them the goods.

"One minute, sixteen seconds. Damn, brother, that's fine work." Tank is wide-eyed. Frankie's heard that Tank has dreams of moving from stall to mechanic, but he's got big, meaty fists, so it's probably not going to happen. Michael, still refusing to be impressed, just glares at him.

Now it's Nick's turn. Frankie scans and finds DS Leonard's mark at the ATM, stuffing an envelope with cash.

"That woman in the red scarf," he tells Nick. "Wallet and phone."

"Nah, too easy. See that tall guy behind her? He's just put an envelope of cash in his inside pocket. I might even split the dough with you."

Frankie shrugs, but inwardly he's pumping high five. He nods. "And the phone," he says, striving for cool.

"Sure," Nick says and strolls off. Frankie drifts forward, the guys hot on his heels. Tank's running the timer, they're all watching Nick closely.

Nick moves in. Frankie is impressed by how smooth Nick is. He moves alongside the mark and lifts the envelope within thirty seconds, the phone a few moments later.

"Fifty-six seconds." Michael's grin is broad, radiating triumph as Nick performs a theatrical bow. "You lose, Frankie boy."

Frankie shrugs, but his heart rate is escalating. Two breaths later, the crew are hemmed in by cops. DS Trish, still wearing her red scarf, flashes her badge and whips out handcuffs. While she's still reading them their rights, Frankie melts away into the crowd.

"Excellent job," DS Leonard says the next night. They're sitting outside a McDonald's this time. "A clean collar, well done."

"Art." Frankie throws him a grin.

"I'm grateful." DS Leonard nods. "And you're good, I'll give you that. In fact, if you like, I can hook you up with another crew." He takes a bite of his cheeseburger. "My guys this time. Now we've got rid of Nick's lot, we get our territory back again."

"What?" Frankie stares at the DS, who shrugs and wipes his mouth.

"So I make a bit on the side. Who doesn't, these days? You in, boy?"

"You're asking me to join a crew *you* run? Pick pockets—steal— for *you*?"

"That's a bit blunt, but yes."

"Wow," Frankie says. "You're not worried I might tell your cop buddies about this?"

DS Leonard shakes his head. "Who you gonna tell? Trish and Don are with me."

"Wow." Frankie removes an iPhone from his pocket and holds it up.

DS Leonard laughs. "You're not catching me like that again—"

"No, I'm not." Frankie stands. "This is a recording of you solic- iting me to become part of a criminal enterprise."

DS Leonard laughs, then stops in disbelief as Frankie produces handcuffs out of thin air and snaps them onto his wrists.

"What—" he begins, but Frankie cuts him off.

"You have the right to remain silent," he says, then reels off the rest of the caution as DS Leonard listens, open-mouthed. Frankie takes the cheeseburger out of the DS's hand and drops it in the bin. He smiles.

"When the mark—that's *you*—doesn't see the anti-corruption cop —that's *me*—coming, it's true art."

# donalee Moulton

**donalee Moulton's** first mystery *Hung Out to Die* was published in 2023. *Conflagration!* (2024) won the Daphne du Maurier Award for Historical Fiction. *Bind* and *Melt*, both published in 2025, are the first in a new series, the Lotus Detective Agency. donalee has numerous short stories in anthologies and magazines. Two were shortlisted in 2024 for a Derringer Award and an Award of Excellence. donalee is a member of the Crime Writers of Canada, Sisters in Crime, the Short Mystery Fiction Society, The Writers' Union of Canada and, wait for it, the League of Canadian Poets.

Find her at www.donaleemoulton.com.

# Maladaptives Anonymous

### donalee Moulton

Marla Porter is a life coach. I don't know what a life coach is, but it clearly makes Marla happy. She's on minute seven of describing how she helps people find purpose, enhance creativity, manage stress, and...

To be frank, I've stopped listening. While Marla continues unabated, I check the exits, the crowd, and the outside activity. It's what I was trained to do as a cop. I'm no longer a cop, but the training comes in handy as a private detective and during moments of boredom.

Marla takes a second to inhale. It's my cue. "Something tells me we're not here to chat about the joys of life coaching."

It's not a rebuke, and my tone makes that clear. Still, Marla abruptly stops mid-syllable. Her head drops. Shoulders round. I give her a minute. People don't reach out to a private detective because they have pleasantries they want to share. Marla reaches for her coffee, takes a quiet sip, and exhales more slowly.

"I think a client of mine is missing. Brian Cormier."

"What makes you think he's missing?"

"We had a scheduled appointment. Brian didn't show up for it, and he didn't answer any of my messages. I thought I'd see him at our weekly group. Mindful Matters. He always comes."

He didn't this time. According to Marla, Brian has his own business as an accountant who specializes in Canada-U.S. tax. It's not tax season, so Brian has a lot of free time on his hands. That's part of the problem.

"Brian finds it difficult to be present. He has a mild form of what health professionals call maladaptive daydreaming. We're working on this in our sessions and in group. I'm worried Brian may have given in to his daydreams."

"What does that mean?"

Apparently anything from running naked down the streets of Pamplona in search of a bull to sailing around the world solo in a forty-foot sloop to finding a cure for foreign accent syndrome. (I did not make that up. That is a direct quote from Marla and one of the many reasons I will not be using a life coach.)

Marla is reluctant to call the police. She doesn't want to sound a false alarm, but her gut is telling her something is wrong. I believe in the power of the gut.

Brian's condo is neat and neatly put together. Furniture, art, knickknacks are well placed to give a sense of roominess without sparseness, style without discomfort. I assume this reflects the man, and perhaps the man's profession.

The super let me in. He really shouldn't, but I've found when you ask nicely and make it clear the situation could be very serious, rules and people bend. I promised to be out in fifteen minutes. I have seven minutes left. Here's what I've found so far: nothing.

I've checked inside drawers and cabinets, under the couch and the bed, in closets and vents. Zip. Then again, I'm not sure what I'm looking for. The bookshelf holds my attention the longest, and I don't know why. There are three deep shelves, and the books on each shelf are contained by bookends that resemble peepholes, made using a piece of Plexiglas about the size of a standard piece of paper with a hole at the top. I peek through every hole. Nothing.

There is an eclectic collection of books, everything from *Cross-Border Taxation* to *Death, Taxes, and a French Manicure* to *The B and E Book*. Fiction appears to be on the bottom shelf and tax books in the middle. How to be a master criminal takes top spot. I pull a few books out randomly, leaf through the pages, and shake them. Still nothing.

I'm missing something. And I'm sure it's right in front of me.

When I'm trying to figure something out, what often works best for me is to stop trying to figure something out. It's advice I'm taking to heart. I grab a smoothie—nothing with kale—and head to Point Pleasant Park. I've recently become interested in birds and the park is a great place, particularly for songbirds and shorebirds. I'm up to twenty-seven on my list. All with pictures. (Mind you, this does include the ever-present House Sparrow and the American Black Duck.)

I'm trying to determine if what I'm looking at is a Hairy Woodpecker or a Downy Woodpecker. I snap a pic and start scrolling through bird sites on my phone. It occurs to me I could be doing the same thing for the bookends in Brian's place. It takes me about six minutes to find what I'm looking for. The bookends are a symbol for accounting; some say it's an inside accounting joke. When placed side-by-side, the two holes resemble a double-ring binder. But only if the holes are on the bottom. Someone has moved Brian's bookends.

That's not all they've moved. I scroll through the pictures of the bookshelf. It's right there in front of me. Three books have been shelved incorrectly. Spine in, not out. Brian has had a visitor who doesn't want their visit to be known.

We're meeting in Marla's west end office, and the life coach is listening intently to my recap. Concern is etched on her face. So is something else. She may be trained to listen. I'm trained to detect lies.

"This means someone was in Brian's place who shouldn't have been." Marla has also been trained to summarize.

"It could mean a number of things. But most likely it's not good news."

"What do we do now?"

"I need to talk to people who know Brian. You need to tell me what you're holding back."

Marla's mouth makes a neatly formed O. Her eyebrows rise to meet the top of her forehead. Her pupils dilate. She gets up from her chair and goes to a locked filing cabinet to her right. When she returns, she's holding a thick green journal with metal binding and a zip bookmark. It looks well worn.

Marla holds the notebook to her chest. Both hands over it. "This is Brian's journal. It should be private."

I've been here before. The reluctance to share secrets because they are not yours to share. I wait for Marla to work through her ethical dilemma. I know how it will end. She already made that decision when she took the binder out of the file cabinet. She just has to accept what she's about to do.

Marla hands me the journal. "I recommend everyone who comes to the Mindful Matters group keep a journal. It's a way to record daydreams, to acknowledge their reality and their lack of reality."

"Did this work for Brian?"

"Brian likes order. He likes rules. He wrote in his journal every day. I don't know that it helped him from daydreaming his time away."

Part one of the plan is for me to spend some time with Brian's journal, to get to know him better through his writing, and to identify anything useful or potentially ominous. Part two is to attend the weekly Mindful Matters group tomorrow morning. That poses a bit of an ethical concern for Marla, but at this point we are adroit at sidestepping those. Marla will simply welcome me to the meeting. I can decide what to say as questions and conversation arise.

I haven't yet opened Brian's journal, but I ask Marla to put into context what I will find inside.

"Brian is a complex man."

So, whatever he wrote isn't good.

I settle down after supper, Brian's journal in hand. I'm about four pages in when it becomes quite clear I will need wine. By my second glass of merlot, I have a much better sense of Brian the accountant and Brian the daydreamer. Complicated doesn't even come close.

It may be because Brian's day job requires him to play by the rules that his daydreaming is focused on breaking those rules. The accountant-by-day wants to be a villain-by-night. He has page after page filled with schemes to steal money, steal jewels, steal anything of value. Lobster, for example. To give the would-be-thief credit, many of these schemes are clever. Some might even work. Others would land the master criminal in jail in a split second.

What I don't find in the journal is an encrypted message or a repeated phrase that is a clue to the missing man's whereabouts. Nope. The journal is an honest account of the daydreams Brian has. Even now, he is playing by the rules.

I have been to numerous AA meetings as a guest of friends celebrating a sobriety birthday. Marla can call this a therapy session, a process group, a psychoeducational meeting, or whatever cool term works for life coaches. It's Daydreamers Anonymous. Or should I say, Maladaptives Anonymous.

Marla offers a quick welcome to me as a new addition to the group. She does not do this well.

I smile and nod, a mixture of relief and insecurity. I do this well. We spend twenty minutes discussing why maladaptive daydreaming is a coping mechanism, twenty minutes exploring healthier coping mechanisms, and the final third of the meeting sharing stories. Cassie and Julian are on deck. The former fantasizes about being loved in all the ways a woman can be loved, the latter a business tycoon all the other tycoons look up to.

At last, the main event—coffee and Timbits. I hover at the snack table. It's a technique I learned in the police academy. Wait for them to come to you. It's also respectful. I did not learn that at the police academy. In less than three minutes, Julian is at my side. This may be because he is the pushiest of the group or the default leader others are waiting to make the first move.

"Welcome. We're glad you came. I hope you found today helpful."

"It was certainly eye-opening."

Julian laughs. It's a deep-throated, genuine sound. I smile without pretense. "We all come with issues. You won't be judged here."

"That's good to hear.

"How do you know Marla?"

"I don't. A friend told me about the group. Brian Cormier."

Julian doesn't miss a beat. Either he has no idea what's going on or he's very good at hiding his reactions. "Brian is a regular. I thought he'd be here tonight."

"So did I. That was the plan."

Julian looks across the room and waves to Cassie, a tall woman with short brown hair. She makes her way to us and holds out a hand. "Welcome. We're glad you came." It must be the group's mantra.

"We've done that already," Julian says, and grins. "Em Montgomery meet Cassie Burke." He sees my surprise at the use of last names. "It's on the sign-in sheet."

Julian turns to Cassie. "Em is a friend of Brian's. We thought he'd be here tonight."

Cassie shakes her head. There's a look on her face I think is concern. "I haven't heard from him in days."

I wade in. "Is that unusual? You seem worried."

Cassie and Julian exchange a look. After a few awkward seconds, Julian answers my question. "It's easy to get caught up in the world inside your head. Sometimes we prefer that to the real world, so we pretend the real world doesn't exist."

"Still," Cassie says, "I can't believe I haven't heard anything from Brian. Nothing at all."

I'm up early the next morning and on the phone to Selin Cormier, Brian's ex. Despite my lack of concrete details, she agrees to meet me. Reluctantly.

The aroma of Turkish coffee greets me when I arrive at Selin's apartment. Hospitality trumps unwillingness. I thank her for taking the time and the delicious coffee. "I'm here because it's been several days since anyone appears to have heard from Brian. His friends are concerned."

I watch Selin's face carefully. She reacts with the classic features of surprise: eyebrows raised high, horizontal wrinkles across the forehead, open eyelids with the upper lid raised and the lower lid drawn down. Surprise quickly becomes something else. Worry. That is just as quickly replaced by another emotion. Indifference.

Selin shrugs. "This will sound cold. But I cannot get caught up in Brian's endless drama. It's why we divorced."

"I take it you haven't heard from him in the past week."

"I haven't heard from him in the past year. I prefer it that way."

"But you know Brian. Do you know anyone who would want to hurt him?"

The surprise is back. "You think someone wanted to hurt Brian? He hasn't just run away to savor his fantasies?"

I admit I don't know the answer to that question. "But there is no sign of him anywhere, and everything is intact at his condo."

It takes Selin a minute to wage whether or not she should share information with me. "There's a man you should talk to. He's a biker, and he's despicable."

His real name is Zane Rowe. He goes by Ryder. And he's meeting with me because I'm paying him $100 an hour. This will not take that long. Either Ryder will have no helpful information, or he'll be involved. If the former, I'll thank him and leave. If the latter, I'll get the hell out of here.

We're meeting in a north end coffee shop. Ryder arrives twelve minutes late (which I am not paying for). I know it's Ryder because the man is at least 6'4", 250 pounds and sporting leather and the Black Schooners insignia everywhere. Several customers exit soon after Ryder plops down with a pumpkin spice latte (which I did pay for).

I haven't said why I requested to meet, only that I was formerly but no longer law enforcement and I would pay him for his time. Ryder stretches out his long legs and takes the most genteel sip of coffee I swear I have ever seen. "What do you want?"

"Do you know Brian Cormier?"

"Nope."

"Accountant who likes to daydream about committing crimes."

"Ahh, the nutjob. I took his money, too."

"What did he want?"

"He wanted me to show him how to do these damn stupid ideas he had written in his damn stupid book."

"Did you?"

"Nope."

"How did he take the news?"

All six foot-plus of Ryder sits up and leans forward. "Look at me. Would you argue with me?"

Point taken. Ryder takes a long, quiet sip of his latte. "To give the nutjob credit, he didn't put up a fuss when I said no or try to change my mind. Kinda like he knew what was coming."

"It was a strange ask."

"I've had stranger."

Not going there. "Did you get a sense from Brian what his next step might be?"

"Didn't ask. Didn't care. Like my good friend Axl Ross once said, 'Let sleeping dogs lie.'"

Pretty sure it's Axl Rose. Pretty sure he never said anything about sleeping dogs. I keep my mouth shut. That earns me a grin from the giant in the chair across from me.

I need to know more about Brian's journal and why everyone and their sleeping dog seems to have seen it. "Aren't journals supposed to be private?" I ask the life coach.

"They are what the owner wants them to be. Some people treat their journal like a diary. Others like a blog."

"I take it Brian was a blogger."

I can feel Marla's smile down the fibre optic cable that connects us. And her sadness.

"Brian was very open about what was in his journal. Literally. We all knew his innermost thoughts."

"Do you approve?"

"It's not about my approval. But we all have a need for reflection. Privacy fosters that."

So Brian ignored his life coach. "How did you end up with his journal?"

"He gave it to me. Asked me to keep it safe." Marla hesitates.

"Why did he think it wasn't safe?"

"It's not as uncommon as it sounds. When you get caught up in a fantasy, you often come to believe the dreams you're writing about."

Got it. Brian wrote about committing crimes. It's not a stretch to believe people wanted the criminal mastermind's brilliant ideas.

"Does anyone else know you had Brian's journal?"

"Only you."

That may work to my advantage.

Thursday night is bowling night. This is relatively new for me. Crown prosecutor Darnell Sparkes, a sometimes client, roped me into joining his team, Justice Strikes (I kid you not). I'm actually good—top female scorer—and I convince myself I need the balance. Better than a life coach. We're up against Strike Force, a team with two cops I know well, Mike Donovan and Darius Brooks. Mike was my partner for seven years.

Bowling involves a lot of chest thumping, catcalling, and occasionally throwing a ball. Darnell is on the lane warming up his throw. This will take a while. The rookie on the lane beside him can't take his eyes off the contortions. Mike, Darius, and I are on the bench and we're not even trying to stop laughing.

"You busy?" This is Darius attempting small talk.

"I am." This is me attempting small talk.

"Jeezus." This is Mike letting us know how lousy we are at whatever this is.

"I do have a few interesting tidbits from a current case." This is me changing the subject. I launch into some of Brian's harebrained schemes without naming Brian. There's the one where he plans to put crap into cars on a dealership lot, then have minions show up the next day as detailers to clean the cars offsite. There's the one where he dresses as a maintenance man, removes a valuable portrait from a hotel wall, and replaces it with a fake. There's the one where he dresses up like a clown to rob banks so—

Before I can finish my riveting tale, a hand is under each elbow and I am being propelled toward the bar. I look up in time to see Darnell watching. "Need a hand?" he asks.

"No," Mike says.

"Maybe," Darius says.

Darnell gets to the bar ahead of us. "Whatever this is, you don't have time now. We'll meet back at Em's place."

This is a tradition that started a few cases ago. It better not throw my game off.

The boys have opted for decaf coffee over a Propeller IPA, so whatever is up is serious.

"Tell us about the clowns again," Mike says.

It's not a long story.

"Who's the mastermind?" Darius asks.

"An accountant addicted to daydreaming." That requires a little more explanation.

Darnell and I look at the two cops. "Your turn."

"Well, this is either one helluva coincidence or your accountant is doing more than daydreaming," Mike says.

"No banks have been robbed. I would know," Darnell says.

"So would the nightly news," I point out.

"Prince Edward Island." This is Darius.

"Dammit." This is me.

We spend the first cup of coffee going through the case files online but there isn't much more to learn. Someone in full clown attire strolled into four banks on the Island, got a few laughs from customers, and more than $100,000 from tellers uncertain whether to be entertained or afraid.

"No one saw a damn thing outside of a big red nose, orange curly hair, and giant feet," Mike says. "We got the first alert about two weeks ago, but the Charlottetown police are stumped. Two more since then."

"When was the last one?"

"Three days ago," Darius says.

"Then it probably wasn't Brian Cormier. He's been missing for a week."

Over second cups, we toss out theories. *Brian has gone rogue. Ryder took Brian up on his job offer. Brian sold his mastermind ideas. Someone stole Brian's ideas.*

It's the last one that lands. It's the only one that explains why someone is searching for Brian's journal.

It's 8 a.m., the appointed hour. The favorite time of day for the Halifax Police Department detectives and their chief to meet. Today we're joined via Zoom by the Charlottetown deputy chief of police and a detective. On *Law & Order* they'd call this a joint task force. We just call it a Zoom call.

By 9 a.m. and my fifth Timbit, it's decided the bank robberies in Prince Edward Island have a direct link to a daydreamer in Halifax and investigations will continue in both locations. On our end, the focus will be on finding out who broke into Brian Cormier's condo looking for his journal. We have a plan.

Marla has agreed to call a special meeting of Daydreamers Anonymous for tonight. I'll attend, I'll share—and I'll let everyone know I have the journal. Then we'll wait.

In the meantime, the two HPD detectives and I do a deep dive on all the DA members. When you're looking to find information about people, there is no better resource than a police department. By noon we have two suspects. Frankly, the same two I started with six Timbits ago: Cassie Burke and Julian Grimes.

They may both be daydreamers, but they're doing something right. Cassie has a condo in downtown Halifax worth more than $1.2

million. Julian drives a Porsche. It's not leased. Somewhere they're getting money. On paper, Cassie is a licensed massage therapist who runs her own business. She has no assistants, and her online calendar has plenty of openings.

Julian is an entrepreneur. When we boil that down, it amounts to several retail operations selling everything from baby wipes to sandbags to paper cups on Amazon. Nothing that screams Porshe.

"We're looking for a nightingale." This earns me a look from both Darius and Mike. Since I've taken up birding, I've discovered the hobby can work its way into more conversations than you would think.

"The common nightingale is a small bird with a beautiful song."

"Em, you're losing it."

"But Mike, the common nightingale has an uncommon habit. It's a trickster. What you see is not what you get."

It's a full house. Marla is pleased, despite the subterfuge. We begin with a discussion of intent. Maladaptive daydreamers can often deliberately move into an intense daydream, in other words feeding the addiction. We look at why and how this happens. Then we explore ways to avoid it.

Now it's time to share. I don't jump in. After someone called Cheyenne tells us she wants to be a cowboy (go figure), I stand up. "This is my first share, so please be patient." I get warm smiles and encouraging nods from the group. I tell them I've been daydreaming all my life but it's getting worse as my life falls apart. I thank my friend Brian for introducing me to this group—and to journaling. "Brian is so kind. He's given me his journal to read, so I'll have a sense of what he felt was important to record. It's sitting on my kitchen table. I read an entry or two every time I sit down. Thank you, Brian."

Both Cassie and Julian beg off the after-meeting coffee klatch. I make sure they hear I'm going and looking forward to a relaxing conversation. I also let everyone know I have to stop at my sister's on the way home. I don't have a sister.

By the time coffee is over, Julian Grimes is in handcuffs.

Julian is cagier than I think any of us gave him credit for. He admits he broke into Brian's condo but contends he wanted to retrieve the journal to see if it could help him figure out what has happened to his friend. Mike is still in the interrogation room with him, but Darius has stepped out. I know what's coming.

"We can't hold him. We have him on a B&E, but he stole a single journal. A journal that belongs to a missing friend. And nothing ties him to the robberies."

I'm deducing. It's what detectives do. If Julian is smart enough to talk his way out of a criminal charge and smart enough to recognize a criminally good idea when he hears one, he's smart enough to know two things. First, there are more good ideas where the clown heist came from. Hence the interest in Brian's journal. What do you do if you can't find the journal? You go to the source itself. That's why the source is currently missing.

The other thing I've deduced is that Julian is too smart to carry out these crimes himself. But he's not criminally connected and you're not going to get just anyone to put on a clown suit and commit armed robbery. For that you need a criminal.

Ryder agrees to meet with me. This time the price is $200.

The biker leans over the small café table and looks at the picture on my phone. "Yep. That's him. Nutjob."

Ryder gives me a grin. "Easiest $200 I ever made."

Not quite. I have another pic. Ryder takes my phone, looks at the screen, looks at me. "So you figured it out."

"I'm getting there. I have figured out that you had nothing to do with this."

"The idea was stupid when nutjob one came calling. It didn't get any smarter when nutjob two arrived."

I have what I need but Ryder doesn't look like he's given me all he has. His long, muscular frame is resting against the back of the chair, head tilted casually, a latte in his hand. I'll wait.

"This guy," Ryder points to the photo of Julian Grimes, "wasn't like the first one. Slicker. Nastier."

Ryder can see the surprise on my face. "Oh, he didn't give anything away. I just know nasty."

"I should have you on my payroll."

That gets me another grin. "None of my business, but I'd steer clear of nutjob number two."

"Let me guess. Do what Axl Ross would do and let sleeping dogs lie."

This gets me a hoot that reverberates throughout the café. Two people get up and quickly leave.

I'm updating Mike and Darius. Somehow we're back at my place. I'm serving herbal tea. I do know how to get rid of guests. Darnell arrives as I'm pouring the last cup. I give the two detectives a look. They shrug. Darnell reaches for his mandarin orange brew.

"My favorite."

Once the laughter (at my expense) dies down, I tell everyone what I've learned, which isn't much. We toss a few ideas around half-heartedly. I blame it on the herbal tea.

"Do you know Ryder?" My question earns me two nods and one eyeroll. "What do you think of him?"

"Good god, Montgomery," Mike says. "You can't date a biker."

More laughter at my expense. "Let me be specific. Is he smart?" I get three reluctant yesses.

"Do you know who Axl Rose is?"

More laughter. "We're not that old," Darnell says.

"So if old law enforcement guys and one old lawyer know who Axl Rose is, how come Ryder doesn't?"

Three mugs land on my coffee table at the same time. "We're getting really desperate," Mike says.

"Do you think it matters?" Darius asks.

"I think it's unusual. He called him Axl Ross."

"Goddammit." This is one word ushered simultaneously from three mouths. The guys are now doing a backslapping, high-fiving jig in my living room. I'm sipping mandarin orange herbal tea. It really isn't bad.

It takes a few minutes for the dancing to stop. Darius looks at me with a grin that stretches across his face. "Axl Ross is president of Le Cercle Noir."

Thank you Ryder.

Le Cercle Noir is a biker gang out of Montreal. Apparently, if at first you don't succeed...

I doubt Axl Ross would have copped to anything, but Julian Grimes is no biker president. He saw the writing on the wall and signed a plea deal that would put him in jail but keep him alive. Once Julian admitted what he'd done, police had enough to descend on Le Cercle Noir's clubhouse. They found guns, heroin, and Brian Cormier.

Marla Porter paid my bill without any questions. Then she shut down Daydreamers Anonymous.

# Edward Lodi

**Edward Lodi** draws much of the inspiration for his fiction, poetry, and nonfiction from his experiences growing up and working on cranberry bogs on Cape Cod. He has written and edited more than thirty books, including six Cranberry Country Mystery novels featuring feisty septuagenarian Lena Lombardi. In his responsible years he was a college English instructor, a social worker and trainer of social workers, and a publisher and editor. In his irresponsible years he was a hippie and a bum. He is a member of the Short Mystery Fiction Society and lives with his wife, Yolanda, in Hingham, Mass.

Find him at www.amazon.com/stores/author/B0BH4VZ6MB/.

# Watch Your Step

## Edward Lodi

**B**randon Whitby eased the boredom of his days as the desk clerk of a seedy motel by alternating between daydreaming of what it would be like to be rich, never having to work again, and cooking up schemes to achieve that goal—without, of course, actually having to put in any real effort. Brandon was constitutionally lazy.

He also suffered from insomnia, probably because he didn't get enough exercise. One night as he lay in bed tossing and turning it occurred to him that there was a means at hand of getting rich quick, or at least, quicker, if only he had the nerve.

His uncle, Philbert Whitby, was a miser whose chief enjoyment in life was hoarding money and watching his bank account grow. As his uncle's sole heir, it was only natural that Brandon would want to see the old man dead. If Brandon could get rid of his uncle by entering into a pact with the devil, he'd do so. But apparently the devil had no interest and nothing to gain from such a transaction—in all likelihood Brandon had already forfeited his soul. Which meant Brandon would have to take matters into his own hands. But how?

If the old man died by other than a natural cause, Brandon would be the obvious—probably the only—suspect. To avoid suspicion, he'd have to make it look like an accident. But no matter how much he wracked his brain, he failed to come up with a foolproof method.

Uncle Philbert lived alone. One evening a mishap occurred which, if not for a meddlesome neighbor, would have made Brandon's wish come true. After frying a pork chop on his gas stove the elderly man forgot to turn off the burner, then fell asleep watching television. Noticing smoke billowing from the windows, the nosey neighbor called 911. Fire fighters arrived in time to save Philbert, but the cottage, badly damaged, was condemned by the Board of Health.

Though disappointed that his uncle hadn't perished in the fire, the incident gave Brandon an idea. Why not invite the old man to move in with him? He'd already proven himself careless. Who knew what opportunities for further mishaps might arise if they shared the same domicile?

"You can't stay here any longer, Uncle Phil."

"I ain't moving."

"Suit yourself. But it'll cost a fortune to repair this place and clean it up."

"I don't have no other place to go."

"Move in with me."

His uncle looked at him with disdain. "Move into your studio apartment? You ain't got room for a cockroach, never mind me."

"It will only be temporary, Uncle Phil," Brandon assured him. "I'll look for a place where the two of us can live together in comfort." He held up his hand to stave off the old man's protests. "You can no longer be trusted to live alone. It's me or a nursing home."

His uncle eyed him with suspicion. "Why would you do this for me?"

Brandon shrugged. "If you go into a nursing home, they'll take every cent you own. There'd be nothing left for me to inherit."

"Humph," his uncle grunted, but acquiesced.

Brandon helped his uncle pack and installed him in the studio apartment, along with a cot for him to sleep on. His uncle's one vice was that he smoked a pipe, a vile mixture of latakia and other noxious tobaccos. The resulting black smoke reminded Brandon of burning rubber. No matter. He could put up with the smell, given the knowledge that each month the old man deposited the bulk of his pension check in the bank. Most misers fondle their money. Philbert Whitby fondled his bank book.

To make his scheme work, Brandon had to find a bigger place. But where? He couldn't afford to buy a house. Or could he? Wasn't his cousin Sarah a real estate agent?

As far as he knew, Sarah, a young divorcee with no children, was his sole surviving relative. A second cousin twice removed, or something like that. What difference did it make? The only relative Brandon wanted removed was his uncle.

Seeing as how they were kin, maybe Sarah would cut him a deal.

When he dropped by her office, he found her seated behind a bare desk engrossed in the pages of a paperback novel. As she hastily shoved it into a drawer he caught a glimpse of the cover illustration—a satyr in hot pursuit of a naked nymph.

"Brandon, what a pleasant surprise." She rose from the desk flashing a smile like a used car salesman spotting an easy mark.

After a brief exchange of pleasantries, he explained what he was looking for—the cheapest house possible. She eyed him shrewdly as he spoke. When he suggested a reduced commission based on their kinship, she readily agreed. Too readily?

"I've got just the home for you," Sarah said.

"Inexpensive?"

"A steal! It's been on the market for some time now and the owners are eager to sell."

"What's wrong with it?" Brandon asked, suspicious.

Sarah seemed hurt by the question. "There's nothing wrong with it, Cousin. Just that it's an antique with some, uh, quaint features." She shook her head sadly. "Buyers these days want modern. They don't appreciate the skilled workmanship that went into homes in the past. But let's go look at it so you can see for yourself."

They drove into the outskirts of town. Some of the houses they passed were in decent shape. Others weren't. When Sarah pulled into the driveway of a weathered saltbox, Brandon's heart sank. The roof, in dire need of shingles, sagged in the middle. Strips of clapboard siding hung loose.

"Don't be deceived by the exterior. Nothing leaks," Sarah assured him. They began the tour in the living room, where patches of mold, leprous spots on the walls where damp caused the yellowing paper to peel, and a crack that ran like a bolt of lightning the length of the ceiling were the salient features.

To divert his attention from these obvious blemishes, Sarah said with feigned enthusiasm, "See this door? A door like this is rare. A fine conversation piece."

His cousin stood beaming at the door like a proud parent. To Brandon, it looked as if it belonged on a barn. What was so special about it? Had it come over on the Mayflower?

"Do you know what it is?"

Brandon shook his head.

"It's a cooling board door."

At his blank stare she explained. "Look at how wide and sturdy the planks are." She let her crimson-tipped nails dance across the boards. "In the days before funeral parlors, bodies were prepared for burial at home."

Bodies? Funny—Brandon had been thinking about a body. His uncle's.

"House builders included a wide-planked door—like this one— that could easily be lifted off its hinges and laid over a pair of sawhorses, ready to receive a corpse."

She swung the door open. "As you can see, this side of the door is plain, to receive the body, and the other side has two parallel boards nailed across it, to be fitted against sawhorses while the body was being...washed and dressed, I guess. The body would then be left on the cooling board in the parlor for viewing by friends and relatives.

Once the body was safely in its coffin, the door was re-hung on its hinges."

Brandon nodded politely.

"There's one other feature I must show you."

What now? A window box for the temporary storage of cadavers when the ground was frozen? A bed sheet that doubled as a funeral shroud?

"This way. Up these stairs."

The uncarpeted stairs—steep, narrow, worn—led to the second-floor hallway. Before they had climbed two-thirds of the way, Sarah stopped.

"This is what I want to show you." She pointed at the step immediately before her, then mounted beyond it so that Brandon could properly examine it. "See the riser? It's three inches shorter than the others. That was done on purpose."

"Why?"

"All the stairs in this type of house would be of the same height, except for one. The trick step. Family members and servants quickly learned which one it was and took care not to trip on it."

"But why a trick step?" Brandon asked. "Why so obvious a hazard?"

"A trap for burglars! This was before electricity or flashlights, remember. Long before burglar alarms were invented. An intruder mounting the stairs at night, in the dark, would trip on the uneven step, making a noise and alerting the sleeping household."

"A trap for burglars," he echoed. "And for unsuspecting guests." He thought of his uncle, who had wide feet like a duck and shuffled when he walked.

Contrary to Sarah's expectations, her baldheaded cousin, with a minimum of dickering (after all, the asking price was absurdly low), snapped up the white elephant she'd been attempting to unload for months.

The creaky old house, with its antiquated kitchen, diminutive dining room, and shabby parlor downstairs, its impossibly small bath with pull-chain toilet upstairs, and two cramped bedrooms, drafty in the winter and with poor ventilation in the summer, suited Brandon Whitby just fine.

Philbert Whitby began grumbling the moment he crossed the threshold.

"How much did you pay for this dump?" he asked, eyeballing the peeling wallpaper and cracked ceiling.

"It's the best I can afford, Uncle Phil," Brandon said, all innocence. "At least we won't be crowded. We each have our own bedroom."

"And stairs to climb," the old man griped.

"Oh, but that shouldn't be a problem, Uncle Phil. We can have a chair lift installed. Of course, it won't be cheap, but you can afford it."

"Me? It ain't my house."

"I'm sorry, Uncle Phil, but I plunked down every cent I have for the down payment. Besides, the lift will be for your use, not mine."

"I can manage these damn stairs just fine without some modern contraption."

And that settled the matter. Except that Brandon piously pointed out the built-in burglar alarm, the trick step two-thirds of the way up the stairway. "You're growing forgetful, Uncle Phil...don't forget that step." He glanced at his uncle's clumsy duck feet.

Philbert Whitby soon adjusted to his new quarters. He even went so far as to suggest that Brandon might want to replace the faulty wiring downstairs. He could hear it sizzling, or so he imagined. Brandon, however, was not about to pour more money into the house than was absolutely necessary. He had plans for the money—when no longer encumbered by his uncle.

With luck, he'd soon be rid of the old skinflint, one way or the other.

A booby trap might speed things up. He could stretch a string across the top of the stairs. But what if his uncle noticed it? He'd have to do the old man in then and there, then try to make it look like an accident. Too risky.

He thought of another, simpler way. Sneak up behind his uncle at the top of the stairs and give him a shove. Grieving, he'd point out the trick step to the police and say that he'd warned the dear old man about it, to no avail.

Again, too risky. Brandon was not a good liar. He was bound to get tongue-tied and betray his guilt. Best thing was to let Nature take its course—Nature being the trick step combined with his uncle's growing senility.

The old man spent much of his time seated in a rocking chair in his bedroom puffing on his pipe, gleefully mindful that his nephew detested the reek of latakia and other tobaccos that seeped through the cracks in the doorway, permeating the upstairs and, eventually, the downstairs as well. Occasionally Philbert became confused and forgot where he was. Most of the time, though, he functioned just fine.

Brandon, having great expectations, cheerfully catered to his uncle, cooking an occasional pork chop or rib-eye steak, cleaning his room, making up his bed, and pulling the chain on the toilet when his uncle forgot. Of course, he had to leave the old man alone during the day while he put in his hours at the motel, or on the evenings when he visited certain establishments in Boston where a lonely bachelor could find companionship, for a price.

One day at the end of October Brandon returned home from work to find the old goat lying at the foot of the stairs, head-down as if paying obeisance to Moloch, the god of avarice. Brandon flipped him on his back to make sure he was dead. His wide feet were aimed toward the ceiling, like signposts pointing to heaven. The old man's accusing eyes stared and seemed to follow his nephew's movements as he called 9 1 1.

Brandon had his uncle cremated. The ashes the funeral director presented in a cardboard box smelled faintly of latakia. Less faint was the odor of pipe tobacco that perpetually clung inside the house, or floated through the hallways, upstairs and down, at odd hours. Wafted by a draft? But what was the source?

Brandon got rid of his uncle's ashes by dumping them into the toilet bowl and pulling the chain.

Soon, he'd pull the chain on the house, so to speak. With his uncle's life's savings now his, he could quit his dead-end job and move closer to Boston and the establishments he frequented.

In the meantime, he stayed on. Save for the reek of latakia, living in the derelict house was bearable. Brandon felt no guilt over his uncle's fatal mishap. The old man, too cheap to install a chair lift, had been duly forewarned.

One night, after Brandon had retired to bed, a loud crash resonated from below. Startled, he sat bolt upright. The thought crossed his mind that his uncle had fallen down the stairs. Then he remembered—his uncle had fallen down the stairs. And was blissfully dead as a result.

Had a housebreaker stumbled on the trick step? Terrified, he slipped out of his room, flicked on the hallway light, and peered down. There was nothing on the stairway. Emboldened, he crept down to the first floor.

In the hallway, flat on the floor, lay the cooling board. Somehow the "architectural gem" had come unhinged. The irony of the expression was not lost on him. Though not enough to unhinge him, the occurrence did shake his complacency. Somehow the old-fashioned flat nails that held the hinges to the doorframe had loosened and fallen out, causing the door to collapse.

It's an old house, Brandon reminded himself. The place was falling apart when he bought it. Leaving the cooling board where it lay, he went upstairs and crawled into bed. But sleep eluded him. He thought he heard noises. And he could smell it: latakia. That burnt-rubber stench. The reek kept him awake all night.

In the morning, he hung the cooling board back onto the door frame, using the original nails. But how long would it remain in place? The three-hundred-year-old wood was dry, the nails thin and rusty. If the damn thing proved troublesome, he would have a professional carpenter secure it more firmly.

As a treat to calm his nerves, he made a trip into Boston.

When he returned home late that evening the reek of tobacco was stronger than ever. A sulfurous stench, as if demons loosed from Hell had spent the day lolling about the place. That did it. He'd move out the next morning. He'd rent a room in the motel where he worked and bide his time until the house sold.

He went to bed determined to sleep. And he did sleep, until a loud crash from below jolted him awake. The cooling board had fallen off its hinges again.

But was that the only thing that woke him? No. There was also the smell. Stronger than ever. But wait, it wasn't just the smell, it was actual smoke that infiltrated his nostrils. Black, blinding smoke, acrid, filling his bedroom, displacing the air, like sewage crowding into an underground cistern. The house was on fire!

His uncle had warned him about the faulty wiring.

He scrambled out of bed and yanked open the bedroom door. Smoke filled the hallway, billowing up the stairs from below. The entire house was ablaze.

In his panic to escape he repeated his uncle's blunder. He forgot about the trick step. Barefooted, he bounded down the stairs until, part way down, he did a flip-flop, head over heels through the air. He landed hard, just as his uncle had, and broke his neck.

Neighbors smelled the smoke and called 911. Two of them, breaking down the door, spotted Brandon's body at the foot of the stairs.

One felt his pulse. "He's dead."

"I can't breathe," the other shouted. "We gotta get outta here."

"We can't just leave the body. Look, here's a board. We can use it as a stretcher."

They rolled Brandon onto the cooling board—unwittingly using it for the purpose for which it was intended—and carried him out into the night. Fire engines arrived shortly after.

Although Brandon died intestate, Sarah quickly stepped forward to declare herself his only living relative. Once the Commonwealth of Massachusetts proved to its satisfaction that this was indeed the case, she inherited what was left of the house and—more important— Uncle Philbert's lifetime savings.

Sarah put the money to good use, abandoning her foundering real estate business and moving to a tropical island, where she spent her days on the beach sipping pina coladas and dreaming up ways to meet wealthy men, doddering old fools she could seduce and marry, then dispose of, one way or another.

# Julie Hastrup

---

**Julie Hastrup** grew up in the Appalachian region of Ohio, but after traveling the world has settled in a small fishing village in Denmark. Her writing stems from her travels and business career prior to becoming a fulltime writer. Julie's work has been published in multiple anthologies, including her Derringer award finalist story in the Superior Shores Anthology, *Larceny & Last Chances*, as well as *Shotgun Honey* and *Mystery Magazine*. Julie is a member of Sisters in Crime, International Thriller Writers, the Short Mystery Fiction Society, and Mystery Writers of America.

Find her at https://hastrup.com/.

# Dinner at Angelo's

## Julie Hastrup

Charlie's Buick crunched into Angelo's gravel parking lot. The single bulb dangling over the entrance cast a narrow cone of light through the fog that had swallowed the night. The place was packed, as usual, and he found a slot in the last aisle, seven rows from the door.

Angelo's had no marquee. Word of mouth—that's how the restaurant filled every table every night. It wasn't the kind of joint Charlie and his friends typically went to on a night out. Too expensive. If he hadn't been coming here since he was a kid, tagging along with his father, he wouldn't have known the place existed.

Charlie slammed the car door shut and snaked through the sedans, trucks, and station wagons filling the lot. He passed Mean Mickey's Chevy and Uncle Joey's Caddy. Without looking, he knew his father's cousins, Old Tommy and Pauley Short Arms, were there as well.

The restaurant's red-curtained windows protected its patrons from curious glances. Charlie didn't care about them. He only had eyes for Ellie, leaning against the closed door where he knew she'd be. The tip of her cigarette glowed as it moved from her mouth. He'd watched her every Tuesday when she took her eight o'clock break outside under the blue awning. And this Tuesday, it was Charlie's turn to approach her.

"A beautiful girl like you shouldn't be out here in the cold." Charlie shrugged out of his jacket and placed it around Ellie's shoulders.

She took a final drag, then threw the half-smoked cigarette to the ground. Her red pump crushed the life out of it.

Charlie stared at her tight skirt, shapely calf, delicate ankle.

Ellie lifted his chin with her manicured finger. "Eyes up here, handsome."

He so rarely had Ellie to himself. Now was his chance. "What's a smart girl like you doing here? Do—"

"Aww... Get out of here."

"Do you—"

"Seriously, Charlie, get out of here." Ellie cocked her head toward the restaurant's door. "Allen Todd's in there, and he'll be coming out any minute."

"Todd's here?" Charlie tried to hide his fear.

"Every day this month. He's not coming for the carbonara, if you catch my drift. The big boys are waiting for you. You know where the back door is."

Charlie hightailed it around the side of the building, the black night broken up only by the dining room windows' red glow. He silently slipped into the building and joined the white-haired dons gathered for their weekly grandstand.

Ellie let herself into the buzzing restaurant and made a beeline toward the kitchen. Her hand brushed the fat envelope waiting for her in the jacket pocket. She ignored Todd and the tables of men waving a finger to get two minutes of her attention. Weaving between tray-laden waiters, past the dishwasher, and into the office, she closed the door and clicked through the safe's combination. Ellie eyed the beige package that had been transferred to her, confirmed its contents, placed it in the safe, and shoved a slimmer white envelope back into the pocket.

With the jacket draped over her arm, Ellie found her father and both her older and younger brothers enjoying a plate of pasta in the rear corner of the restaurant. Their three heads bent toward each other, no doubt discussing her father's latest scheme. "Papa, Charlie lent me his jacket. Could you take it to him? He's in the private room."

Angelo, the restaurant's namesake, did the same thing every Tuesday when the envelope exchange took place. He swallowed another bite of his dinner, rested his fork on his plate, tilted the remainder of his red wine down his gullet, and wiped his lips. This time, instead of rising with a belch and a groan, he said, "I've retired."

Ellie's brothers stopped chewing, their forks freezing over their plates. This was obviously not part of the plans they'd been discussing.

"Francis," Angelo nodded at Ellie's older brother, "you take the jacket this week."

Eyes wide, Francis followed his father's routine before rising from the table. Again, as was customary, Francis said, "Ellie, you need to thank the gentleman."

Ellie didn't think anyone ever overheard their code, but, as a good daughter, she played along and accompanied her brother down the hallway toward the back room.

"Can you believe it?" Francis whispered to her.

"That he retired? No. That he named you to head the family? Well, you're the oldest, so, yeah."

"I don't want the title. I'm supposed to deploy tomorrow."

"And you haven't told Papa yet? Sheesh, Francis. Are you dim?"

"I was planning to break it to him tonight."

"Tell him in the morning." Ellie tucked her hand through her brother's arm. "Tonight, follow his instructions, or there'll be hell to pay."

"What am I supposed to do in there?" Francis nodded at the room reserved for private parties. "I haven't been to one of these meetings since before Mama passed."

Ellie sighed. She'd been taking care of both her brothers—and her father, if she was honest—for what felt like forever. "This is how it works. We'll both go in. I hand you the envelope and give back the jacket. You tell me to bring you and your friends tonight's special pasta."

"But I already had two bowls."

"How'd you think Papa became Big Angelo?" Ellie puffed her cheeks. "Then you take the seat at the head of the table and bring out the ledger."

"Where's the ledger?"

"In the cabinet behind your seat. Each of them will brag about how much they 'invested' this week. You mark it against what they promised they'd bring in at last week's meeting."

"That's it?" Francis scratched his head. "Why do I remember these lasting forever?"

"No, that's not *it*. They'll each have made bets on who'd get the most, and of course they'll bluster and brag. Your job is to make them commit to bringing in even more next week."

"You should be the one handling things for the old man."

"I wish." Ellie gave her brother a half smile. "Maybe when you're protecting the free world..."

"You should. As the next oldest, it's only natural." Francis took a deep breath. "Okay, then at the end of the evening I hand out the bank checks for their cut of last week's take? We still get forty percent?"

"Forty-five. And you do that after I clear the plates, but don't let them leave until I knock on the door, signaling the dining room is clearing out. You want these guys getting in their cars as part of the crowd." Ellie put her hands on her brother's shoulders. "You got this."

Big Angelo hadn't taken the news of his eldest's deployment well, and Ellie steered clear of him, cleaning whichever room he wasn't in. She'd taken over all household duties after her mother's death but had hired someone to replace Mama in the restaurant's kitchen. Ellie's cooking was even better than Mama's, but she wasn't stupid.

Men took up three-quarters of her dining room each night. And while Mama always said, 'The best way to a man's heart is through his stomach,' Ellie's version went more like, 'The best way to a man's wallet is through his hunger." And she knew what the men hungered for.

Ellie had become an expert at working the room, making each patron feel like he was the center of her universe. She made sure to seat the warring butcher and grocer in opposite corners, the mayor and Father John with each other so their hands would stay where they belonged, and Todd next to her hostess stand where she could keep an eye on him.

That Tuesday, Ellie accepted a jacket from Old Tommy, confirmed it contained an acceptable amount, and exchanged its envelope with one from the safe.

"Papa, Old Tommy lent me his jacket. Could you take it to him? He's in the private room." Ellie waited for her father to swallow his pasta and empty his glass.

Angelo cleared his throat. "Leo, you take the jacket this week."

Ellie grabbed the back of a chair for balance. Leo? Her father couldn't be serious. It should be her. She'd earned her position in the family.

Her younger brother smirked at her. "Ellie, you need to thank the gentleman."

Teeth clenched, she followed him to the private room. Papa had made his decision, and there was nothing for her to do. Outside the door, Leo stretched his hand into the jacket and withdrew the payment meant for the dons.

"I'll take that." Leo deposited the envelope in his pocket, then opened the door and ushered her into the room. "Be sure to thank Old Tommy, then instead of today's special pasta, bring my friends a T-bone and a good Chianti. None of that schlock you normally serve."

Ellie fumed all the way to the kitchen and altered the dons' standing order to what Leo had demanded, took a deep breath, and resumed her place working the tables. Nearing the end of service, Ellie tapped on the door to alert the men it was time to leave. No one acknowledged her, so she knocked harder and returned to the dining room to wish her customers a good night.

The last of her guests had exited, and the headlights popping on in the parking lot attested to only a few stragglers. Still the back door remained shut. She put her ear against the wood panel and heard nothing. Violating protocol, Ellie pushed it open. "Leo—"

Seven empty bottles of her best Chianti and the cake for tomorrow's Elk's luncheon sat half-eaten between a table full of snoring men. Her brother must have snuck into the wine cellar and stopped by the walk-in while she tended to business.

Ellie pounded one of the bottles on the oak slab next to her brother's ear. "Wake up. They need to leave."

Leo yawned and struggled to focus on his watch. Face red, he barked, "You're late *and* an idiot. They can't go now. They'd be sitting ducks for the Feds."

"Give me your keys, and I'll get your cars to the employee lot next door." She held out her hand in front of each man. "You can exit with the staff."

With the last don ushered out between her chef and the head waiter, Ellie went looking for her little brother, ready to give him a piece of her mind. She didn't find him until she arrived home.

She charged to the couch where he lay passed out, but Angelo's beefy arm stopped her. "Leave him be. The boy worked hard tonight."

*He* worked hard? "I haven't seen Leo work at all, much less work hard, his entire life." She took another step toward him, and Angelo raised his hand, ready to strike. Ellie remembered the mess he'd made of her mother's face for no reason and backed down. "Yes, Papa."

Ellie snatched her brother's jacket from the floor and flung it onto a wingback chair. Something solid thudded against the upholstery. She fished an envelope out of Leo's pocket, still full of bank checks.

*Bastard.*

The following Tuesday, Mean Mickey arrived during her smoke break and placed his jacket around her shoulders. "I expect last week's checks to be delivered tonight. With interest."

Ellie flinched. You didn't mess with Mean Mickey, not if you wanted to keep walking with both legs. The colossal man rounded the side of the building as Ellie's shaking hand discarded her cigarette.

The restaurant door opened before Ellie turned the knob. Leo stepped out into the night.

"After last week, I thought I should check on you." He reached into the jacket. "You're always messing things up, so I better take care of this."

Before Ellie could say anything, Leo had disappeared into the restaurant.

Ellie smiled at a few of her guests and promised to stop by the mayor's table before he left. She hightailed it through the dining room, trying to not give away the trouble she felt brewing. Todd stood as she passed, and the kindness in his eyes almost broke her façade.

Ellie paused at her father's side, the chair next to him empty. "Papa? Have you seen Leo?"

Big Angelo grunted and, mouth full, pointed to the kitchen.

Leo waited in her office. "Open the safe."

She looked at him, trying to parse what was happening. Was he robbing her?

"Are you slow?" Leo tapped her forehead. "Give. Me. The. Checks."

"Leo, you can't cheat these men." She whispered, despite her staff being too busy to eavesdrop. She handed him the week's freshly laundered money. "Give them last week's checks along with these."

"What checks?" Leo's innocent expression unsettled her. "Those fine gentlemen never saw you give me any checks last week and won't see an exchange today. You must be keeping it all for yourself." He smiled and held his hand out for the jacket. "I'll be sure Mean Mickey gets his jacket back."

"You can't do this. They'll take it out on me." Seconds ticked by as visions of the coming punishment rolled through her imagination. A plate crashing to the floor jolted Ellie back to the present with Leo no longer next to her. She hurried through the kitchen and out to the dining room. "Papa?"

His table stood empty, his plate of pasta half finished.

Ellie ran to the hallway. Big Angelo lumbered along, several yards ahead, with his fleshy hand draped across Leo's shoulder.

Her brother turned. "Bring us steaks and champagne. We're celebrating."

Big Angelo patted his son's back and continued into the private room without acknowledging her.

Frantic, Ellie checked her watch. The restaurant had begun to clear. Despite knocking once, the private room's door remained closed. Based on last week's scene, Ellie knew her brother was trying to get them too drunk to realize they'd been cheated. And she'd be the one to pay.

Ellie crouched at the table next to the hostess stand. "Excuse me, Mr. Todd? Could I have a word with you? Outside?"

"Never thought you'd ask." Special Agent Allen Todd rose and followed her out into the night.

The pounding registered somewhere in Charlie's alcohol-numbed brain.

"Hey, kid, you getting that?" Mean Mickey pointed toward the entrance.

Focused on standing without toppling over, Charlie stumbled away from the table and cracked open the door. "Yeah?" He wanted to come up with something smarter to say to Ellie, but his brain and his mouth wouldn't cooperate.

"Charlie, your car lights are on." Ellie tugged at his sleeve.

"Lights?" Charlie sensed the urgency in her voice but couldn't understand what she expected him to do.

"The pretty girl wants some time with the kid." That was Old Tommy shouting from the far corner.

Ellie pulled his ear closer to her mouth. "Go to your car. Now, Charlie."

He staggered the few steps from the private room to the back porch, the cold wind clearing his head a bit. *Car, lights... Right. Forgot to turn them off.*

He loped around the side of the building to the parking lot. A stream of police cruisers and official-looking black sedans sped toward the back of the restaurant, kicking up gravel in their wake. Fully alert now, he ducked between the remaining parked cars and inched his way to his Buick, determined not to get caught up in the raid. His lights weren't on. Ellie must've made a mistake.

*Ellie!*

Charlie took a step toward the restaurant. He had to warn her. That's when he saw light spill from the front door. Out walked Ellie, Todd behind her. She wasn't in cuffs, thank God. Charlie crawled inside the Buick and ducked low. Barely more than the top of his head showed above the dashboard while the love of his life dealt with the Fed.

Todd leaned in and lit Ellie's cigarette.

Could they be together? *No way. Not Ellie. She's one of us.*

Todd put his jacket around her shoulders and said something in her ear.

*She's laughing?*

Maybe they'd been seeing each other all along.

Eyes fixed on Ellie and Todd, Charlie told himself to leave, but remained frozen, staring at what played out before him. She'd warned him. That's the only explanation for what she'd done. But why would she do that if she and Todd...?

The Fed disappeared into the building, closing the door behind him and thrusting Ellie into semi-darkness. When she stepped away from the dim overhead light, all he could see was the glow of her cigarette.

Shaking his head, Charlie started his car. His headlights illuminated the entrance as he turned in the parking lot. Even though she couldn't see him, Charlie waved goodbye to Ellie.

Special Agent Allen Todd had been hanging around Angelo's for weeks. Everyone knew that's where the dons cleaned their cash. He'd planned to shut the operation down, but once he got a look at Ellie, he didn't feel a need to rush things.

Todd didn't think Ellie had caught on to him being a Fed. He'd been discreet, left his badge in his car, and, hell, everyone in the restaurant packed heat. Her intelligence came as a nice surprise, and Ellie's plan for tonight was pure genius. Out with the old, in with the new.

Todd had never planned to change occupations, let alone teams.

But sometimes you got an offer you couldn't refuse.

# KM Rockwood

**KM Rockwood** draws on a varied background for stories, including working as a laborer in steel fabrication and fiberglass manufacture, and supervising an inmate work crew in a large state prison. These positions, as well as work as a special-education teacher in alternative education and a GED instructor in correctional facilities, provide material for numerous short stories and novels, including the Jesse Damon Crime Novel series. She currently volunteers in a personal care facility in a retirement community.

She is a member of the Short Mystery Fiction Society, Crime Scene Writers, Writers Who Kill, and Sisters in Crime, including the Chessy Chapter, Emerald, and Guppies.

Find her at www.kmrockwood.com.

# Evening Escapade

## KM Rockwood

Timing was everything.

If we were going to stage a breakout, we would have to time it for when it was most likely to succeed. Under the cover of darkness.

I'm Howard. We are domiciled in the Health Care wing of the gravely misnamed Oak Creek Retirement Home. No creek. No oak. Closest we came was a dusty courtyard with a defunct fountain, sandwiched between the dingy multistoried building and an embankment leading up to the railroad tracks. Even that was fenced off.

Sometimes they called us "guests," a total absurdity. Sometimes "patients," which could reasonably apply to the more disabled among us. Usually, "residents."

But "inmates" was what we felt like.

Days dragged on endlessly.

Up that embankment, and beyond the main line, a few railroad sidings branched off toward aging warehouses. Train whistles sounded day and night as freight cars were shuttled around. Switching, moving, going places, having adventures. Or at least potential adventures. Mocking the confines of our dull and utterly predictable daily routine.

If we wanted some adventure, we would have to create our own.

The five of us were at lunch idly discussing our limited options when Curtis, his long fingers nervously drumming, suggested we abscond and catch a train somewhere. Didn't much matter where. "Hop a freight," he said. "I used to do that when I was younger."

We all used mobility devices. Powerchairs, fancy walkers with wheels and seats called rollators. Curtis and Sharon mostly used canes, although Sharon also had both a walker and a powerchair.

"Hopping a freight" felt like an unrealistic goal, but absconding might be possible.

Margarite volunteered that her old house was just a few blocks away. She'd kept it in case she got well enough to move back, and her son had reluctantly agreed.

We knew how unlikely it was that Margarite would get back to her house. Hardly anybody ever got better enough to go home, especially in the eyes of the all-powerful social worker.

But Margarite's son had promised not to sell the house while she still had any hope.

She had even insisted that her son leave a key to the house with her.

A place we could go made the entire idea of absconding a bit more viable. Except Margarite was dependent upon her powerchair, and the house had stairs. Including a steep flight from the street to the front door.

Margarite maintained that she could power up the driveway and enter through the garage, though Curtis, the most mobile among us, would have to use her key to go in through the front. Once inside, he could go to the door between the kitchen and the garage to let the rest of us in.

We decided our best bet was on a night when Nurse Nancy was on duty. She worked seven p.m. to seven a.m. three days a week.

Some in our group questioned whether Nancy was a real nurse.

She didn't act like it. But I pointed out that she dispensed medications and didn't report to anyone else during her shift. She *had* to be a real nurse. Just not as conscientious as most nurses.

First, the entire staff on that shift was pretty lax. Call buttons could go unanswered for hours, until just before the daytime workers arrived.

In addition, things disappeared when she worked. Things like goodies brought in by visitors. Luxury toiletries. Pieces of jewelry.

But even worse was Enrique. Nurse Nancy introduced Enrique as her fiancé and said he came to see her. He did, but he also spent time visiting with some residents. We noticed it tended to be the older, more confused folks. Especially the ones who had no visitors and no family to look out for them. And who might have a little money left after paying the totally outrageous cost of care here.

When someone mentioned that to Nurse Nancy, she said of course the people who needed Enrique's visits most were those with no one else to come see them.

That made a certain amount of sense. But at nine o'clock at night? Well past regular visiting hours and as everyone was being put to bed.

Sometimes he carried a briefcase.

Curtis, who often got out of bed and wandered the hallways, said he had seen Enrique sitting with a bedridden lady just before she died. Some paperwork was spread out and she had a pen in her hand. Enrique was helping her write something. We suspected he was having her sign over her assets.

Margarite said darkly that she had seen her son talking to Enrique. They were up to no good, she was sure.

We began to plan our adventure.

The overnight shift had fewer employees than the day shift, and since the residents spent most of the night sleeping, the staff had a lot less to do. They often gathered in the dining room/lounge, where they brewed a large urn of coffee.

Sometimes we detected a whiff of cigarette smoke, although by the time the next shift came in, the only scent was sanitizer and disinfectant.

The elevators that we would need to make our escape opened into this area.

Curtis and Sharon thought maybe we could leave through the emergency stairs at the end of the hallway. I was pretty sure most of us had no chance of being able to do that, what with the powerchairs and walkers. But Curtis wanted to check it out.

I grabbed my walker and followed him to the door.

He opened it and stepped inside the stairwell.

We expected an alarm—after all, the door had a sign saying "Alarm will sound"—but we weren't prepared for the ungodly wail it gave off.

Startled, Curtis let the door slam behind him.

With an audible click, it locked from inside the stairwell.

Nurse Nancy came bustling down the hall. She saw me with my walker, gawking at the door.

"What did you do?" she demanded.

Some of us are slipping cognitively. Some of us are still pretty sharp. But often the staff doesn't pay much attention to that, especially on this shift. Life is much easier if we let them assume we're all victims of muddled thinking.

People with cognitive impairments can't be blamed for much of anything.

"I need to use the restroom," I said.

She shook her head. "That's the emergency exit, not a restroom. What's the matter with the toilet in your bathroom?"

"Nothing. I just thought this was closer."

"Well, it's not."

"Oh, okay. I'll head back to my room."

She watched me until I got to my room.

Curtis later told me he hobbled down the stairs to the utility basement. He did discover that on most floors, the doors were locked, but he could get out on the ground floor in the lobby.

He came back up in the elevator and went to his own room. He didn't do much hallway wandering that night.

We decided that if we collected some of the pain medication, sleeping pills, and tranquilizers that were prescribed to some of the residents, we could put them in the coffee and maybe everyone working would fall asleep. Or at least be too groggy to stop us.

Missing one little pill shouldn't hurt anybody. We hoped.

First, we tried with Curtis. Everybody was used to his wanderings. Eventually someone would guide him back to bed in his own room, but the staff didn't worry about it too much.

When Nurse Nancy set out with the medication cart one night, he meandered along in her wake. As she was in a room dispensing the pills, he'd liberate a few out of the little cups on the top shelf.

She was supposed to wait and supervise the administration of the medication, and she did for people who couldn't take it on their own. But for the others, she left it with a cup of water for them to take it themselves. When she did that, it didn't leave much time for Curtis to act.

It wasn't long before Nurse Nancy realized Curtis was hanging around the cart, and she started to take it into the room with her.

He had gotten a small assortment of pills before he'd had to give up. We identified them by looking them up on Gwenda's computer.

Gwenda's family seldom visited, but they gave her the latest electronic gadgets for Christmas and birthdays. Most of the gifts had never been removed from the boxes, but she used the computer all the time.

Our next idea was to try Sharon. We had a few reservations about recruiting Sharon. She also tended to wander the halls, but since she sometimes tried to get into the wrong bed or open other people's closet doors, the staff paid more attention to her than they did to Curtis. However, she seemed to understand what we wanted when we told her to go get the pills from bedside tables. We gave her a pillowcase to empty the pill cups into.

She was successful, in a way. She brought back dozens of pills in the bottom of the pillowcase.

Unfortunately, she had also emptied the denture holders on everyone's night table into the pillowcase.

This not only dampened the pills, turning them to mush and making them hard to identify, but also meant that the next morning, the day shift supervisor had to call in the dentist to sort out the dentures.

For the next week, the staff on Nurse Nancy's shift kept a much better eye on the hallways.

Finally, they slacked off again.

Gwenda had been tasked with looking up directions from Oak Creek Retirement to the address Margarite gave her. She said she could print them out for us to take along. Margarite insisted that she knew how to get there, but she insisted on a lot of things that turned out to not be true. We weren't confident she would remember.

Around eight o'clock on the Monday night we'd decided upon, I grabbed my walker and headed for the lounge.

Nurse Nancy was out dispensing meds. Other staff members were preparing residents for bed and cleaning up any messes that the day shift would notice when they came in. Old folks can create messes of an amazing scope. Often truly disgusting messes.

These were essential tasks that they finished up before they started their hours-long coffee break.

The urn would be set to brew the coffee.

I had some crushed-up meds from our raids wrapped in a tissue in my pocket. I intended to dump them into the coffee urn.

But when I rounded the corner into the lounge, I saw a woman sprawled on the floor, right in front of the serving counter. She looked like she had been grasping for the edge of the counter as she collapsed and ended up lying on her side.

My vision isn't good any more, but inching closer with my walker, I realized she wasn't a resident. She was one of the aides. I couldn't bend down enough to check if she was still breathing. Not unless I wanted to fall on top of her. She seemed to be mostly still, but her arms and shoulders twitched.

None of the staff was in view. Who knew how long it would be before someone noticed? This wasn't a feeble older person who had passed out. This was a vibrant young woman. The situation must be serious.

I fumbled in the pouch of my walker for my phone and hit the emergency button. It automatically dialed 911 and relayed location information.

Cautiously, I backed up, mostly hidden behind a large plastic plant, and watched.

We were only two blocks away from the fire station. I heard a siren.

Nurse Nancy came by with her now-depleted medication cart. "You get it all?" she asked.

The aide scrambled to her feet, clutching a towel. "I think so. I had to lie on my side and reach all the way under that damn counter."

"Thanks for taking care of it." Nurse Nancy bent over and picked up a small bucket from the floor. I hadn't noticed that. "If you don't get every drop of milk, it'll stink to high heaven."

The siren stopped outside the building.

The night doorbell shrilled.

Nurse Nancy and the aide looked at each other. "What the...?"

I slunk back to my room and pretended I'd been in the bathroom.

The next night we tried again.

The lounge was empty. No one lay on the floor. The coffee urn sputtered. Guiding my walker, I eased up to the table with the urn and tried to yank the lid off.

It was stubborn and refused to release. Perhaps it screwed on instead of pulling off straight. I gave it a serious sideways-and-upward tug.

The lid zoomed up and flew out of my hand.

I braced myself for the tremendous crash the metal lid would make as it hit the floor.

But it landed on the back of a couch, slid down to the seat, and quietly onto the floor. I took that as a good sign.

I emptied my supply of crushed pills into the urn.

Now to get the lid back on.

Clutching my walker, I bent down, but when I tried to grab the lid, it slid in one direction and the walker in the other. I fell backwards on the couch, fortunately landing on my rear.

From there, I could reach the lid. I put it on the seat of my walker.

Struggling to my feet, I inched back to the urn, replaced the lid, and left.

I just got into the hallway when Nurse Nancy and Enrique came out of the office.

"What are you doing out here?" she asked, glaring at me.

I drained any expression from my face. "I was coming to see if breakfast was ready."

Nurse Nancy rolled her eyes. "It's bedtime. You just had your supper."

"Oh. Did I get ice cream for dessert?"

She had no idea what I'd eaten, but she answered, "Yes, yes. You got a nice scoop of ice cream."

"Chocolate?" I asked.

"Lovely chocolate ice cream," she said. "You can't possibly be hungry, can you?"

"I guess not."

"Do you need help to get back to your room?"

"No. I'll just get ready for bed."

"You do that. Someone will be in to help you in a few minutes."

As I started slowly toward my room, I overheard a bit of conversation between Nurse Nancy and Enrique.

"I'll get the paperwork and come back later," Enrique was saying. "I don't want to wait until next week."

"Good idea," Nurse Nancy said. "I'd be surprised if he lasted more than a day or two."

Enrique went down the elevator and Nurse Nancy hurried to get her medication cart.

I changed into my pajamas, but I left my underwear on. One problem with our plan was that, since we were supposed to be sleeping at the time we made our escape, we had to actually go to bed. I could get back up and change into my clothes again, but not everyone could. We'd just have to go in whatever attire we could manage.

After I climbed into bed, an aide stuck her head inside the door. "You need any help?" she asked.

"No, thank you."

She left.

The sounds of staff bustling around getting everyone ready for the night died down, and the hall lights dimmed. I swung my feet onto the floor and was putting my pants back on when Curtis appeared in my doorway.

He was fully dressed. "They're pretty much asleep. I think it's time to go."

Enrique had said he would be coming back. I was worried about that, but there wasn't much we could do about it. Just leave as soon as we could.

Four of us gathered in the lounge. Sure enough, the staff was sprawled in the upholstered chairs, several of them snoring lightly.

"Do you think we may have given them too much?" Margarite was ensconced in her powerchair, wearing a flowered bathrobe and covered with a knitted afghan.

"Nah. They're tough old birds." Curtis clutched his cane. "Besides, who cares? And where's Sharon?"

"She was pretty confused," Gwenda clutched the map with the directions to Margarite's house. "Maybe we should leave her."

"No," I said. "She might be confused, but she did her share. It wouldn't be fair to leave her. Besides, she knows our plans. She'd probably tell them where to look for us."

Curtis nodded. Since he was the spryest among us, he went to find Sharon.

Turns out she had her walker and was waiting for us by the fire stairs. Fortunately, she hadn't opened the door and set off the alarm.

Since we couldn't fit all of us with the powerchair and walkers into an elevator at once, we had to take a few trips to get down to the lobby.

Curtis then took the elevator to the basement. He pressed the "hold" switch so the elevator would be stuck there with its door open. Then he called the other elevators in turn to the basement, and did the same thing to them. He climbed the fire stairs to the lobby, leaving the elevators stuck on the basement level.

Since only employees were supposed to access the basement, that door to the stairs wasn't alarmed.

But the front door was. When the reception desk in the lobby wasn't staffed, an alarm would be set. It might sound not only in the building but also alert a security service that would dispatch someone unless they got an immediate message to cancel.

That meant we needed to leave the area around the building as quickly as possible.

When we opened the front door, the shrill alarm sounded.

The powerchair was the fastest, so Margarite went first, followed by the walker contingent. Last was Curtis with his cane.

As he got to the door, Curtis grinned and pulled something from his pocket. I glanced back at him.

It was a cigarette lighter.

"Where'd you get that?" I demanded.

"Nurse Nancy's purse," he said. "She was asleep."

"Well, put it away."

"Nah. I figured I'd just light up the drapes here. Make a little smoke."

"You can't do that. Suppose it turned into a real fire. You could kill everybody in the building."

"So what?"

"How about the other residents? The ones who weren't able to join us?"

Curtis shrugged and flicked the lighter.

"It will set off the smoke alarm," I said. "The fire department will be here in a minute or two. They'll catch us before we have a chance to get away."

That sank in. Reluctantly he headed out the front door and let it close, still flicking the lighter.

As planned, we headed around the corner of the building and down the alley next to it. The sound of the alarm faded as we moved away.

Curtis continued to play with the lighter. I said, "Curtis, that thing is going to get us in trouble. All this planning and you're gonna ruin it with a stupid lighter."

He shrugged again, but he tossed the lighter into a dumpster as we passed it.

Margarite, who said she had a pretty good idea of how to get to her house, surged ahead on her powerchair. She turned a corner and sped under the railroad bridge.

Curtis clopped ahead with his cane. Gwenda, Sharon, and I followed, struggling with our walkers on the rough pavement.

I saw Margarite stopped ahead. I thought she had decided to wait for us.

She hadn't. The power chair had lost traction on a railroad siding.

We caught up with her.

Furiously, she slammed the controls into forward and reverse. The chair yawed, slipped sideways, and stalled with one of the wheels jammed tightly in the space between the rail and the pavement.

Curtis surveyed the situation. "That's stuck pretty good. Maybe we should just leave her and go on ourselves."

"You can't do that!" Margarite shrieked. "I won't give you the key."

He sighed. "Okay. Can you get off so it doesn't weigh so much? Maybe I can pry it out with my cane."

"I don't think..." she started to say.

A train whistle screamed. It was much louder out here than in our building.

We looked at each other. Surely the approaching train was on the main tracks up above, not on this minor siding.

But we heard an ominous clunking noise and saw some red lights next to a warehouse, way down the tracks.

Margarite grabbed onto my walker and hurled herself out of the powerchair.

I moved out of the way so she could land on the seat. Then I aligned the wheels at a ninety-degree angle to the tracks and shoved hard.

The walker bounced and fought me, but I managed to maneuver it off the tracks and onto the pavement beyond.

Curtis said, "I need this," and snatched Sharon's walker away from her.

Sharon tottered over to join us beyond the rails.

Positioning his cane on one of the walker's support rails, he used it as a lever to pry the stuck wheel of the powerchair free.

The red lights along the track moved slowly, but they were definitely moving in our direction.

Curtis hopped on the powerchair. "How the hell does this thing turn on?" he asked, frantically fumbling with the controls.

Finally, he pushed the right button, and the chair powered up. He steered it diagonally across the rails and to the other side.

Gwenda stood on the other sides of the tracks, gaping at the red lights.

"Get over here, Gwenda," I said. "Now."

She shook herself and hobbled over.

Curtis dashed back and pulled Sharon's walker off the tracks.

The train's whistle shrieked again. The red lights lurched to a stop. Slowly, they started up again, this time pulling away from us.

Curtis retrieved his cane. He scowled at the bend it had acquired, but continued to use it, although he had to lean over.

Sharon's walker now had a distinct tendency to veer to the left.

Margarite wrestled herself off the seat of my walker and back onto her powerchair. She looked around. "I'm not sure where we are."

Gwenda pulled some papers from the storage pouch on her walker. "I have the map. And the directions."

We set off across another set of tracks and emerged on a city sidewalk.

The sky was dark, but our way was illuminated by streetlights. We made a strange sight, struggling along. Fortunately, traffic was light. When we heard a car coming, we gathered into a group rather than leaving ourselves stretched out like a ragtag parade.

One thing Margarite had been right about. Her house was only a few blocks away. It still took us a long time to navigate the distance.

"We're here." Gwenda stopped in front of a tall house on a hill, raised above the sidewalk.

Lights spilled out of the windows.

"Nonsense." Margarite stared. "That can't be my house. There are people in it."

Curtis checked Gwenda's directions, then checked the house number painted on the curb. "It looks like the right place."

"Well, it doesn't look like my house at all."

We stared at the steep steps leading up to the front door. And the driveway that ended at a garage. Just as Margarite had described.

"When was the last time you saw the outside of your house after dark?" Curtis asked.

"Well—maybe a few years ago."

"This has to be it."

"Then why is there someone living in it?"

"You'd have to ask the people who are living in it," Curtis said.

"It's *my* house. They don't belong here. I'm going to find out what's going on." She spun her powerchair around and started up the slope.

A car screeched to a halt just beyond the driveway. A man hopped out.

I recognized Enrique.

What was he doing here?

"Stop right now." He charged up the driveway after Margarite.

She ignored him and continued her ascent.

But the powerchair was struggling. It climbed more and more slowly, eventually shuddering to a halt.

Enrique was catching up to her.

The chair began to slide backwards, Margarite still in it.

At first, Enrique didn't seem to notice.

Then the chair gained momentum.

Enrigue tried to scramble out of the way.

And slipped.

The powerchair smashed into him.

He let out an alarmed cry as the chair rolled over him, then lay motionless on the driveway. The chair continued backward down the driveway into the street.

Another car was approaching. This one a city police car with its lights activated.

Margarite's chair plowed into the side of the patrol car, leaving a big dent.

Two police officers climbed out and surveyed the scene.

One bent down to look at Enrique's still form. "We'll need an ambulance for an injured party. And tell dispatch we found the missing patients."

His partner murmured into his radio. Then he said, "We're supposed to hold these folks here."

"For how long?"

He shrugged. "I dunno. Sounds like it's a real dumpster fire."

I was a bit insulted to hear our adventure described like that, but maybe it was accurate. After all, we got caught pretty quickly. We didn't even get into Margarite's house.

We gathered in a huddle. The police just stood there watching us.

An ambulance arrived to pick up Enrique. It left.

"What are we supposed to do now?" one officer asked.

"Just wait. As soon as they can, they're sending a van to pick up these folks and take them back to the nursing home." He nodded toward us.

"What's the delay?"

"They closed the street and the alley. Not gonna open it until they get that dumpster fire completely extinguished."

It dawned on me that they meant a *real* dumpster fire. I looked over at Curtis. He was staring up at the sky.

A few things changed after our attempted adventure.

Margarite found out her son, rather than letting the house sit vacant, had rented it out. To Enrique.

We never saw Nurse Nancy again. Or Enrique. The entire staff on the overnight shift was replaced.

It's my understanding that there are now more security camaras and alarms throughout the building.

They hired a new activities director, who sets up a couple of trips every month. Restaurants for a lunch, museums, and some shows. It made our lives a lot less monotonous.

The train whistles still sound in the night, but they no longer seem to be mocking us.

We did have our adventure, even if we had been thwarted. I don't think any of us are anxious to repeat it.

# Joseph S. Walker

**Joseph S. Walker** is the President of the Short Mystery Fiction Society and a member of Sisters in Crime and the Mystery Writers of America. He has been a finalist for the Edgar, Derringer, Thriller, and Shamus Awards, and is a two-time winner of the Al Blanchard Award.

Find him at www.jswalkerauthor.com.

# Quincy and Crow
## Joseph S. Walker

When Helena Vasquez's great-grandfather bought the lot at the corner of Quincy and Crow, there was still farmland within walking distance. The city was only beginning to stretch its arms west, but he was a farsighted man who knew how to bring a daydream to life. The intersection was within two miles of three cemeteries, and Quincy was going to be one of the major traffic arteries of the coming urban sprawl.

An ideal location for a funeral home.

The area boomed. Helena's grandfather added an on-site crematorium and offered generous payment plans to his working-class neighbors, in their one-story ranch homes and walk-up apartments. He became well known for his sensitivity and skill in handling bodies mangled in the local factories.

Her father added a second location, farther south. Not long afterwards things started to go bad around Quincy and Crow. As factories closed, the neighborhood developed a reputation—gangs, drugs, police cars racing by at two in the morning with sirens wailing. Through it all, the Vasquez Funeral Home stood proud, the brick edifice untouched by graffiti. Even the most vicious gangbangers nodded respectfully to Helena's father on the street. If they fell, it would be him gently lowering the casket lid and sealing them in darkness forever.

By the time Helena took over, things were turning around. The neighborhood remained shabby, but most of the truly bad actors were either dead or permanent guests of the state. When a new coffee shop opened down the block, next to a store selling organic groceries, Helena hoped a wave of artsy young people seeking cheap accommodations just might be on their way to save Quincy and Crow. She imagined cutting-edge galleries. Gourmet food trucks.

That was before she ever heard the name Norman Graff.

"You'll be given fair market value for your properties. We will also assist in relocation opportunities." Norman Graff, the town's new City Planner, leaned too close to the microphone on the stage of the high school auditorium, and his voice was distorted and crackling. Sitting in the front row, Helena couldn't see his eyes behind the circles of light reflected from his rimless glasses.

The movie screen behind Graff cycled through images of an enormous stadium with a retracting roof. In some the stadium was set up for baseball, in some for football, in some for concerts. Acres of asphalt surrounded the huge building. Parking lots, laid down over the homes and businesses of the people who filled the auditorium.

Graff seemed oblivious to their murmurs. "Of course there will be many jobs at the stadium itself," he said. "Vending. Security. Parking operations."

"Who determines fair market value?" someone behind Helena yelled. She didn't bother listening for the answer, which would just be a longwinded way for Graff to say *"me."*

"What if we don't want to sell?" asked another voice.

"Change can be traumatic," Graff said. "The principles of eminent domain, however, are well established. This project is vital to the continued growth of the city's tax base and tourism industries. It will ultimately benefit everyone."

After the meeting, Helena waited in line half an hour to speak to Graff directly. "My name is Helena Vasquez," she said, not offering her hand. "I own the Vasquez Funeral Home on Quincy and Crow. It's been a family business for four generations. I'm not selling."

Graff shrugged minutely. She wondered if the glasses were designed to always reflect whatever light was available. "I would suggest consulting an attorney, Ms. Vasquez, about the advisability of fighting city hall."

Helena tapped the map handed out at the meeting. "Your parking lots cover large sections of two cemeteries."

"The remains will be relocated." Graff scrolled through emails on his phone. "Respectfully. Carefully."

"I'll see you in court."

"No, you won't. In the unlikely event you get to a courtroom, Ms. Vasquez, you'll be seeing people several levels below me in the city bureaucracy." Graff looked over her shoulder. "I have many other people to speak with. Have a pleasant night."

The first three lawyers Helena hired all made elaborate promises, then quit within a week. When the fourth did the same, she stormed into his office, seeing everything in shades of red. Only when she grabbed his shirt and shook him did he respond to her demand for explanation. "It was made very clear my choice was to drop you or never win any case in any court in this city again." He shook her off. "If you tell anyone I said so, I'll sue you myself."

She spent hours every night after work scouring legal websites and forums, snatching a few hours of sleep only when her eyes got too watery to read. Representing herself, she sued the city and the county and, in desperation, Graff personally, though that suit was dismissed immediately. At the few court dates she could get, she sat alone at the table on her side of the aisle, never looking at the ranks of smartly attired lawyers opposing her.

Three months in, the citations started. Her landscaping was not adequately maintained. Her parking lot lacked sufficient drainage. Her electrical system wasn't up to code, in some vaguely defined way.

Six months in, the city started tearing down other buildings on her block. Enormous yellow machines rumbled past all day, disrupting services. Mourners glowered at her.

Nine months in, Helena realized that families the Vasquez Funeral Home had served for decades were taking their dead elsewhere. A hospice nurse she was friendly with whispered that the city hospitals were steering the bereaved to her competitors.

One year in, Helena gave up.

A month later, she sat in her office at the southern branch of the Vasquez Funeral Home—now, Helena reminded herself, the only branch. She had never liked it. Her great-grandfather set the corner-stone at Quincy and Crow with his own hands. That building had been beautiful to her, a warm haven where the living could give the lost a dignified exit. By contrast, the southern branch felt modern and sterile and impersonal. It was newer and bigger, with state-of-the-art facilities, but it had all the personality of a blank envelope.

The midnight world outside was dark and deserted. Everyone else had gone home hours before. She should go home, too. But *home* to Helena Vasquez still meant the three-room apartment above the building at Quincy and Crow, not the anonymous beige duplex where her few possessions sat in unopened cardboard boxes. *Home* was now a tumbled pile of bricks and two-by-fours, ready to be hauled away.

There was a noise behind her. Helena turned and Nathan Graff was in the doorway, a fat briefcase dangling from one hand. The only light was from her small desk lamp, but his glasses gathered it into the flat meaningless disks she remembered from the auditorium. That was the last time she had seen him in person. True to his word, he had never appeared at any of her dozens of hearings and trials.

"Ms. Vasquez," he said. "I was going to come see you tomorrow, but I was driving by and saw the light in your window."

Helena stayed silent and motionless.

Graff stepped forward. "I came to say I underestimated you. You proved resourceful and smart and determined. You dragged out the inevitable far longer than I thought possible." He sat in one of her client chairs, perching close to the edge. "I respect that. I came to enjoy countering your efforts."

Helena was surprised by the sound of her own voice. "Like a cat enjoys playing with a mouse?"

"I hoped we could end any sense of hostility between us." Graff reached into his briefcase, pulled out a bottle filled with amber liquid, and set it on her desk. "I brought a peace offering. A bottle of Pappy. Quite difficult to obtain. For most people."

"You're not most people."

His mouth turned upward. "I am not."

"Most people don't need to crush dreams." Helena spoke more harshly than she intended. "Things other people built."

Graff sighed and pinched the bridge of his nose. "I build, Ms. Vasquez. I'm building this city. Someday someone else will build over everything I create. I accept that."

"I don't."

He spread his hands. "Your location was vital. Have you even looked at the blueprints? What was once the corner of Quincy and Crow will now be the exact location of a major league pitching mound." He leaned forward, his glasses glinting. "Isn't there some pride in that? We could have a plaque made, if you'd like. Identifying the location of a once-treasured local establishment."

Helena's voice was back under control. "Take your plaque, turn it sideways, and shove it up your ass."

Graff shook his head. "I can see there's no purpose in continuing to talk." He stood and turned for the door. He didn't see Helena reach for the bottle, didn't see her coming around the corner of her desk, moving fast. He didn't see her swing it directly into his temple.

Helena watched Graff struggling up into consciousness through layers of awareness. There was the pain first, no doubt, the side of his head a swollen, pulpy mass. Then the awareness that he couldn't move. His wrists and ankles were tied together, a rope running between them. Something cloth was shoved deep in his mouth. Then, finally, the realization that he was on his back in a cushioned box. Helena leaned on the side, looking down at him.

She waited until she was sure he was fully aware of her before she spoke. "You know, Norman, there are some very unscrupulous people in my line of work. They'll sell you a casket for a couple thousand bucks, then put Granddad in a cardboard box when it's time for the fire." She ran her hands along the velvet lining surrounding Graff. "No Vasquez ever played that game. I'm giving you the top of the line."

Graff started thrashing. Helena stepped away from the casket and fiddled with the controls of the incinerator. It, too, was the top of the line. She opened the door at the end of the conveyer belt Graff rested on, and a blast of heat surged through the room. The new urgency in Graff's contortions and muffled screams told her he felt it.

When he'd exhausted himself, she picked up the bottle of Pappy and went back to peer in at him. She tucked the bottle between his arm and his torso. "You can take this with you," she said. "I was never much of a drinker."

Graff moaned and beat his head against the pillow.

Helena reached in and took off his glasses. She tilted her head critically. "You have bad eyes, Norman. Weak. Watery." She dropped the glasses on his chest. "Maybe you'll need these, where you're going."

He was trying to say something, or maybe just scream. Helena ignored him. She pulled the lid of the casket toward her and let it drop, then hit the button to start the conveyer belt.

"Don't worry, Norman," she yelled, as the box slid smoothly into the fire. "I know just where I'm going to scatter your ashes. The pitcher's mound. And I'll do it respectfully, Norman. I'll do it carefully."

# Bethany Maines

**Bethany Maines** is the award-winning indie and traditionally published author of romantic action-adventure and fantasy novels that focus on individuals who know when to apply lipstick and when to apply a foot to someone's hind-end. She also holds numerous screenplay and writing awards and is a member of the Pacific Northwest Writers Association. She can usually be found chasing after her daughter or glued to the computer working on her next novel or screenplay.

Find her at www.BethanyMaines.com.

# Front Desk Staff

## Bethany Maines

I was about to lose a hundred dollars to a douchebag named after the blonde himbo from *Saved by the Bell*. I tried to hurry Mrs. Martin into the elevator and shot a glare at Zack Sherman. Zack ignored me.

Mrs. Martin tottered along, still chattering, and I smiled, lifted her shopping bags, and tried to look like I gave a damn. She didn't need the help, but she liked to be waited on. Technically, the bellhops should have been carrying her bags. It was well known that front desk staff didn't carry anyone's anything. The bellhops thought we were stuck-up bitches, and we probably were, but I was paid to be the face of this establishment, and I had earned the right not to lift things.

I tried to make eye contact with Maurice, the third front desk staff member, but I could tell he was trying not to bitch please the guest who was complaining about needing a reservation for our spa that was booked out for the next six months. Maurice, his luminous umber skin glowing even under the hotel lighting, always had an appointment or six booked. If she tipped him properly, he might relinquish one of his spots.

Meanwhile, I was stuck with Mrs. Martin. I knew Mrs. Martin

would tip, but I hadn't counted on Mr. Louis—the guest I had stayed late to help—stopping by the front desk to check out at that exact moment. Or Zack snaking my tip out from under me.

Mrs. Martin's procedure this month had been lip injections. She always stayed at the hotel to recover. She had to be seventy-five but looked somewhere between fifty and 812. I wasn't sure at what age plastic surgery stopped working and just made you look like you'd been encased in plastic wrap, but she had definitely reached it.

"Oh, honey! Of course!" I couldn't hear what Zack was saying, but I could lipread that much, and the limp-wristed hand flap that went with it told me that Zack was leaning into his gay stereotype voice as Mr. Louis stuffed cash into a tipping envelope.

Next to him, Maurice gave Zack so much side eye that he could have been a meme. Unlike Maurice, Zack wasn't gay. As far as I knew, he wasn't even bi. Zack's sexual orientation was money. And he would code switch to the language of whatever got him cash the fastest.

I finally got Mrs. Martin into her room and hustled back down to the front desk. I usually worked the day shift, but I'd decided to help a co-worker and make some extra cash on the four-to-midnight shift. I probably would have said no if I'd realized I'd be working with Zack.

"Where is it?" I demanded, keeping my voice low. Front desk staff did *not* make scenes—not if they wanted to keep their jobs. Employees were not allowed to make guests uncomfortably aware that staff had lives outside of the hotel. We were serene extensions of the *brand*.

"Where's what, Camila?" asked Zack, pronouncing the *L* in my name like the dumbass white boy he was. He consciously smoothed his hair. It was a maneuver that showcased his highlights, nails, and thousand-dollar watch. His blonde tips were an after-hours courtesy of one of the stylists at the spa. His manicure was, too, but the two women didn't know about each other. Don't ask me how he managed that. The watch he claimed was a gift. Privately, I would have bet he'd lifted it from one of the guests.

"My tip," I hissed. Tips and side hustles were the only way any of us paid rent. Most of us had roommates. At twenty-seven, that felt embarrassing, but at least I wasn't in my mom's basement. Not that she had a basement. No, my mom had a third-string bad choice of a boyfriend and was scraping by on rent just like I was. But I swore I wouldn't end up like that at her age. I had plans. I had dreams. And I would do whatever it took to make it.

"I don't know what you're talking about," Zack said.

"Mr. Louis left me a tip. You took the envelope."

"That's not how I remember it," Zack said.

I opened my mouth to argue, but two guests approached, and Zack practically leaped to the counter to assist them. I pretended to busy myself entering morning call times, waiting to finish the discussion. I was getting that money, even if I had to pull it out of his pocket through his nose.

The new guest was your typical Wall Street-Suit-Bro. The kind of fifty-ish guy with an ex-wife he met in college, a trophy wife he met someplace cooler, and a girlfriend he met at the strip club. But unlike the typical man in finance, his date was *not* younger than me. She was maybe thirty-five and looked flawless in an Armani pantsuit. It was almost enough to make me believe they were actually married —except that she was only packing her oversized Birkin. That bag retailed for forty grand. Zack was clearly aware of the price of purses because he smiled at both of them and attempted to make small talk.

I could see the screen of Zack's computer from where I was standing, and watched him scan the black card of Mr. Aaron Green. The woman was distinctly not interested in Zack's chatter and distanced herself, looking at her phone. As she turned her back, I saw that she was using Scruff. The queer-centered dating app seemed like a surprising choice for someone who looked like she embraced the male gaze. She flipped from Scruff straight to Tinder, then Grinder, and then posted a message on WhatsApp before finally turning back to the desk. She visibly rolled her eyes at Mr. Green, who was still talking to Zack.

Zack promised to be at their beck and call before handing over the room keys. Green seemed receptive, but the woman, who remained nameless, wasn't interested. I took out my phone as Zack walked them all the way over to the elevator. Zack didn't come back to finish his argument with me, but that was all right. I was about to make a mint off his new favorite guests.

It took only five minutes to find Mrs. Aaron Green. She was definitely the trophy wife and definitely *not* the woman who had just entered the elevator.

> Hey girl.

I hit her DMs on Instagram first.

> This is awkward, but I would want someone
> to tell me. I work at a hotel. Your husband
> just checked in with someone who
> wasn't you.

I snapped a picture of his check-in info on the computer screen and hit send.

As usual, there was a surge of people checking in after dinner, but Zack, of course, managed to avoid returning to the front desk, so Maurice and I had to deal with prime time by ourselves.

It wasn't until a few hours later when I saw Mr. Green's lady friend standing on the curb and reapplying her lipstick, that I remembered to check my phone. I pulled Instagram open as I watched Ms. Armani Pantsuit get into a cab. Sure enough, a string of angry messages were waiting for me. But it was only the last one that mattered.

> Do you know how many infidelity clauses he
> put in our prenup?

My hand tightened around my phone but I felt the ever-present tension between my shoulder blades ease a fraction. It was the calm that only came from knowing that all my bills were getting paid this month. Hell, if I played my cards right, maybe I could get some money in savings for once.

> Hey… this is going to sound like a weird idea, but if it's in your prenup, doesn't that mean that if you got proof of him cheating, you'd be making bank?

I waited. Then my phone chimed.

> Go on.

> I'm just saying that if you were to hit me with some cash, I could probably get pics and hotel check-in information.

The messages went dark for a few minutes. Then they pinged through in happy succession.

> My lawyer says that this arrangement is perfectly legal.

> I will pay you two grand for photos.

> Plus copies of all the hotel charges.

I grinned and headed for the security office. A hundred bucks PayPal'd to Mike, the head of the security night shift, purchased time-and-date stamped still frames of my target couples. Mike liked me and had hinted a couple of times about going out for drinks.

I wasn't so sure about that. I wasn't going to work at a hotel forever and I didn't want a hotel guy as a boyfriend. I was going to be a real estate agent. I was halfway through my 119 hours of education and staring down the massive test at the end, but someday I would be selling houses to all of the people who rented these rooms.

I typed back to Mrs. Green as I walked. Might as well see if she wanted the deluxe service.

> Toss in an extra thousand, and I'll spray his
> sheets and towels with poison ivy.

The string of laughing emojis filled my entire screen.

> Send me your Venmo when you're done.

With the security camera shots of Mr. Green and his girlfriend procured, I popped into housekeeping and grabbed two towels before heading down to the staff locker room in the basement, where I kept a spray bottle filled with distilled urushiol oil inside my locker. Also known as the stuff that makes poison ivy poisonous.

My grandmother's yard was covered in the stuff, and I'd spent my childhood being warned not to touch it. Once I'd learned how to make limoncello, I realized I could use the same process to distill poison ivy. My side hustle in high school was selling small spray bottles to ex-girlfriends for twenty dollars a pop. So many boys in our school had come down with an unexplained rash that they'd closed the building for two days to do a deep cleaning. I was kind of proud of that.

I spritzed the towels using rubber gloves and then refolded them so the sprayed sides were to the inside. I carried them gingerly as I headed back upstairs, careful not to make too much skin contact.

"Hey Camila," called Maurice as I crossed the main lobby. "Have you seen Zack?"

"Not in a couple of hours," I said.

"Probably taking foot pics for his OnlyFans," muttered Maurice, and I snickered. I didn't know if Zack actually had a foot channel, but it seemed like something he would do.

I rode the elevator up to the eighth floor. Mr. Green had requested a business suite. Usually, that was used by families with young kids. There was a sitting room area with a convertible couch, and the bedroom area could be closed off with a sliding panel. And because the hotel had been built fifty years ago, the architects had included adjoining doors between suites. We have one request for them a year and it's usually a married couple who don't want to listen to each other snore.

I readied my cell phone under the towels and hit record. I probably wouldn't get anything since the girlfriend had left already, but I might catch something incriminating. I did work in customer service after all—I always deliver excellent value for the money.

I knocked on the door and heard a quick step and then a pause that told me Mr. Aaron Green was looking through the peephole.

"Can I help you?" Green asked, opening the door and smiling, although his voice was chilly.

I knew what I was supposed to say, but the words stuck in my throat. With his jacket off and his shirt sleeves rolled up, he looked a lot less Wall and a lot more Street. On one wrist, I could see three faded blue-black dots. *Mi vida loca.* It didn't mean much in this zip code, but where I grew up, everyone knew that was a prison tattoo.

I cleared my throat and tried again. "Your wife asked for extra towels."

"Oh," he glanced over his shoulder before turning back to me with a broad grin. "That was nice of her. Lana's not my wife, though. We're just business associates."

"Oh," I said, trying to sound cheerful, "well, she businessly suggested you needed more towels."

Green laughed. "I am planning on having a few friends up tonight. That probably is a good idea. Thanks." He reached out to take the towels, and I angled my phone to get a shot into the room. As he took his hand off the door, it swung wide, and I could see straight through into the bedroom. I couldn't see the face of the man on the bed, but the hand that hung limply off the side was well-manicured and wearing a thousand-dollar watch.

I could see on Green's face that he knew what I'd seen and I dropped my hand to my side, hiding my phone. We stared at each other, Green holding the towels. He wasn't smiling anymore. Without the smile, I could see that his eyes were cold.

"Five hundred bucks," he said. "You were never here."

If it were me on that bed, would Zack help me out? Absolutely not.

"Cash," I said, holding out my empty hand.

The grin on Green's face returned. "Not a problem." He set down the towels and came back with his wallet.

"Now," he said, laying a hundred in my hand, "some of my special friends are going to come up here for a visit."

Another hundred was placed on top of the first. Men like him got violent when you told them no.

"And if any of them are stupid enough to ask for me at the front desk..." he continued, putting down another bill.

Three hundred. Green would be worth a lot less money to his wife if he got arrested. She might not pay me.

"I will personally direct them," I said. Four hundred. "We don't make a note of our guest's visitors."

The hotel wouldn't like this kind of press. They might even fire me. The last crisp one-hundred-dollar bill was added to the pile.

"It's just a little fun," Green said with a wink. "And you know he's into it."

My insides twisted like I ate something bad for me.

"Mister, I don't actually care. I'm just here for the money."

His grin became absolutely shark-like. "You know, if you're interested, we could use someplace with a long-term arrangement. My clients like classy places. And honestly, when he wakes up, he won't remember a thing. It's not like anyone is getting hurt."

I tilted my head like I was thinking. Meanwhile, beneath my uniform shirt, sweat slimed my sides, coating me like I'd been sprinting.

"Talk to me when you check out," I said. "Let's see how this goes."

"Practical," he said with his ready smile. "I like that. I'll see you in a couple of hours."

"See you then," I said, tucking the cash into my back pocket with a nod. Green swung the door shut as I walked away. When I got to the elevator, I pushed stop on the video recording on my phone. My heart was jackhammering in my chest. I felt light-headed and a little dizzy. The five-hundred-dollars felt like a rock in my back pocket.

And it was going to stay right there. I wasn't going to miss out on doubling my monthly income for Zack. I took a long breath and let it out slowly. I could do this. All I needed was a plan.

Because I also wasn't about to let Zack get raped.

Hotel carpets were designed to muffle footsteps, but I still tiptoed all the way back to the adjoining suite. I used my master key card, the ratchet sound of the door unlocking as loud as a gunshot. Inside the room, I hurried to the desk and used the house phone to call Maurice. Then, it was a matter of waiting. I crouched behind the adjoining door, clutching the physical set of keys we were all required to carry on shift, and sweated through my shirt while I waited for Maurice and the security team to make their move.

The fire alarm went off first, and then I heard Maurice's voice in the hall, answering questions and knocking on doors.

"We're having everyone wait in the lobby. Please take the stairs. We think it's a faulty switch, but we need to have everyone out while the fire department checks."

Maurice knocked on Green's door, and I waited, my hand clamped around my key. Once Green was out, security would come in.

"Sir, I'm very sorry for the inconvenience. It should only take about fifteen minutes."

Maurice sounded confident and calm. Exactly how he did when one of the guests didn't get their latte on time and raged out on housekeeping.

I couldn't hear Green's response, but Maurice reassured him again, and then I heard the door swing shut and latch. I slammed my key into the door and yanked it open. The door on the other side would also be locked, and I fumbled my key, trying to turn it in the second door. Holding my breath, I swung the door open. Zack was still on the bed, totally unconscious, his shirt half-unbuttoned.

On the desk, three glasses, one with lipstick, formed a little trio. I paused to snap a pic, then tucked my phone away and grabbed Zack under the armpits. His feet thumped onto the floor like a sack of potatoes, and I panted as I pulled him toward the adjoining suite. Hopefully, when Green got back up to the room, he'd just think Zack woke up and wandered off. Mike and the security team had wanted to call the police, but I didn't think they could have gotten there fast enough and they would have been too loud to please our hotel overlords. All I wanted was Zack out of that room. Justice and legalities could wait.

"Camila, *mi reina,*" a voice said from behind me, and I jumped with a scream, dropping Zack. His head made a clunk noise on the floor. Mike and the other security guy laughed like this was what they did every Thursday night. I was too jacked to find it funny. Besides, Zack didn't have the brain cells to lose.

"Why don't I just get that for you?" Mike asked, shooing me out of the way. He was big, the way security personnel were supposed to be, but liked to wear his hair long and shaggy as if he was auditioning to be authentically brown Jesus. Or maybe he never actually booked a day at the salon. I glared at him, unable to come up with an appropriate flirty comeback, and hated myself for it. They hefted Zack off the floor, and I locked all the doors between the rooms behind us. Then, we hurried down the hall to the service elevator.

Mike swore we wouldn't be in trouble, but I couldn't help but worry about what management would say. I messaged Mrs. Green while I waited. I didn't want to tell her about the arrest until the money hit my account. But when the police did arrive, they were able to collect Green and all his special friends without making a scene. They took them out through the service entrance, with the other guests none the wiser. They said they were picking up Lana, his business associate, at a separate location. That was fine by me.

I stood on the loading dock next to Mike and watched the perp walk. Green might have looked pissed if he weren't too busy trying to scratch himself while handcuffed. His entire face and neck were covered in a bright red rash. I snapped a pic as they tucked him into the police cruiser. I sent Mrs. Green that one for free.

"Thanks for coming to help," I said to Mike as the police cars pulled away.

"Well, I had to," Mike said. I gave him a questioning look. I supposed it was his job, but no one liked Zack, and carrying his dead weight was something Mike could have passed to the police to do.

"You're front desk staff." Mike cracked a grin. "You don't carry things."

# Debra Bliss Saenger

**Debra Bliss Saenger's** writing and publishing hats include print and digital editor, journalist, marketing professional, English teacher, and public television director. She enjoys writing fiction and poetry as a Sisters in Crime, Short Mystery Fiction Society, Poetry Society of Virginia, and Arlington Writer's Group member. Her short stories and poetry can be found in print and online publications, including literary journals. She lives in Northern Virginia with her family and a fetching rescue dog.

Find her at www.dblisssaenger.com.

# Checking Out at the Live Free or Die Motel

## Debra Bliss Saenger

Deputy Sheriff Connor Fisk was ending the graveyard shift before being relieved by the daytime crew. Parking his car kitty corner next to the highway, he tuned his aging county-issued radar at the sparse oncoming traffic. Midnight ticked past long ago and boredom was setting in, a hazard for law enforcement personnel in this remote site. Leaf peepers were plentiful, but crimes were uncommon in Pine Top County.

"Doggone it," the deputy grumbled as a potato chip escaped his sizable fist.

A jarring awareness stopped his search for the snack. It was the lack of light. As his gaze shifted beyond the passenger seat, his eyes swept across the darkened horizon. The faint profile of a local motel to his right emerged.

He surveyed the Live Free or Die Motel—the origin of his disturbance. The ever-present neon vacancy sign cast a yellowish glow, but no other lights were visible. Usually, the owner, Gunther Dekker, kept his motel lit up at this hour for the infrequent tourists driving by.

Fisk did not move from his patrol car. He was not impulsive, and his deliberate nature marked him years ago. Even though he packed a gun these days as a county law enforcement official, he relied on his bulk as his weapon of choice. His gun remained holstered as he reviewed the building.

The picture of the motel framed a sad scene. It was nearing fifty years old, just like its owner. The structure sprouted more weeds in the parking lot than guests in the less-than-sweet suites. A different scenario stood before him, replacing Fisk's childhood memory of a bustling business. The unraveling of the motel had been gradual, but continuous, and the once-charming structure now exposed decades of decay.

Just as the motel's exterior facade crumbled under the onus of time, so had its host, Gunther. The motel owner, discouraged by the deterioration of both his building and his body, sought solace in a bottle. His alcohol of choice was cognac, and he shared a glass with any companion who would join him.

As Fisk assessed the site before him, he found the comparison with Gunther unsettling. After all, if someone compared the molded body of Fisk's youth to his now robust waistline, they might laugh at the fact that Fisk's fist was no longer the biggest part of his body. He sucked in his belly for a minute as he regarded the motel, relieving the pressure from his belt.

A dim light flickered on in the motel's lobby. Fisk exhaled with relief as his stomach extended over his belt. With the movement of a law enforcement veteran, the deputy knocked the car into gear and banged a scorching U-turn across the highway into the motel's near-empty parking lot.

The front door to the motel's office opened as he climbed out of the patrol car, and a sheet of white fluttered on the threshold. It was Elyse, the owner's wife. She paused at the motel door, a nightgown draped to her knees, sheathing her body. Her gray-blonde hair, usually pinned into a severe bun, hung in loose waves to her shoulders. Her rotund body filled the gown, and Deputy Sheriff Fisk fixated on her ample figure.

"Deputy!" Elyse said.

A slow burn spread across the back of Fisk's neck.

"Excuse me, Elyse. There were no lights on. Maybe an intruder..."

Fisk's voice trailed off and his face settled into a sheepish grin. Elyse had a way of chastising him. And a memory from years ago magnified that feeling.

Fisk had been a rookie cop when he first saw Elyse, her face pressed against the bakery shop's window. Even then, at eighteen, curves rounded her figure, and her face, as fair as a vanilla wafer, had captivated him. Within a few weeks, he had persuaded the young woman to accompany him to Lucille's Diner for lunch. Months later, he persuaded Elyse to accompany him to a well-known lover's spot.

On their first rendezvous, Elyse permitted Fisk a few discreet kisses before insisting that he take her home. Hooked, he pursued her, bringing her small gifts, regaling her with tales from his scant experience on a county law enforcement team. After murmured pleadings, Elyse would relent and allow his kisses to wander to her shoulders, but that was all.

Fisk wondered if he might go mad, but Elyse's mind ruled her body, and she had made it clear that she had more planned for her life than the role of a deputy sheriff's wife. Fisk's obsession with her deafened his ears to her warnings. When he reached over to caress more intimate areas, she froze to his touch, removed his hand, and demanded he drive her back home. Once there, she closed the car door and leaned through the window.

"You're not enough."

Fisk put his hand to his cheek as though he'd been slapped. A month later, Fisk heard that Elyse was dating Gunter Dekker, a newcomer who had purchased the Live Free or Die Motel. Three months later, the regional newspaper posted their wedding announcement.

Despite her marriage to Dekker, Elyse had never left Fisk's head or heart. He thought of her every day he passed the motel, hoping to catch a glimpse of her. On patrols, thoughts of her wafted through his mind. At night, visions of her tormented his dreams. Now he was at the motel on official business.

"The lights were off, Elyse. I came to check the premises, make sure you're okay…"

He stopped at Elyse's expression.

"Come inside," she said. "There's a problem."

He followed her into the dimly lit motel lobby. He stopped gazing at Elyse and scanned the room. Mismatched chairs lined the interior walls, and a lobby desk defined the check-in area. On its surface, a small lamp emitted a spotty circle of light. The aroma of aged carpet and upholstery added a smell of neglect.

Behind the desk lay the body of Gunther Dekker, blood pooling beneath his head. The desk lamp could not illuminate the dark orbits of his eyes. But then Gunther's eyelids closed and opened. He was alive.

"Call nine-one-one," Deputy Fisk ordered Elyse. "And for God's sake, hurry."

Elyse opened her mouth, then pursed her lips. She reached behind the motel's counter to scoop out an old push-button phone and punched in the number.

A gurgling noise came from deep in Gunther's throat. The deputy sheriff grabbed a clean rag from his back pocket, forming a crude compression around a small bullet hole near his jaw.

"Hold on, Gunther. Medics will be here soon," Fisk said.

The deputy sheriff continued to note the details of the scene: an overturned Styrofoam coffee cup dribbling its contents and mixing with the bright red stain on the rug, a blood-soaked, handwritten note, an empty bottle of cognac, and a wastepaper basket filled with trash.

Only the wail of an ambulance cried out that night. The technicians transported Gunther to the nearest medical facility twenty minutes

away. His prognosis was undetermined, but Elyse elected to stay behind at the motel.

"I can't leave," she told Fisk. "We have guests, there is no other help."

"Okay, Mrs. Dekker, the lights were out, and your husband sustained a severe injury, possibly by an intruder," Fisk repeated for the third time. "What, if anything, can you tell me?"

Elyse sat stiffly in an old high-backed wooden chair. Her tightly closed lips confirmed her unwillingness to talk.

Fisk slammed his hand on the countertop, frustrated by her lack of cooperation. "You leave me no choice but to call the Sheriff."

Elyse remained motionless, and Fisk turned to use the phone to call his superior, Willard Tucker, the Pine Top County Sheriff.

Tucker did not appreciate being woken up before dawn. Before he left Fisk listening to a dial tone, he gave strict instructions to leave the crime scene untouched and the witness alone until he arrived. And, next time, to keep his damn fingerprints off the phone.

Surveying the scene as he loped through the motel lobby, Tucker zeroed in on the one person who discovered the crime scene.

"Mrs. Dekker, my name is Willard Tucker. I'm Pine Top County's Sheriff. We've met before at the community center's fundraiser."

Elyse shrugged.

Tucker sighed. He stepped closer, hands on his hips, his eyes locked onto hers. "Let's start with your movements last night. Did you see anyone, hear anything?"

"I went upstairs early last night with a migraine," Elyse said, her voice flat. "Less than an hour ago, I found Gunther lying on the floor behind the check-in area. I had come downstairs to start breakfast. He had a gun against his cheek. There was blood everywhere." She paused, shaking her head. "I'm not sure the carpet stains will ever come out."

As the interview between Elyse and Tucker continued, Fisk searched the motel lobby area for clues, his fingerprints dotting the scene.

The check-in desktop revealed a utility bill stamped with a red "PAST DUE" notice. He lifted the envelope and saw more overdue bills. He imagined the pressure of a collection agency pushing the motel owner to settle his debts.

Next to the stack of bills, a list of repairs detailed needed work, including a leaky shower stall, un-shimmed doors, and a broken faucet. Holding the paper up to the lamp's light, Fisk spotted the barely visible stain of a fingerprint. He slipped the paper into his uniform pocket.

"Gunther could be careless, very careless," Elyse was telling Tucker. "I cover the morning shift to make sure guests get checked out. After that, I head up to our quarters on the second floor. A buzzer on the reception desk alerts me if I'm needed in the lobby."

Fisk heard her exhale. "I suspect Gunther spent his evening dipping into the cognac. When I came down before dawn, I found a bottle on the floor and another hidden behind the cabinet. Then I saw Gunther lying behind the lobby's desk. But the gun he was holding wasn't his. It belonged to the guest in room eight. He'd asked for his gun to be locked in the motel safe." She rubbed her forehead. "The stupidity of this was that Gunther's repair list included fixing the broken lock on the safe."

Tucker folded his arms. "Are you saying the gun wasn't locked up?"

Elyse nodded.

"In that case," Tucker said, "anyone would have access."

Sitting in his vehicle, Fisk reviewed the evening. Sheriff Tucker had accompanied Elyse to headquarters for further questioning, though it appeared to be an open-and-shut case of suicide. He had dismissed Fisk, ordering him to return to duty.

Fisk leaned back in his seat to better observe the unlit Live Free or Die Motel, with the two guests relocated to another motel in town. An update on Gunther's condition wasn't promising. He remained on life support, the prognosis bleak, his brain permanently damaged by the bullet that had traveled from his jaw to his brain.

Fisk slipped the repair list out of his pocket, fingering the edge of the paper. Like Elyse, Sheriff Tucker was unaware that his deputy was a regular visitor to the motel. Nightly stops during his graveyard shifts included sipping cognac with Gunther, the patrol car parked discretely behind the motel.

Last night, seeing the itemized repair list, Fisk knew the broken safe held an answer for his future. Instead of money, it contained something better—a gun. No one would be surprised to hear that the motel owner had tried to commit suicide. The community was aware of his money problems, and his glum disposition added to the aura of a man teetering near the edge.

It took little effort to retrieve the firearm from the broken safe and take advantage of the motel owner sodden with cognac. Wrapping Gunther's hand around the weapon's handle, Fisk aimed it upward at the man's head. Gunther's hand had jerked, causing the aim to veer to the left. Fisk hoped the outcome would soon be deadly.

Before he used the rag to staunch Gunther's blood flow, Fisk had used the same cloth to wipe down his fingerprints from the gun and the safe. Thanks to his search of the scene during Tucker's interrogation of Elyse, the repair list with his fingerprint had been discovered and safely stashed in his pocket. He'd made sure his DNA and fingerprints were also scattered throughout the lobby, obscuring any indications of his earlier social visits.

Fisk prided himself on his handy skills, and he would step in to help with the motel repair list and any other needs.

Elyse would be his if everything went as planned—maybe not today, but soon.

He would be enough.

# Clark Boyd

**Clark Boyd** lives and works in The Netherlands. His short stories and essays have appeared in a variety of online publications and anthologies, including *This Time for Sure,* the 2021 Bouchercon Anthology, and *Moonlight & Misadventure,* a previous Superior Shore Anthology. In a previous life, he spent twenty-two years covering international news for U.S. public radio and the BBC World Service.

Find him at www.linkedin.com/in/clarkboyd.

# Hopscotch & Pop Tart

## Clark Boyd

opper McTaggart, his formidable bulk crammed behind the wheel of a pink Fiat 500, stared into the wall-eyed face of the rubber chicken hovering outside the passenger window. The veteran FBI agent, now only a few months shy of retirement after forty years at the Bureau, winced from a place deep in his soul. He knew how quickly a simple plan could devolve into a hair-brained scheme before completely dissolving into existential absurdity.

The chicken was held by one William Munz, and McTaggart was laying eyes on him for the first time. Munz's threadbare sweater, McTaggart noted, was covered with what looked suspiciously like cocaine. Ever the sleuth, he followed the trail up to the kid's mouth, which was also ringed with white. Then there were Munz's blood-shot, yellowed eyes and his crooked nose, all of which perched precariously above thin, cracked lips and a wispy mustache. It was, McTaggart decided, the face of a tweaker framed by equal parts mullet and rat tail.

Munz grinned more than a little maniacally and pointed at the chicken. McTaggart's wince transitioned seamlessly into a full grimace. Then came a low groan of regret and pure despair.

"Friggin' comedians," McTaggart mumbled to himself.

He shifted his 6' 6," 275-pound frame and reached for the door lock, his sciatica sending skitters of pain down his right leg. After hearing the lock pop, Munz put his chicken away in a beat-up messenger bag, opened the passenger door, and piled into the car next to McTaggart.

"You Hopper?" Munz asked.

"I'm Special Agent McTaggart, yes."

"They ever call you Hopscotch? Shorten the first name, play up the Scottish thing."

"No, never. I thought you were kidding about the rubber chicken, Mr. Munz."

"That's how everyone recognizes me. I'm a prop comic. Call me Billy. Or Pop Tart. Like the breakfast food, except without the hyphen."

*Without the hyphen. Jeezus.* McTaggart let an uncomfortable silence fill the car.

"It's my stage name. Breakfast pastries are another signature part of my act," Munz said.

"So that's icing and not, say, a few grams of blow all over your sweater and your face?"

Munz did his best Ed McMahon by way of Phil Hartman. "You are correct, sir. Yes!"

McTaggart's hand reached automatically for the hip flask hugging his right leg.

"What's with the clown car?" Munz asked.

"The rental place at the airport was out of sensible sedans."

"And every other vehicle, apparently. How are we going to lay low in this ride?"

*We?* McTaggart thought. He touched the cold metal of the screw top. He'd been sober five years now, but he still kept the empty flask in his front right pocket as a reminder of how bad things had once been. He also found that it kept things in perspective when the going got rough. In this case, however, McTaggart noticed an unhealthy amount of doubt creeping in. He glanced at his watch. 11:40 p.m. In less than an hour, he might be making the last collar of his already faded career— an aging, mid-level mob boss named Alfonso Ancona, who liked to call himself "The Neapolitan Nightmare." Or, and McTaggart found this far more likely, he'd be left empty-handed inside a casino comedy club called The Upside-Down Frown in this Midwest hellhole, watching a tweaker named Billy Munz wave a rubber chicken in the air while a crowd of twenty drunks angrily chucked their drinks and burgers at him. McTaggart looked at the sign above the entrance to the club. A set of red neon lips continuously alternated between the frown and the upside down. A drop of cold sweat ran from McTaggart's armpit down to his waist.

"So, Hopscotch, should we go over the plan again?" Munz asked.

"Jesus wept," McTaggart said softly. "Why am I here?"

Reluctantly, he cast his mind back, looking for a reasonable answer.

The road to hell, they say, is paved with good intentions. But is the path to a purgatory like The Upside-Down Frown? That sad trail, McTaggart knew, was blazed by a random call to the Bureau's tip line and the ensuing, probably unwarranted hopes of catching that crapsack Ancona, who was the FBI agent's white whale.

His partner, Chad Stevens, had brought him the tip line recording a few weeks back.

That was the first time McTaggart had heard Munz's nasal whine.

*Hey, hey, hey, FBI. My name is William Munz. Billy. I live in French Lick, Indiana, and I work at a comedy club in town that's attached to the casino. Well, not work fulltime or anything. I do a set there once a week sometimes. Prop comedy. Tuesdays, usually. The frickin' worst night. Barely clear two hundred bucks. Anyway, I was mailing some money home to my mom in Florida a few days ago and saw a Most Wanted poster in the post office. For some guy named Alfonso Ancona or Anaconda or something. Heh. Wow. Bad looking dude, right? And that leather jacket he's wearing in the photo. Anyway, I think I might have seen him in the club, and he was wearing that same get-up. The poster said there's a reward and I'm hoping to leave this hick town and go to someplace a bit nicer, like Rock Island. Or maybe Branson. They got three comedy clubs there, wicked, right? Call me back. Peace out.*

"Kid sounds high as a kite," Stevens said after they'd listened twice.

"How else would you have the guts to out yourself publicly as a prop comic?"

"He's probably just some internet goon trying to prank the Bureau for clicks." Stevens wrinkled his brow. "Wait, your dad was a comedian too, right?"

"No. He was a mediocre CPA with delusions of comedic grandeur. And Ancona *did* always wear a leather jacket."

Stevens stifled a laugh. "Really, Tag? C'mon. No one's seen Ancona for years."

McTaggart knew all too well his partner was right. The picture on the wanted poster was more than five years old. Plus, Ancona had a penchant for changing faces and places. The informant grapevine had him in and out of Los Angeles plastic surgery clinics at least three times. The only credible sighting in the last five years? A waiter in Vanuatu claimed to have served a dirty martini to a "criminal-looking man" who vaguely resembled Ancona. The gentleman, said the waiter, sat day after day in a sunlounger by the hotel pool. What gave him the impression that this man was a wanted criminal mastermind taking advantage of the island nation's well-known lack of an extradition treaty with the United States? For starters, the waiter said, the guy called himself "The Neapolitan Nightmare." Also, he kept pulling hundred dollar bills out of a silver briefcase. And finally, the fool wore a leather jacket in 95-degree heat.

Stevens read McTaggart's mind. "Vanuatu? Tag, please. It's ridiculous. The assistant director thinks Ancona's life of crime is dead. Or at least on life support."

McTaggart stared at his young, square-jawed partner. Then he looked down at the half-finished retirement paperwork on his desk. "I might just dig a bit."

"Okay, but you'll have to go solo. I've been asked to assist in New York on that triad raid. I'm not missing my chance to be first through the door."

McTaggart remembered the early days in his own career.

"Well. I guess we'll put the retirement party on hold," Stevens said. "Check out Mr. Funnyman's story. Let Uncle Sam put you up at the resort. You'll have to gamble with your own money, though. French Lick. Sounds classy." He chuckled and headed for the door.

The minute Stevens left the room, McTaggart unlocked the bottom drawer of his desk. There it was. His copy of the entire file on Alfonso Ancona, the criminal who had eluded him all these years. Not the only one, but certainly the one that hurt the most. The one who had made a fool of him time and again by slipping away to the Caribbean or southern Italy. The one who became so great an obsession that McTaggart missed any chance of having a wife and family. The one who eventually sent his career at the Bureau into a tailspin, aided and abetted by that sweet nectar the Scots call Lagavulin. Looking at the file again, McTaggart could almost taste the smoke and the peat. He fingered the empty flask in his pocket and sighed.

His Ancona file, however, included a few things the Bureau's official one didn't—the postcards the mobster had sent to McTaggart's home address every few months ever since the FBI agent got out of rehab five years ago. They always came postmarked from towns with weird place names like Eggnog, Utah and Meddybemps, Maine. Taped to the back, there was the same blurry picture of Ancona in his leather jacket, his face scratched out. McTaggart never failed to notice the middle finger held high in his direction in every photo. Off to the side of the photo, each postcard carried the same message: "Still At Large, McBuzzard."

On the top of the pile of postcards was the latest one, postmarked French Lick, Indiana. McTaggart picked up the phone and dialed Billy Munz's number.

"Holy crap," Munz said, in lieu of "Hello." "The FBI called me back."

"I'm Special Agent Hopper McTaggart, Mr. Munz. Now, you said you *thought* you saw a criminal named Alfonso Ancona while doing a set at a comedy club?"

With whirlwind delivery, Munz told McTaggart that Ancona frequented the club every Tuesday. He knew because the visit always seemed to coincide with his set. Ancona sat down just before midnight and left by 12:30. Besides the leather jacket, he always had a big silver briefcase with him.

"He meets with the club manager in the green room," Munz said. "I overheard them a couple of weeks ago. See, I got booed off the stage early and had to retreat to safety after someone pelted me with a Reuben. I walked in on them. Ancona said something like, 'Here's seventy-five grand to be cleaned.'"

Wow, thought McTaggart, even the mighty Alfonso Alcona was now working a backwater like French Lick. In his next breath, he realized that meant he'd have to work it too.

"Did you talk to the guy?" he asked Munz.

"Yeah, I asked him why he's always here on my nights."

"And?"

"He said, 'What can I say? I love prop comedy.' And that's what I do, Agent McTaggart. I'm a prop comic. I like to use things like Pop-Tarts—"

"Let me stop you right there, Mr. Munz. Could you, without any doubt, point this person out to me in the club during your set?"

"Sure. I'm happy to do it. It's a two-drink minimum, though."

McTaggart felt a familiar itch move up his shoulders towards his neck.

"Hey, Hopper, you think the $5,000 reward is enough to get resettled in Branson?"

"Dream big, kid. I'll call you again with details soon. And it's Special Agent McTaggart."

Through the phone, he heard Munz unwrapping something in foil.

"You'll know it's me in French Lick because I carry a rubber chicken…"

Then the kid started to chew, and McTaggart hung up.

Those same sounds brought McTaggart back to the uncomfortable present and the even more uncomfortable Fiat.

He looked over at Munz, who was devouring a Pop-Tart. "Frosted Strawberry, my favorite."

This op was now, officially, every layer of FUBAR imaginable, McTaggart thought. His hand went back to the flask. Then he checked his watch again. 11:53 p.m.

McTaggart turned and looked directly at Munz.

"It's a simple plan, kid, ok? You start your set just after midnight, right? I'll sneak in and scope out the situation. Then, at some point, you find a subtle way to point out Ancona to me and keep him occupied while I make the arrest. He knows me by sight. If he sees me, he'll either bolt or start shooting. I'm counting on you, Billy."

"Perfect. I've got some great material tonight, partner. Special stuff."

"We're not partners. You're not an agent. You're a comedian. Sort of. One who's helping me arrest an old enemy. Hopefully."

"Got it. Man, the first thing I'm gonna do when that government check clears is buy something nice for my mom. Then I'm catching a bus to Branson. I've heard they've got, like, three clubs. Maybe more."

"Missouri is truly the epicenter of prop comedy."

"Nice one, Hopscotch. Don't steal my thunder, okay?"

Billy Munz got out of the car and gave McTaggart a thumbs up.

As the kid walked away, he reached into his messenger bag and pulled out a fresh box of Pop-Tarts, presumably for use in the set. Just before he passed under the neon lips, Munz turned and grinned at McTaggart. From the messenger bag he pulled out the rubber chicken and started waving it in the air.

"Dammit, Billy," McTaggart mumbled. He sat and brooded.

Then his phone alarm chimed. Midnight. Time for the late show.

"Focus up, McTaggart."

That's what he said to himself as he paid the cover and stepped into the club. At least he had the presence of mind not to flash his FBI badge. Ancona likely had security guys working the floor. The op, such as it was, might have been ruined before it even got started.

McTaggart quickly discovered that focus was in short supply inside The Upside-Down Frown. The club's mix of cheap booze and relentlessly marginal comedy began to overwhelm him immediately. The sound of scattered, skittering laughter knocked his mind back to childhood, to the days when his dad, an accountant by day but aspiring comedian by night, would drag him to clubs like this to watch his act. His father had been a dismally bad stand-up, a man who forever tried to make entire ten-minute sets out of a collection of put-downs he stole word for word from a 1950s joke book. Instead of dinners at home and decent bedtimes, McTaggart's formative years consisted of watching his father ask listless audiences: "Have we got any bean counters in the crowd tonight?" When little Hopper grew up and told his dad he was joining the FBI, his father called him a square and lamented at how the creative gene had gotten lost between father and son.

McTaggart's stomach churned. Flop sweat ran from his forehead down into his eyes as he watched Pop Tart take the stage. McTaggart froze in place along the back wall, trying to stay out of as many sight-lines as possible. If Ancona was there, McTaggart was sure he'd remember the face of the FBI agent who had nearly captured him seven times. He scanned the crowd. The place was full for a Tuesday. A few men and women had already passed out, their heads plastered to the tables. Three guys looked like a match for Ancona's body type. Only two wore black leather jackets. For a split second, McTaggart dared to hope that the plan might work, that he might finally nab the Neapolitan Nightmare, gather his special commendation and a moderately-priced retirement gift, and then escape it all by buying a shack on a secluded Mexican beach. But the two men with jackets were too far away for him to be sure. He desperately needed Billy Munz to deliver.

The kid began his act.

It was the kind of train wreck McTaggart wanted to look away from but couldn't. First, in an attempt to explain the stage name, he pulled a Pop-Tart out of his messenger bag. But Munz didn't use it as a prop. He just ate it on stage as he made jokes about his favorite breakfast foods. Then came the rubber chicken, which the kid used to make a series of tragi-comic jokes about wishing he could afford some real chicken. On and on it went like this, the kid's ten minutes ticking away with few laughs and no hints about Ancona. Finally, Pop Tart took a claw hammer out of the bag and placed a single ripe tomato on a stool near the front of the stage.

"Hey folks, I'm no Gallagher. I can't afford sledgehammers and watermelons. Y'all up front better cover yourselves with bar napkins!"

The crowd tittered nervously.

Pop Tart raised the hammer, aiming to smash the tomato.

In the back, McTaggart lost his mind. This was clearly Munz's "showstopper," and he still had no idea if Ancona was really in the crowd.

Pop Tart swung the hammer down but stopped midway. The crowd groaned.

The comedian looked over at one of the guys in a black leather jacket, the one seated in the front row off to the left. McTaggart broke out of his daze, quickly moving along the bar to get a better view. He thought he glimpsed a silver shine, maybe from a briefcase, at the man's feet.

Then Pop Tart pointed at the guy and did his best Henry Winkler, complete with the thumbs up. "Hey Fonzi, nice jacket. Ay-y-y!"

For the first time in the entire set, the crowd— at least those who were still awake— broke into mild laughter and applause. A few hoots rang out from the back. The target of Munz's burn stood up and pointed an angry finger at him. Those in the crowd who remembered *Happy Days* joined in the teasing, further infuriating the man in the black leather jacket. As soon as he turned to confront the crowd, McTaggart got a good look. Definitely Ancona.

Defying both his years and his lack of fitness, McTaggart moved swiftly between the tables, his hand already reaching for his gun. Ancona had turned back to the stage, ready to heckle, or possibly shoot, the snot-nosed punk who had made him the butt of the night's only half-decent joke. McTaggart knew it was perfect. Ancona was so angry and so distracted that he hadn't clocked the giant FBI agent descending on him.

But Pop Tart, feeling the rush from the laughter, got cocky. He wanted another laugh, and he decided to get it at McTaggart's expense.

"We got any law enforcement in the crowd this evening? How about you sir? The large man with the gun heading our way. Federal agent, I'm guessing. Have you ever noticed how—"

"Munz, you friggin' idiot!" McTaggart yelled, waving his gun at the comic. Those still conscious either dropped to the floor or ran for the exits. Everyone began screaming. Amid the mayhem, McTaggart smashed into a table, sending drinks and greasy food in all directions. By the time he recovered and refocused on Ancona, the mobster had a gun drawn and was taking aim at him. Three quick pops followed. McTaggart felt one bullet part his hair. Another almost clipped an earlobe. The third smashed into his right thigh, and he fell hard, face down, onto the alcohol-soaked floor. His tongue could taste the pools of rancid gin and cheap beer.

"So much for my six-year chip," he said to no one but himself.

He reached down and felt the giant hole created when the bullet ripped through his pocket, the empty flask, and then his leg. He watched his own blood streaming out onto the floor. The club began to flicker and fade at the edges of his vision. He was aware, though, that Ancona was advancing towards him, a righteous grin on his face, anticipating the kill shot. McTaggart shook his head, lifted his chin, and stared the Neapolitan Nightmare right in the eyes.

"So long, McBuzzard," Ancona said, taking aim at McTaggart's face.

But before the mobster could pull the trigger, Pop Tart leaped from the stage and landed on Ancona's back. McTaggart watched in awe as the wily little prop comic used his claw hammer to quickly beat Ancona into submission. Within half a minute, Ancona was down and out, Pop Tart was standing over him, still clutching the hammer.

"Good night, French Lick, you've been great," Pop Tart yelled.

McTaggart, the light fading in his eyes, looked at Ancona, battered and beaten. "Now who's still at large, crapsack?" He was only vaguely aware of the trio of local cops that burst into the club, guns drawn, completely flummoxed by the chaotic scene in front of them.

Pop Tart pointed frantically at McTaggart. "That man's a federal officer. He's been shot. And that guy over there—that's Fonzi Anaconda. He's a mob boss. Arrest him!"

"Don't move, man," one of the cops screamed. "Put your hammer down."

Ignoring both directives, Pop Tart leapt back onto the stage and grabbed the rubber chicken. As he did so, one officer let loose a volley of shots that didn't come close to hitting anyone or anything. Except the tomato, which disappeared in a showery mist.

One more leap and Munz, his face dripping with tomato juice, was at McTaggart's side.

"Hang in there, Hopscotch. Eyes up here. Stay with me."

He wound the chicken around McTaggart's bleeding thigh and pulled the neck as tight as he could. Then he used the hammer as a torque wrench to tighten it further.

McTaggart groaned in pain. "Don't call me Hopscotch, dammit."

Before he passed out, the last thing he saw was Pop Tart smiling wide, arms raised in triumph, as if waiting for the cops in the now-empty room to break into applause.

It was still dark when McTaggart woke up in the hospital bed. He looked down at the heavy bandage on his leg. Above it, he could see the purple bruise left by Billy Munz's makeshift tourniquet. McTaggart tried to shake his head, but it felt like his brain might explode, so he stayed as still as possible. He noticed the button by his side that allowed him to self-administer morphine. He treated himself to a double shot and went back to dreamland.

Later, he opened his eyes and found his partner, Stevens, hovering over his bed.

"How long have I been out?" McTaggart asked.

"Thirty-six hours, give or take. You did it, Tag. You got Ancona. He's looking at a welt the size of a softball on his head and two broken collarbones. Not to mention thirty-five-to-life in one of our least desirable correctional facilities."

"The kid helped. Munz, I mean."

"I watched a YouTube video. His act is seriously unfunny."

"Yeah, but his prop work is on point."

"Still, Tag, it's you who's getting the commendation. Nice way to go out."

"What's the kid get?"

"The Bureau's undying gratitude and a modest reward of about four thousand bucks after taxes."

"Enough to get the hell out of French Lick, Indiana. Lucky bastard. Any chance we could give him an extra thousand for saving my life?"

"I'll check with the assistant director," Stevens said. "See you back in DC."

McTaggart put his head back on the pillow. Stevens stopped short of the door.

"By the way, the kid says you have a new nickname. I told him we'd put it on your commendation. What do you say to that, Hopscotch?" McTaggart wearily raised his hand and extended one finger. Stevens chuckled and then was gone.

McTaggart laid back and stared at the ceiling. One corner of his mouth rose up involuntarily in a half-smile, but he managed to stop himself. Then the pain overwhelmed him. He pushed the blessed morphine button and drifted off again.

Two hours later, the doctor arrived, clutching an iPad in one hand and something yellow and red in the other. "This saved your life," the doctor said, lifting up Munz's rubber chicken so that McTaggart could see it. The distended neck was covered in dried blood.

McTaggart shook his head, working hard to stop the grin that crept across his face.

"Actually, it was perfect," the doctor said. "Snug enough to stop the bleeding. Pliable enough that even an amateur could tighten it easily."

"I'm sure it got a big laugh down at the club, too."

"It's no laughing matter. The bullet glanced off your flask and hit your femoral artery. You would have bled out if it hadn't been for El Pollo Loco here. And the comic. What's his name? Pop Tart?"

"So he says."

"You owe him one, Agent McTaggart."

"Two, actually. But who's counting?"

The doctor tried to toss the chicken onto the little table beside the bed, but instead it landed squarely on McTaggart's lap. Its googly eyes stared daggers into what was left of McTaggart's dignity. Something between a cough and a bark rose up in his throat, but he managed to swallow it. He closed his eyes and slept again.

"Choking the chicken, partner?"

Munz's whiny wisecrack and subsequent giggle brought McTaggart out of a deep sleep. He had been somewhere far away from French Lick. There was a shack on a beach. A cloudless sky and a jasmine-scented breeze. McTaggart was in a hammock, drinking something ice cold and eating a chicken quesadilla. On a nearby palm hung a dartboard with Fonzi Anaconda's smug face tacked to the middle of it. In the dream, McTaggart launched dart after dart, each projectile miraculously landing right between the mobster's eyes.

But now McTaggart was awake and once again staring at Billy Munz.

"You know. Because of the chicken? And it's in your lap, too. Do you get it?"

"Yes, Munz, I get it."

"They gave me a bunch of money."

"Did they?"

"They also said you're retiring."

"That's the plan, kid."

Billy Munz then went somewhere entirely new for him—silent. McTaggart watched the gears working in the kid's mind. He figured Munz was gearing up for some terrible zinger. Maybe a quip about "no plan survives contact with a rubber chicken," or some cringeworthy burn about the way McTaggart's giant clown feet dangled over the edge of the tiny hospital bed.

Instead, the kid looked directly at him, deadly serious.

"Come with me to Branson. We can partner up on new capers. Bag some more bad guys. The crusty old lawman and the smart-ass prop comic turned dynamite PI duo. Hopscotch and Pop Tart, fighting crime in their pink Fiat. C'mon, that's a show you'd watch, right?"

McTaggart turned toward the window. The sun streamed in and bathed his face. It felt warm, like that dream of Cabo. He had to admit it, though. He'd watch that show.

"Tell you what," Munz said. "I'll throw in the rubber chicken as your retirement present."

McTaggart grinned. The kid's plan sounded no more ridiculous than the one that somehow netted Ancona. Plus, anything to save this well-meaning little bastard from the fate of his own father, right? And besides, McTaggart knew that Cabo would get so boring so quickly that it might be hard to stay reliably sober.

"Sure, Pop Tart. Why the hell not?"

"You finally called me by my stage name. Let's ride, Hopscotch. Branson or bust!"

# James Patrick Focarile

**James Patrick Focarile** is an award-winning writer and Derringer finalist who resides in the American Northwest. He holds an undergraduate degree from Rutgers University and an M.F.A. from Brooklyn College. His work has appeared in numerous publications, including *Mystery Tribune*, *Guilty Crime Story Magazine*, *Shotgun Honey*, *Close To The Bone*, and *Thrill Ride Magazine*. He is a member of the Short Mystery Fiction Society.

Find him at www.JamesPatrickFocarile.com.

# A Promise to Pete

## James Patrick Focarile

Two small white socks were left on the front doorstep. That was the only clue. The baby was missing. Taken. Now, all we could do was wait. The kidnappers had been explicit. No cops.

That's how I got involved—Dirk Masterson, Private Investigator. The boy's father, Pete, came from my old neighborhood and I bumped into him regularly at the track. Not jogging, horses.

I'd handled only one kidnapping case before, but it wasn't human. A pet chihuahua taken by a vengeful, but beautiful, ex-wife. This was different. Serious.

Was I up for the challenge? My meat and potatoes were stakeouts on cheating husbands, not matters of life and death. But I'd promised him. Promised his wife, Maggie.

"I don't think I can wait another minute," Maggie said. "Why don't they call us, or text us?" She had blue eyes, brown hair in a bob, and legs like a Rockette. A black and blue mark caked in makeup marred her left cheek.

Pete put a hand on his wife's shoulder. She pushed it away. Glared at him. "This is your fault."

Pete's face tightened. "I'm trying to make a life for us."

"Running a business like that?"

Pete didn't have time to answer.

"Auto repairs?" she said, shaking her head. "I'm not a fool. It's a chop shop. Stolen cars and parts to the highest bidder. That's not what I signed up for."

"Let's stay on task," I said. "Go over what we know."

"Again?" Pete muttered.

"Better than arguing."

They both forced a nod.

"So, the last time you saw little Pete was yesterday?" I said.

"Yes," Maggie said.

"When you put him down?"

"Yes. It was around seven, just after the news. He went right to sleep. We watched television for another hour and then went to bed."

"And neither of you checked in on him again?"

"No." Spoken in unison.

"Is that unusual?"

"We have a monitor in his bedroom," Pete said. "We heard him breathing. It's been crazy over the last few months with the shop opening. I needed the rest. In the morning, when Maggie went in to get him, he was gone."

"Around six," Maggie said, her voice strained. "We didn't hear a peep from him all night. It must have been the rain."

I held little Pete's two white socks. They were doll-size and damp from the storm.

Maggie pointed to them. Her fingernails were bitten down to the quick. "He hates wearing anything on his feet. They're always hot. He must have pulled them off."

I handed her the socks, but she wouldn't take them.

"Excuse me," she said, fighting back tears. "I need to use the bathroom."

When she was gone, Pete leaned in closer. He was strong with a wiry build and stood a couple of inches taller than me. Thankfully, what I lacked in height I made up for with muscle.

"She's a wreck," he said. "But she's not wrong. The shop attracts some undesirables."

Pete's cellphone buzzed. He handed it to me. I read the text aloud:

> Bring 50K in cash. Tonight at midnight. New Hampsted Train Station. Leave cash in locker #510. Come alone. When we have the money, more instructions will follow.

"Fifty grand!" Pete said.

"Do you have it?"

He hesitated a moment, then nodded.

"In cash?"

Nodded again. "Yeah."

"In the bank or just lying around?"

"In a safe." His voice dropped to a whisper. "In the shop."

I rubbed my thumb and index finger together. "Business has been brisk."

"Yeah, but that's everything."

"You sure you don't have any enemies, Pete?"

"Not someone who would do this."

"What about debts? If not from the shop, maybe from the track?"

"No," he said, raising his voice. "I'm all caught up."

I glanced at his cellphone. Ten p.m. "We have two hours to plan the drop and deliver the money. Let's get to work."

"What do I tell Maggie?"

"Tell her you're going to deliver the money. Alone."

He turned to go.

"Oh, and Pete." He stopped and looked back at me. His face was lit up like a live wire.

"Say something nice. I'm not sure she can handle much else."

Pete and I drove separately to the train station. We arrived five minutes before midnight and parked a few spots away from each other. Pete carried an old football duffel stuffed with cash. I lingered a few yards back and then followed him inside the station. As instructed, Pete placed the duffel in the open locker, closed it, and exited. His job was done. I'd call him if I had something. I found a good stakeout spot at a coffee kiosk across from the lockers. Grabbed a large coffee and kept my eyes fixed on #510.

Now all I could do was wait.

An hour later, someone showed up.

He wore a long, tan trench coat with the collar up, a black ball-cap, and sunglasses. He was a walking cliché, but damn if his disguise didn't work. Other than his medium height and gray hair, I couldn't discern another distinguishing feature. He opened the locker with a key, grabbed the duffel, and headed for the main exit with purpose. I tossed my empty coffee cup in a nearby trashcan and followed.

I hung back but kept him in my sight. Outside, he headed for a dark green Subaru and I beelined it for my rusted Impala. One thing I had plenty of practice with was tailing cars.

He drove steadily, taking back streets through several different neighborhoods. It gave me plenty of time to memorize his license plate. If I lost him, at least I'd have something to go on.

Finally, he pulled into the driveway of a black and white Colonial and entered the house. I slowed the Impala, parked two doors down, and turned off the ignition.

I tapped my fingers on the steering wheel. I didn't have a lot of confidence this guy would text Pete now that he had the money. Maybe we should have involved the police. Maybe I should have passed on this case. A lot was at stake and I was making most of this up as I went along.

Hopefully, little Pete was alive.

I sat and waited for a sign. After ten minutes, the kidnapper rushed out the front door empty-handed. He started the Subaru, slammed it into reverse, and pulled away at a clip.

Decision time: Follow the old man or stick with the money?

Stick with the money.

With my Smith & Wesson in hand, I exited the Impala and skulked into the backyard. While the front of the house was dark, shades drawn, the back was lit up like a carnival. I peered into the kitchen window.

The face was different, but it was hard to mistake the legs. She looked a few years older than Maggie, but the features were the same, cobalt blue eyes and brown hair, hers to the shoulder. She wore a black skirt to the top of the knee, sensible high-heeled shoes, and a fitted red blouse. A little formal for a midnight kidnapping, but who was I to complain. In her arms, she snuggled little Pete. The duffel sat on the kitchen table, the zipper wide open, cash brimming.

I moved to the back entrance. The main door was open, but the screen door was locked. I punched a hole in the screen with the barrel of my 9mm, reached my hand in, opened the door, and stormed into the kitchen.

I waved my gun. "Don't move."

She stood, frozen.

"Who are you?"

She stared at me, lips pressed together, little Pete squirming in her arms.

"Let me guess. Maggie's sister?"

She nodded.

"Anyone else in the house?"

She shook her head.

"If you're lying to me, they'll be trouble."

"I'm not lying."

Her voice was calm. Confident. Surprising, considering she faced a stranger with a gun.

"The boy looks unharmed," I said. "Let's put him down and talk."

She left the room and I followed. We passed the stairs to the second floor. It looked dark. She placed little Pete in a crib and took a seat on the living room sofa. I sat in a cushioned armchair opposite her, my back to the wall, the Smith & Wesson aimed at her chest.

"Anyone else coming?"

She crossed her legs and caught me staring. "No, I live alone."

"Big house."

"I'm divorced," she said. "I got it in the settlement."

"Okay, let's hear it."

"Where do I start?"

"How about the beginning?"

"I'm Faith."

"Does Maggie know you have her son, Faith?"

She hesitated. "Yes."

"She's one hell of an actress."

"If she seems nervous and upset, it's genuine. Pete's a bully and this wasn't her idea."

"Who's was it? Yours?"

"Yes. And my father's."

"The old guy driving the Subaru?"

"Yes."

"I guess it's a family affair."

"You're the detective Pete hired, right?"

"Yeah."

"Maggie texted me. I guess I underestimated you."

"You're not the first."

"Pete hits her," she said.

I nodded.

"And he gambles too much."

"He likes the ponies."

"It's more than that. Pete borrowed a lot of money. And not from a bank."

My sixth sense told me she was telling the truth. "And kidnapping the boy?"

"Taking him and the money is Maggie's only way out. A fresh start."

"What about Pete? He is the boy's father, after all."

"Pete lost his rights a long time ago." Her voice wavered. "My sister and her son deserve better."

"What happens now that you have the kid and the money?"

She didn't answer. I gestured with the Smith & Wesson.

"A week from now, Maggie disappears," she said, finally. "We'll set her up somewhere else. In another town and state. Some place far away."

"And Pete never sees his boy again? Pretty harsh."

"So is Pete," she said, her voice as sharp as a blade's edge.

"Pete's my client. I have a responsibility, obligations."

"Even if it means putting a mother and child in harm's way?"

I didn't know how to respond. Pete and I weren't close anymore, but he called in a favor—and the code of the old neighborhood required an answer.

But what if Pete wasn't the guy I remembered? What if he lied about having debt? What if he hit Maggie? The evidence certainly pointed in that direction.

"What if this was your sister?" Faith asked. "Your nephew? What would *you* do?"

Her words hung there. I didn't want to answer, but that didn't seem like an option. I slid the Smith & Wesson into my coat pocket. "I'd do the same. I'd protect my family."

"So now what?"

I glanced at my feet. "I don't know."

"Are you going to let them go?"

I inhaled a deep breath and blew it out. "What if Pete goes straight?"

She laughed.

"I'm serious. What do I tell Pete?"

"You're a smart guy, you'll figure it out."

"I'll check in on Pete occasionally," I said. "In case he sees the light."

"You do that."

"And I might swing by here as well."

She stared at me. "I'll be here."

I pulled little Pete's white socks from my coat pocket. "You dropped these on your way out."

"Give them to Pete," she said. "A keepsake. In case he doesn't see the light."

I stuffed the socks in my pocket. Then I got up and walked out the front door.

I didn't deliver on my promise to Pete. He was my client and I left him wanting. He was out fifty grand, and a week later, a wife and son.

But codes, like hearts, were bound to be broken. And sometimes, that's the best thing you can do.

# Jim McDonald

**Jim McDonald** is the author of *Altered Boy*, a psychological thriller, *Counterculture Revolution*, inspired by the tragic events at Ohio's Kent State University in 1970, and *Smash Palace*, a collection of thirty-two short stories. While out west, he wrote music articles and concert reviews for Vancouver's *Georgia Strait* and Victoria's *Monday Magazine*. He is a member of the Short Mystery Fiction Society, Crime Writers of Canada, and the Writers Union of Canada. Jim is a math teacher, officiant, and publisher.

Find him at www.jimmcdonald.ca.

# Ticket Out

## Jim McDonald

**The Scheme**

Fourteen months inside is a drag, except for my mopping buddy Deuce, who taught me how to crack the new digital Forte lock. Four hundred and twenty days in Crime University—Brockville Jail to the straights. I hate that Forte lock. During the jewelry store heist, I just couldn't crack it. Didn't have the chemicals. Then the heat was on me, and that's all she wrote. My name's Mikey. If I see a crack in the system, I'm gonna find a way to slip through it. Always been a night hawk. You can't pick a lock at noon.

With a few bucks and a light suitcase, I grab the first bus from Brockville heading for Toronto. It pulls into Union Station early in the morning, the sun's not even up yet, and the driver shakes me awake—a little too rough for my liking. "End of the line, buddy. Let's go." It's 5:30. Is the Pin open yet? Is Bella still working the sunrise shift? I hop on the subway to find out.

The Pinball Café earns a few bucks, but my old boss Pinball Pasko uses it as a front to launder his dirty money.

I see Bella through the big picture window, under the orange glow of its lights. We were a couple when I got arrested. She visits me a few times, then stops. Doesn't matter. I see her face every night as I drift off.

I rattle the door. It's locked. She waves me away, yelling, "We're not open yet. Come back at..." She glances from the ratty suitcase up to my face. Her eyes get big.

"You."

She lets me in and shoves a hot cup of coffee in front of me.

"Mikey, you look like hell."

"I've missed you."

She bends down to look me in the eyes. "Pasko and me are an item now."

I can hardly believe it. Pinball Pasko might be a rich racketeer, but he has the personality of a hyena. "Pinball and you?"

"He gives me flowers, buys me stuff, like earrings, this necklace..." She points to a gold heart on a thin chain. "And, you know..."

I shrug, pretending to let it go. I need a nest egg to get back on my feet. "You think Pinball's got anything I can handle? I've learned about those new Forte digital locks at Crime U."

Her eyebrows shoot up. "We can't talk here. Meet me at the York Hotel at noon."

She has that glint in her eye. The one that got me sent up the first time. I ignore the feeling in my gut.

Instead of lunch, we head to the York's lounge and have a drink. One thing leads to another, and we end up in Room 313. Just like old times. Then her tears start. I know the problem.

"Pinball?"

She grunts a mirthless chuckle, tells me what it's like. He is still the hyena I remember. "I'm just playin' the game for now. He's insane. Thinks he owns me. I can't even look at a man, and he goes wacko." She rubs her jaw. "I gotta get out, get away."

I'm getting the drift. "You got a scheme brewing?"

She does.

On Saturday nights, after the café closes, Pinball has a high stakes poker game. Bella is the main dealer. They have a heavy at the door, armed and dangerous. "Remember Kurt?"

"The psycho?"

"The one and only."

"We'll never get past him."

She has that part covered. The back door is secured by an Apex lock.

"That's kid's stuff," I say.

She nods. "We'll need three guys to pull off the job. A big dude to handle Kurt. Coming in the back, he'll surprise Kurt, disable him, and rob the players. Cash, watches, rings…"

I can see it.

"We'll also need a hotshot driver for the getaway car."

I'm pondering possibilities.

"And you to do the locks."

Locks? Plural?

"Pinball has a safe in his office. Lotsa cash. Maybe a hundred grand. Guess what kinda lock it has?"

"The digital Forte."

"Right on, lover."

There's more. "Take like, maybe ten grand for you and the other two guys, and stash ninety for us. There's an air vent in the office. You'll need a Phillips screwdriver. Put the ninety, or whatever, in the vent. Replace the grille, and I'll slip in when the coast is clear. We'll hook up, and we're off to wherever."

"The Caribbean?"

"I feel you. Sun, sea, and sand."

She sits down on the bed beside me. "I'll rig it, make sure most of the winnings are at my table. One thing. Whatever you do, don't tell the other guys about me. If Pasko finds out, well…"

My lips are sealed.

Bella fronts me scratch to get through the week. I learn that the guys from the botched jewelry store robbery are still in the game. Big Rog is an animal, an ex-heavyweight, who has put a few palookas in the hospital. Bonus, he owns an arsenal. Pumped to have a reason to use his new AR-15. Tommy is a tall drink of water who loves fast cars and faster women.

## The Heist

Tommy leaves the car idling in the alley while I go through the back door Apex in a jiff. Wearing ski masks and black clothes, we wait in the stairwell while Big Rog surprises Kurt, taking his gun and wrapping him in duct tape. Rog and Tommy burst into the smoky room, waving black AR-15 rifles and barking orders. "On the floor. No talking."

Bella plays her part by screaming and crying.

Big Rog's acting fierce, growling, telling the fish, "Don't nobody be a hero." One glance at his AR-15, even the big guys bow their heads.

Using the micro drill bit with the right mix of chemicals, cracking the Forte is a snap. Thank you muchly, Deuce. A lotta cash in a lotta piles, wrapped in green paper. I cut off the wrapping with my switchblade and count out a pack of one hundred grand. What remains is a bundle about four times as big. I take a huge breath and put aside twenty large for the boys. Stuff the rest into a white garbage bag. Unscrew the grille and slide in the bag. About half a mil? Our ticket out. Me and Bella are gonna live in style for a long time.

I wave the twenty grand in Rog's face, and he grins, then scoops the cash from the tables into his black bag.

Tommy's already gone with watches, rings, wallets, bracelets, earrings, whatever.

Rog grabs Bella, puts his gun to her head, drags her squirming and struggling to the car. Yells. "If anybody follows us or calls the cops, she gets it."

With the .38 in hand, I say, "What're you doing?"

"She's insurance."

Rog throws her in the back seat. Tommy has taken off his mask. She stares at him. He knows her, and she knows him.

Rog freaks out. "Why did you take off your mask?"

"It's itchy," Tommy says. "Besides, kidnapping isn't part of the plan. Do you even know who she is?"

I'm silent, staring at Bella, willing her to keep quiet. She stares back, understanding. We'll figure a way out.

Rog shakes his head.

"She's Pinball's girl."

He stiffens, like a new deck of cards. "*Pinball's* girl? Let's get outta here. Floor it."

## The Hideout

The hideout is an auto garage out in the country. We have three getaway cars there, one for each of us. The garage smells like oil, rubber, mildew, urine, and cigars. Car parts are everywhere. A pickup is up on the four-post hoist, its motor sitting in the truck's cargo bed.

Rog ties Bella to a chair in the filthy john. Slams the door.

Tommy's trembling. "What're we gonna do? She saw my face."

Rog dumps the money out of the black bag. "She won't talk."

"What do you mean?" Me asking now.

Rog grabs Kurt's gun from the bag and points at the bathroom door. "I said. She. Won't. Talk."

I finger the switchblade in my pocket. "I gotta take a whizz."

"Don't do nothin' I wouldn't do in there."

Bella's wide-eyed hopeful look crumples when she sees my switchblade. Expecting the worst, she clamps her eyes shut. She half-whimpers, half-whispers as I cut the ropes. "Oh, thank, thank you. I, I—"

"No time for that." I shove her out the window above the sink. "Run. Meet you at the York."

One sharp glance back at me, eyes moist. Rips the gold heart from around her neck and drops it in the sink. I stuff it in my back pocket. Fire a bullet into the ceiling, and then another. "Stop," I yell, and blast the window, shattering the glass. Rog and Tommy rush in, guns ready. The curtains flap in the wind.

"I'll go after her," I say.

Rog glares at me. "No, you won't. Tommy, go get her."

"No way, man. Gimme my cut first. How do I know you guys won't rip me off?"

Rog huffs. "Know what? Forget the chick. She's gone. Let's split the take and we're outta here."

I suppress a sigh of relief. "Let's do it. This place is too hot. My guess—she's talking to Pinball right now."

A rumbling in the distance, getting closer.

Tommy's at the window. "Three cars, one is Pinball's Mercedes."

Rog kicks the table—the watches, jewelry, and cash fly every-where. Crouches behind it, aiming his AR-15 at the door. I hastily grab a watch and a stack of bills and shove them in my pocket, climb up the hoist, and into the cargo bed beside the motor, with the .38 Special in hand.

Rog cuts down the first men through the front door, Tommy sprays the closed back door. Two men poke their guns through side windows and fire. Tommy's dead before he hits the floor. I shoot back, getting them both.

Gunfire cracks below me. It's Pinball Pasko. I take careful aim at the center of his skull and pull the trigger.

Click.

Damn, where's my backup clip? I push the motor with all my might, and it topples over the edge. Pasko never knew what hit him.

Rog catches one in the shoulder. I think, *the hell with this noise,* and climb over to the windowsill and through the opening, landing in a dumpster.

That's when I hear the Mercedes fire up, then speed away,

kicking up a cloud of dust, Bella at the wheel. I think she sees me, but maybe not. I figure she's heading to the York.

I walk for a long time, finally flagging down a taxi to take me there. Wait in the lounge.

Nothing.

Nobody.

Go to the Pin. It's surrounded by black and yellow tape. Cops are questioning the gamblers.

I slip into the grocery store across the street. The owner is watching the action, shaking his head and tut-tutting. I buy a six pack. "What's happening?"

He snickers through yellow teeth. "Heh-heh, the poker game got robbed. Serves 'em right."

"Poker game?"

"Yeah, they think it's a secret, but everybody around here knows about it."

"Doesn't Bella work there? The morning shift?"

"Sure, but about an hour ago, she shows up in Pasko's car and comes out with a suitcase and some garbage."

"Garbage?"

"A white garbage bag."

I return to the York. Waiting, nursing a beer until midnight. Pay cash, part of my cut. Count my stash in the men's room. Nine grand. A watch worth a couple hundred bucks. And in my back pocket, a memento.

I lift her necklace, the gold heart dangling on a broken chain.

# Peggy Rothschild

After losing their home in a California wildfire, **Peggy Rothschild** and her husband moved to the central coast. Peggy is the author of three Molly Madison Dog Wrangler mysteries and her short stories have been included in various anthologies including two prior Superior Shores Anthologies. Peggy is a member of Sisters in Crime National and Los Angeles, Mystery Writers of America, the Short Mystery Fiction Society, and the Dog Writers Association of America.

Find her at https://peggyrothschildauthor.com.

# Ghost Wolves
## Peggy Rothschild

We approached the house from the back, both dressed in dark jeans, jackets, and beanies. The rain clouds weighing down the sky all day had moved on and moonlight shone on the still-damp streets like a beacon. When Gus presented his plan, I'd suggested we not go in on the night of a full moon. But he said the owner rarely traveled. This was our chance.

The wooden stairs groaned as we climbed to the door above the garage. Gus did nothing to minimize the noise he made as he huffed and puffed at my back. I'd checked out the door earlier and knew it was guarded by a key-in-knob and deadbolt and opened onto the kitchen. I had both unlocked in under sixty seconds, then slipped inside and dealt with the alarm.

Not for the first time, the security struck me as rinky-dink for the neighborhood. Maybe the owner had convinced himself the exterior's peeling paint—along with its location in a tangle of narrow winding roads—would keep his home from being targeted by burglars. Still, it was strange. Especially since he supposedly had a small fortune stashed here. But I kept that opinion to myself. Gus didn't know I'd learned what we were after.

Growing up at my Uncle Rick's place in the valley, I'd thought the world was divided into wolves and sheep. Sheep backed out of their driveways at seven a.m. and mainlined coffee on their traffic-riddled commute downtown or to one of the studios. Lucky sheep only had to power through a forty-minute drive. The unlucky ones had to grind their way for twice that. Wolves like my uncle made their own hours and rules, eventually taking everything a sheep owned—including their wool. He said we were ghost wolves, neither seen, nor trapped, our existence inferred through what we'd taken.

I moved deeper into the kitchen, then froze. Moonlight poured through the two skylights, haloing a body spread-eagled on the floor. A needle hung from his pale arm while a bloody swamp pooled beneath his head.

This already wasn't going as planned.

I retreated until I bumped against the center island.

Gus pulled out his gun.

"What're you doing?" I whispered.

"Whoever took out this guy could still be inside."

I shifted my gaze from him to the man on the floor. "I think he took himself out." I pointed at the dangling needle, then at the drug paraphernalia on the counter. "Looks like he shot up, lost consciousness, and hit his head on the way down."

"You think the dude got high standing in the middle of the kitchen?"

"Seems that way." I set down my tool bag and approached from the side. The coppery scent grew stronger as I crouched beside him. Heart pounding, I held a gloved finger against the man's tattooed neck then exhaled, feeling calmer. Shaking my head, I straightened.

"What about the frying pan?" Gus pointed at the island top where a cast iron pan sat full of uncooked bacon.

"Maybe he was hungry, but decided to shoot up first?"

"He was gonna eat a whole pan of bacon?" Gus's eyebrows disappeared beneath his shaggy hair.

"If a guy has a needle in his arm—and it's not full of insulin—I'm thinking healthy living isn't his main concern. The bigger question is why is he here? I thought the owner was out of town."

"This ain't the owner. Maybe he's a house sitter. Or guest." Cocking his head, Gus shifted his focus from the pan to the body. "Shit. I think this guy is Hunter Hart."

"Who?"

"The drummer? For HartSong?" He widened his eyes at me. "*Billboard* magazine called his music thought-provoking. Forget the other three members, he and Jenna Madrigal *were* HartSong. Before Jenna OD'd, Hunter was banging both her *and* the drums."

"You're a classy guy. And since when do you read *Billboard*?"

"What you don't know about me could fill...a...a—it's a lot."

"I'm sure it is."

In full lecture mode, Gus wagged a finger at me. "Hart was a kick-ass songwriter. Wrote *Hit It, All for You, Smack Down*. You gotta know that last one." He pointed at the tattoo I'd touched when checking the man for a pulse. "That heart thing's like his trademark."

I stared at the red heart and EKG rhythm line on the side of his neck. "Right. I always liked their music."

"So, there's hope for you after all." He gave an emphatic nod. "But after Jenna Madrigal died... You remember her?"

"I guess."

"She was HartSong's lead singer and so damn hot. She died maybe...six months ago?"

I shrugged.

"Doesn't matter. The point is, after she died, Hunter left the band. Completely dropped out of sight. Everyone said he had a drug problem too." Gus nodded toward the floor. "Looks like 'everyone' was right."

"Now that you mention it, I heard he was planning to get another band together and do some kind of redemption tour."

"Half of what you hear in this town is BS. You should know that. But if it's true, his fans are going to be disappointed. A goddamn shame."

For a second, I thought I saw a hint of a smile on Hunter's face. I glanced at Gus, but he said nothing. "You think he was staying here?"

It was Gus's turn to shrug. "No idea. You ready?"

I nodded, then held a finger to my lips. Gus returned my nod. I closed my eyes and listened.

When I was nine or ten, my doctor declared I had "golden ears" because I could hear extremely soft sounds as well as high frequencies. The downside was that some noises—like crinkling foil, chewing, or Gus's raspy breathing—set my teeth on edge. Back then, I hadn't realized my natural ability would serve me so well.

Gus had gone through this drill with me before and remained silent—other than his wheezing. As far as I could tell, no one else was in the house. After a solid minute I said, "Place sounds empty. Guess your source had things partly right and the owner's out of town."

He nodded but kept his gun out.

"Where's the safe?" I picked up my tool bag.

"Office upstairs. Under the kneehole of a desk."

"Sounds uncomfortable."

"Better you than me." Gus waved his gun, indicating I should lead the way.

I backed away from the body to avoid the dark red pool. A huge fishtank in the adjacent family room provided enough ambient light to find my way to the next set of stairs. Once I was shielded by the staircase wall, I clicked on my penlight and climbed. Gus followed panting, knee creaking. He was way too noisy to ever be my chosen B&E partner.

Acute hearing and a great sense of touch were my only true gifts. I'd learned the rest of my skillset from my uncle and cousins. Growing up, everyone I'd known was a criminal. Except my brother. When he was nine, he'd seen our dad gunned down during a failed robbery. I suspected that was why he'd steered clear of the family business.

When I reached the upstairs hall, I paused. A soft hum. Sounded electronic, nothing to worry about.

"It's to the right," Gus whispered.

I turned down the hall. The office curtains were open, giving a clear view of the blocky white house next door, as well as a potential view of us inside. I clicked off my penlight. Moonlight shone on the street below. Approaching the first window from the side, I eased the curtain across until it hit the center support bracket. I ducked below the sill, then closed the other side. After doing the same with the second window, I turned on my light again.

Paintings hung on three of the walls. A Kandinsky-like abstract, an impressionistic river scene, and an amateurish painting of a horse. A squat wooden desk sat in front of the horse. I moved behind it, set down my bag of tools, and dropped to my knees. I ran the light in a grid across the carpet until I spotted the seam. The flap of carpet folded back as if it had been lifted hundreds of times.

Beneath was an old Sentry safe. I peered closely at its markings. Make that really old—practically ancient. "This must've been installed around the time the house was built." I backed up to look at Gus. "It's at least fifty years old."

"Meaning, easy-peasy?"

"Yep. Not going to need my drill or borescope." I ducked under the desk again and spun the combination lock, getting a feel for the tumbler notches. Then I got to work dialing for dollars. When the final tumbler clicked, I twisted around to face Gus. "This is it, right? The last job?"

"Depends."

Though I'd expected an evasive answer, fury still heated my face. "On what?"

"On whether what's supposed to be in there really is. And if I can get enough from selling them."

Gus had told me I owed him three jobs, then I'd be free. This was job number six. I'd hoped he would keep his word but was now convinced he was never going to let me go. He'd disallowed all but two, saying they hadn't brought in enough money. A stupid move on his part. Gus was a tough guy, but he was no wolf.

My own stupidity during a burglary had caught me in this leg-hold trap. Though I'd disconnected the security system—including the cameras—I hadn't processed how out of place the teddy bear propped against the headboard was in the master bedroom. Damn nanny cam. That's what happened when you worked distracted. At the time, my brother was circling the drain, and I was trying to figure out how to help. Gus was my punishment for trying to do the right thing.

Lucky for me the homeowner was a business associate of Gus's and went to him rather than the cops. He gave Gus the recording—complete with a clear shot of my face—and told him to get back the goods and teach me a lesson. I'd returned everything that hadn't already been sold, then Gus started doling out my lesson—threatening to take the evidence to the cops if I didn't do the jobs he presented. While I doubted Gus would voluntarily enter a police station, I could picture him sending the footage of me along with an anonymous note. Equally concerning was the risk of him getting caught on a job with his regular crew. If that happened, Gus would rat me out to save his skin, making him not just stupid, but a threat. I didn't want to be on the cops' radar for any reason.

Despite its age, the safe door swung open noiselessly. Someone kept it well-maintained. I shone my penlight at the contents. Beneath a couple of passports and a stack of papers, the glow of gold greeted me. Pulse racing, I crawled from under the desk.

Gus shoved his gun into the waistband of his jeans and waved me farther back. With his bum knee, his descent to the carpet looked awkward and painful. But he wasn't going to let me be the one to handle the goods. After wedging himself under the desk, he loaded the gold bars into his satchel. There were only four but, at approximately twenty-seven pounds each, would make a substantial load. According to the research I'd done before the job, the bars were valued at over $800,000 each, though Gus would only be able to sell them for a fraction of their worth.

We were stealing them from a guy who bought the bars at discount from Gus's fence. There'd likely be no police report about this job. But that didn't mean people wouldn't be hunting for the gold and the thieves who took it. They just wouldn't be cops. Gus's fence was a different kind of thief, one I'd never deal with. We'd get more money working though my cousin, Moose. He knew investors who could sit on a take like this until the heat died down. But Gus and I didn't have the sort of relationship where I would share the names of my family members, let alone one who was a trusted confederate.

Having gotten what he came for, Gus closed the safe and smoothed the carpet back into place. When he scooted from beneath the desk, his eyes practically vibrated with excitement. "Let's get out of here."

It took him forty seconds to get to his feet and another ten to shake out his legs. Hoisting the satchel, he ran the strap from his right shoulder down to his opposite hip then limped from the room.

Nerves kept my heart racing. Mouth dry, I followed two steps behind. When Gus was halfway down the flight of stairs, I grabbed the rail for support, aimed my foot at the center of his back and pushed. He lost his footing. His hand reached for the wall, but the weight of the gold bars pulled him forward. Down he fell, tumbling all the way to the bottom. He gave a low groan, then tried to rise.

A bloody Hunter appeared at the base of the stairs and smashed Gus's head with the iron skillet, raw bacon strips flying. He looked down at Gus and hit him again. Pan hanging at his side, my brother gave me the smile that always tugged at my heart. "I think he's down."

"Looks like." I stepped over Gus and gestured at Hunter's hair. "What's with all the blood? That wasn't part of the plan. For a minute, I actually thought you were hurt."

"Figured your pal would be less likely to check for a pulse if I looked bloody. You mentioned he was squeamish. It's just corn syrup and red dye. Plus, penny shavings for the smell."

"Thorough." I looked at a pink and white strip of meat slowly sliding down the wall. "Maybe you should've emptied the bacon from the pan before hitting him."

Hunter gave another half-smile and shrugged. "I'm new at this."

"Rookie mistake."

Hunter had changed his last name before his rise to fame and never mentioned family in any of his interviews. Though he dabbled with drugs, being related to a bunch of thieves and killers was a whole different level of criminality—and not something he wanted advertised. When he fell in love with Jenna Madrigal and the two formed HartSong, he'd followed her down the hard drug rabbit hole and got hooked on heroin. Jenna's death had scared him. He quit the band and disappeared for four long months before running to me, his thieving sister. I made up the guest bedroom and began researching rehab facilities. Hunter tried to stay clean. He'd keep off the junk as long as he could, then slink away to score. Four nerve-wracking weeks passed before the right job appeared.

Five hours earlier, I'd driven Hunter to a street overlooking this house. We watched it until sunset. When the last fingers of light faded from the sky, I'd driven to a twisting street and parked, then walked to the house, and rang the bell. Several times. After returning to the car, we waited some more. Then two hours ago, I'd let Hunter inside where he'd remained until it was time to fake his death. Just before midnight, I'd driven back to the neighborhood to meet up with Gus.

Hunter freed the satchel from Gus's body. "We get enough?"

"More than. But we're only taking two of the bars."

"Why?"

"I ran the numbers with Moose yesterday. Our share from two will cover the cost of your rehab. You'll be able to stay as long as you need and still have money left. Maybe even enough to set up a small comeback tour. If we take all four, it'll look like someone robbed Gus instead of a dispute between partners."

"Won't that scenario point a finger at you?"

"I'm Gus's secret weapon. His crew doesn't know I exist. He's been taking credit for all those locks and safes I've opened for him. My work's been completely off the books."

"If you're sure..."

"I am."

"You know this world better than me. Let's make sure he's down for good." He held out the empty syringe.

I'd been nervous about leaving Hunter with a needle so he could pretend he'd shot up, afraid handling the syringe would send him spiraling. Part of me had wondered whether he'd be here when I returned with Gus—or have left in search of a fix. But he'd come through.

I took the empty syringe and exchanged it for one I'd stored inside a case in my tool bag. Two milligrams of fentanyl was considered potentially lethal. Just to be sure, I'd dissolved and loaded ten milligrams-worth into this syringe.

Hunter retreated a step.

The fear in his eyes was a good thing. "Ready?"

"As I ever will be," he said.

I handed him the syringe.

Getting the money for his rehab was only half the job. Getting me free from Gus had meant involving Hunter in my work. Despite Gus's bad knee, he was way too big for me to take on alone—unless I used a gun. Which brought the risk of him turning it on me—or pulling his own—along with all sorts of forensic questions if I somehow managed to shoot him.

Hunter crouched, pulled the elastic tourniquet from his pocket, and positioned it below Gus's elbow. With a deftness that spoke to his heart-breaking familiarity with injectables, he inserted the needle into Gus's vein, removed the elastic band, and depressed the plunger. He stood and handed me the syringe and tourniquet. Then he lifted two gold bars from the satchel and handed them over as well. He stared down at the unconscious man and said, "I can't watch this."

I put everything into my tool bag. "Let's get out of here."

We went out through the back, leaving the door ajar. At the base of the stairs, I took Hunter's nitrile gloves, peeled off my own, then stuffed them in the bag as well. I looked up at the house, wondering if all that raw bacon might lure scavengers. Or maybe another wolf like me would spot the open door and go inside to see what they could steal, further muddying the scene.

Grabbing Hunter's trembling hand, I guided him along the narrow streets until we reached the car. He stared as if unsure what to do next. I opened the door for him. He practically collapsed into the passenger seat.

"Buckle up."

"Right." His face drained of color and emotion. What we'd done was hitting him harder by the minute.

I started the engine. He stared out the window while I drove surface streets, making frequent rearview mirror checks while we traveled a circuitous route. At the forty-minute mark, Hunter's breath slowed. He'd fallen asleep. Grateful he was getting a respite, I continued until we reached the coast and parked on a quiet street near our destination. Too keyed up to sleep myself, I scrolled through my phone and waited.

A few minutes after eight a.m., I pulled into the parking lot at the Still Waters Recovery Center. I hoped the private suite, ocean view, personal chef, gym, heated pool, and spa would make Hunter's stay feel more like a vacation than medical treatment.

He straightened, staring bleary-eyed at the white stucco building. "What're we doing here?"

"I made arrangements to start your stay today."

"But you haven't sold the gold bars yet."

"I had enough banked to get the ball rolling." Hunter didn't need to know I'd sold all the shares of Apple I'd bought a decade ago to cover his first month's stay. "By the time the next bill comes, I'll have the money from Moose. You ready?"

"I guess. I mean, yeah." He took a deep breath and opened the passenger door, then swiveled back toward me. "What about my stuff?"

"I packed a bag for you."

His mouth dropped open. "When?"

"After I left you at the house last night. It's in the trunk. Along with your drum pads. I can bring whatever else you need when they allow visitors."

"Wow. You were pretty confident this was all going to work out."

"True." Anything else was unacceptable.

Hunter had sworn he thought the job was a fair trade. I'd get him the money he needed to get clean and resume his music career, and he'd help me get free so I could go back to jobs of my own choosing. I'd agreed, knowing I risked turning my brother into a fellow wolf. Unlike me, Hunter had a meaningful gift. His music spoke to people. Improved their lives. He was also a good person. The best I knew. Maybe he'd be okay. Of course, there was always the chance that, like me, Hunter had been born with a wolf already inside just waiting to be set free.

Time would tell. I hoped the music won.

# Beth Irish

**Beth Irish** is a health sciences librarian whose first short story appears in *Crime Takes a Holiday: The Eighth Guppy Anthology* published by the Guppy Chapter of Sisters in Crime. *Friendship Never Dies* is her second mystery fiction publication. Currently working on her first cozy mystery novel, Beth is the President of the Upper Hudson Chapter of Sisters in Crime and a member of the Short Mystery Fiction Society.

Find her on Amazon at https://amazon.com/author/beth_irish.

# Friendship Never Dies

## Beth Irish

How did I end up in this dilapidated joint? I've always wanted to say dilapidated joint, but I'd never been in one until now. The Rustic Shed certainly qualified. It put the "rust" in rustic. From the size of the building, it might have even started out as a shed. I shuddered, imagining what public health violations lurked behind the dark-stained walls and dim lighting.

Maybe coming here was a mistake. My curiosity clearly outmaneuvered my common sense. Since it was too late to turn back now, I texted Victoria.

Made it. Parked van behind Rustic Shed.

Victoria replied within seconds.

Got it. 30 min. away.

Thirty minutes. More than enough time for someone to hotwire my van and leave me stranded. I shivered, the frigid air seeping through the windowsill chilled me to the bone. Even the roaring fireplace and my piping hot coffee couldn't compete with the freezing January temperatures. Or my nerves.

Two months ago, I'd never heard of the remote Upstate New York village of Whiskey-Jack, let alone think I'd find myself there in the dead of winter. That's when Shea's son called to tell me his mother had died when her car swerved into a tree. The first responders speculated she'd fallen asleep at the wheel. The force of the impact sparked such a powerful explosion the flames were visible ten miles away.

Two months? More like a lifetime.

Two weeks after her funeral, the messages started. Stunned, I read the text notification twice before opening. It was from Shea. How was it possible? She apologized for worrying me. Driving home from a conference, she came across a Toyota Corolla, the same make and model as hers, crashed into a tree. She stopped to help, but it was too late. There was no doubt the woman died on impact.

A crazy idea flashed across her mind. An impulsive decision that would lead to regret or to freedom. How often does one get a perfect chance to make a clean break?

With no time to lose, she tossed her suitcase in the backseat and swapped purses. The stench of leaking gasoline filled her nostrils. She barely made it back to her car before the explosion. She sped off, leaving her old life in ashes.

I read and re-read the message. As much as I wanted to believe Shea was alive, the story seemed farfetched. True, the last time we spoke she asked for my divorce lawyer's business card. Even so, I never thought she'd make the call. As tempted as she was to leave, she had grown too complacent. But if presented with a no-strings-attached opportunity, would she grab it?

It seemed more likely someone was playing a cruel joke. Who would do something like that? And why?

The texts continued. Each one written in Shea's distinctive style. Nothing had changed, except, you know, she was gone. I was at the memorial service. I consoled weeping relatives. Heartfelt tributes were read from tear-stained notes. Granted, there was no casket for anyone to comment: "Doesn't she look like she's sleeping?" Only framed pictures reflecting happier times.

Grief overruled my instinct to block the number.

Exactly five weeks and two days after they began, I pulled up Shea's Facebook page.

A post written by Violet that afternoon caught my eye. Violet? Shea never mentioned anyone named Violet to me.

Shea, it feels as if you never left.

Had Violet been receiving messages too? I opened Messenger and began to type.

Violet answered within ten minutes. She introduced herself as Victoria, and that name I knew. Shea and Victoria had been sorority sisters in Montreal many years ago and had maintained a close, if long-distance, friendship. I couldn't remember what Victoria did after university.

Like me, Victoria began receiving messages after Shea's funeral and hoped she wasn't the only one. She posted on Facebook, curious to see if any of Shea's friends responded.

Our phones dinged as we texted. Another message from Shea. She always did have impeccable timing.

Meet me in Whiskey-Jack next Tuesday 7 p.m. Center of town cemetery by the stone angel. I need help. Bring cash.

That single message spoke volumes. Never in a million years would she ask for money. And meet her in a cemetery at night? She always worried when I walked my dog Lucy alone after dark, insisting I text her when I got home.

Something was wrong. Before responding, Victoria and I did some plotting of our own. On the slim chance it was Shea, we decided one of us should agree to meet her. The other would discreetly follow and call 911 for help if it wasn't Shea. If it *was* her, we'd convince her to come home for the help she so obviously needed.

My hands trembled as I typed.

> I can be there. Do you need anything else?

> Just cash. You're the only one who truly cared for me. Miss you. Thanks.

"Cory? Cory, is that you?"

The sound of my name spoken in a broad Lancashire accent drew me back to the darkness of The Rusty Shed. I'd never seen anyone match their social media profile picture so perfectly as Victoria. Blonde hair, warm smile, late fifties, maybe early sixties.

Victoria swept the bench with her left hand. A few crumbs flew to the ground. She grimaced as she slid onto the seat, holding a mug with a piece of string and cardboard dangling from the side.

"I needed a strong cup of tea before we got started, but this mug needs to sit down more than I do."

At my puzzled expression she explained, "Because the tea is so weak."

I liked this woman.

After the obligatory pleasantries, we reviewed our plan. Victoria never skipped a beat. There was a self-assuredness about her that was both comforting and disconcerting. After all, what did I really know about her? How could she drop everything to be here tonight? Is she married, single, widowed?

Me? I come and go as I please.

Or was I reading too much into things? Nothing wrong with being a take charge person, right? Right. Focus on the moment.

"6:40." Victoria glanced at her phone, "We have twenty minutes to find the statue. According to Google Maps, the cemetery is three miles up the road. This is it. Showtime. Ready?"

"Nope. But I don't think I'll ever be ready. Let's do it."

"I'll sneak out the back door when you leave." Victoria must have sensed my uneasiness. "In case you're being watched." She gave me a reassuring smile. "Trust the plan."

I nodded, tossed a $20 bill on the table, then headed out into the night to face the unknown alone.

Fortunately, my van was right where I left it. Out of the corner of my eye, I saw Victoria crouched in the shadow of the bushes. I slid open the back door, tossed in my purse, then pretended to see a problem with my back tire, hoping my little act would distract anyone watching.

I closed the back door, catching a glimpse of Victoria curled up behind the driver's seat. How had she managed to do that without me noticing?

As Sherlock Holmes might say, the game was afoot. Literally, because the cemetery gate was too narrow to drive through. I pulled into one of the unpaved parking spots. Well, if I had to wander through a deserted graveyard after dark, at least I was dressed the part in basic black from head to toe.

We agreed not to talk after leaving The Rustic Shed since I was supposed to be alone. Still, I couldn't stop myself from muttering, "See you soon. I hope."

No answer. I wasn't expecting one.

I hadn't heard her get out of the van. But I hadn't heard the van driving off either. Giving my spare key to a complete stranger—not one of my smartest moves.

Based on the map, the statue should be about half a mile from the gate. Less than ten minutes to make it. Taking a few deep breaths to calm my nerves, I strode confidently down the gravel path. Perhaps confidently is too strong a word, but if I pretended to be confident, maybe I would convince Shea, Victoria, and whoever else might be lurking behind the gravestones not to mess with me.

I might even come to believe it myself. The lack of streetlights made it difficult to see anything ahead of me. The moonlight shining through the trees helped, but it also created eerie shadows. Even worse, I couldn't tell what made them. Was anyone besides Victoria following me? What if she wasn't? What if she chickened out? The quiet was deafening.

And now there were large shapes lurking by the headstones. I walked faster, stifling a scream, then spotted a herd of deer. Startled, they sprinted off, leaving me alone once more.

I stumbled upon the statue with two minutes to spare. A stone angel, arms and wings outstretched, bearing the inscription "Gabriel's Loving Protection."

A silhouette with six legs emerged from behind the statue. *Wait, that's not possible.* The six-legged creature morphed into a man and his German Shepherd. He said something to the dog, but I couldn't make it out.

In case the comment was directed to me, I responded. "Evening."

"Evening Ma'am. Enjoy your walk." They continued down the path, swallowed into the night.

One minute to go. No Shea. No Victoria. Not even a German Shepherd.

And then a figure appeared.

"Cory? Is that you?" The voice spoke barely above a whisper. It didn't sound like Shea, but I wasn't sure. *Where the hell was Victoria?*

"Shea? I can't see you. Can you come closer? Are you okay?"

Shea stopped dead in her tracks. Was it Shea? The person in front of me was the right height and shape, but Shea would have run up for a hug. At least, that's what the Shea I know would do.

I wished Victoria would give me a sign.

"Thanks for coming. I couldn't risk meeting you in Albany." The figure stopped just far enough away to make it impossible to see her face.

"Why, are you scared?" *C'mon already, Victoria.*

"Did you bring money? My name is off our joint bank accounts, me being dead and all. Besides, if I try to access them, they'd find me."

Maybe if I started walking towards her I could see—she's not a woman at all, but a man.

Shea-poster retreated, but we both knew it was too late. His voice shifted from a whisper to a guttural snarl. "Did you bring the money?"

"Yes, but I don't have access to enough cash to keep you going for long. Come back with me. You'll be safe."

"No." Shea-poster put his hand in his pocket. Dare I hope he's just warming his hand? No such luck. He immediately pulled it back out, holding a gun. "We're going to find an ATM and you're going to withdraw as much as you can."

*No way.* At that moment, Victoria stepped out of the shadows. Why wasn't she hiding behind a gravestone calling 911? She was heading straight toward Shea-poster.

OMG. I knew it. In that moment, I knew it. I'd been had. Duped. Fooled. Set-up. How could I have been so stupid as to blindly trust someone I met through Facebook? No police were coming unless it was to investigate a suspicious death in the cemetery.

Mine.

Shea-poster inched closer to me, "Lady, you have ten seconds to start moving. One...two... "

So that's what a trigger cocking sounded like.

"I wouldn't if I were you," a familiar British voice coolly piped up. "Now, put the gun down. I'm an expert shot."

Shea-poster shifted to see Victoria aiming at him. "Don't come any closer. Drop your gun."

"I think not. You drop yours."

Wait. They weren't co-conspirators? Did I miss her calling the police? Who was she?

As if on cue, light flooded the area from spotlights hidden behind aging monuments. State troopers surrounded us, their guns trained on Shea-poster.

Shea-poster lunged toward me.

Victoria flew through the air. A gun fired as she tackled me to the ground. Her body jerked then went limp.

I heard a scream. It took a moment to realize it was coming from me.

"Do you mind? I think you broke my ear drums."

"VICTORIA! You're alive?"

I've never hugged anyone so hard in my entire life. Happiness, fear, confusion, I didn't know what I felt. If I had to choose one emotion it was relief. Tears streamed down my face.

Victoria was alive. I was alive.

"Sorry. Some women wear necklaces, my accessory of choice is a bulletproof vest. I'll be a bit sore in the morning, but no serious harm done. Are you okay?"

"Yes, but no one's told my knees yet the danger is over."

"Here, let me help you up." Victoria steadied me as I swayed a few times before I could stand on my own.

Dozens of officers swarmed around Shea-poster. Even the dog walker was there. The German Shepherd, a well-trained police dog, growled menacingly as two officers handcuffed a struggling Shea-poster.

Not going down without a fight, he protested his innocence. I was the one who demanded money to take to Shea. He was only defending himself.

Victoria interrupted. "Won't work. Here's a hint. If you're going to con someone, make sure she's not RCMP."

*Wait a minute. RCMP?* "You're a Mountie? With the Royal Canadian Mounted Police? Why did Shea never mention that?"

Victoria grinned. "Shea may have shared too much for my liking on social media, but she *could* keep a secret. If you're up to it, we'd better get to the station for questioning. Oh, and I knew if all went according to plan it would be too late for you to drive home. I booked you a room at the B&B. I'll fill you in later, promise. And next time, you may not want to give your keys to a total stranger."

"Thanks, I'll keep that in mind."

"Over here!" Victoria waved me over to a table by a bay window with a lakeside view. In the light of day, Whiskey-Jack didn't look half bad.

"I took the liberty of ordering you a coffee. Cream and sugar?"

"Thanks, black is fine." After savoring the first mouthful, I summoned the courage to ask the obvious. "Shea's gone?"

Victoria nodded. "I'm sorry."

"And you were sure it wasn't her?"

Another nod. "I've known Shea, well *knew* her, for over forty years. You form a special bond pledging a sorority with someone. It sounds cliché, but it's true. She would never have put anyone through what we went through. I verified the death certificate, spoke with the coroner, and checked the car's VIN. There's no doubt."

"But how did he know so much about her?"

"Well, Shea could keep a secret, but her social media privacy settings? Wide open to the public. I kept warning her to strengthen them."

I mentally made a note to review mine later that day.

"He's a lowlife identity thief. His MO is to scan obituaries, then check social media accounts. He scrolls through the friends and selects one or two. This time, he picked the wrong two people to con."

"This time?"

"From what we can determine from registered complaints, we're fairly certain this is the fifth time in the last two years. He took the two of us to be, in his words, 'a couple of old broads who'd fall for anything.' He wasn't expecting either of us to be different from the other women he conned. They gave him money or whatever else he asked for, trying to help their friends."

My face must have been a study. I couldn't remember a time in my life when I'd been so angry.

"Don't worry. He's going to get what's coming to him. I'll say this though," Victoria paused to take a sip of her Earl Grey, "it would make for one captivating thriller, don't you think Dr. Shore?"

Victoria chuckled at my shocked expression. "Guess I'm not the only one with secrets, eh? You didn't think I would trust you without investigating first, did you? Dr. Corinne May Shore earned a PhD in Creative Writing from the University of Houston. Oh, you're also C.M. Shore, *New York Times* bestselling author. With those credentials, I knew you'd meet me here. How could you resist a mystery? Shea mentioned you were a writer. I connected the dots."

"Guilty as charged. But why didn't you tell me Shea was really gone?"

"I'm sorry about that, but I needed you to act as if you thought she was still alive."

As the conversation drifted to memories of Shea, we lost all track of time, switching from coffee and tea to wine as morning slipped into afternoon. I imagined Shea joining us, happy that her two oldest friends were meeting at last.

*"Here's to you, Shea,"* I thought, and I swear I heard the sound of three glasses clinking.

# Gina X. Grant

**Gina X. Grant** writes fiction that leans more light than dark, blending humor, heart, and a hint of mischief. Nestled just north of Toronto, Canada, in a cozy house surrounded by thirty-two trees, she shares the space with Canoli—a rescued Mexican street dog who may be the real boss of the household.

A proud member of Sisters in Crime, the Short Mystery Fiction Society, the Writer's Circle of York Region, and Novelists Inc., Gina is gearing up for the 2025 launch of *The Unlikely Murder Club*, a sharp and witty silver-sleuth cozy mystery series.

Find her at www.ginaxgrant.com.

# Secrets Unleashed

## Gina X. Grant

Casing the joint proved easy. Nobody questioned a middle-aged woman puffing away on a cigarette, casually leaning against ProfitMax Corp's multi-story head office building. *Not coughing is probably going to be the hardest part of the job,* Agatha mused, taking the occasional drag to keep the cigarette from going out.

At six p.m., she got the last of the information she needed. The cleaning staff arrived promptly at the start of their evening shift. Very promptly. Nobody wanted their minimum wage pay docked for tardiness, but not a single person wanted to be there even a minute before they had to. Agatha added a mental note to her growing list: *six o'clock. No earlier.* It joined the other facts, figures, and blueprints she'd memorized, along with the plans and schemes she'd developed to undertake this heist.

The next day, with her temporarily blonde curls tucked under a convincing gray wig, she slipped into the building at 6:15. "Clean. I clean," she said, pointing to herself and making polishing motions. *Wax on. Wax off.* When the security guard opened his mouth to refuse her entry, she pointed to a dollar-store watch on her wrist, crying, *"Tarde. Tarde."* which the internet had assured her was Spanish for "I'm late." The guard began a lecture about badges and sign-in sheets, but Agatha just scrunched up her face, the picture of confusion.

And threatening tears.

With the predictable eye-roll and long-suffering-sigh combo, the guard buzzed her in. He clicked a few keys on his computer, then swiped a visitor's pass through the squat black encoder. The device sat perched on the security console, surrounded by a bank of closed-circuit TV monitors. Before handing it to her, he carefully and loudly enunciated, "This is just for tonight. Tomorrow, you get your boss to..."

Agatha gifted him with an enormous smile, showcasing rotten teeth, hitting him in the face with a blast of garlicky fish breath.

He waved her away, eyes watering.

With security cleared, she took the elevator to the basement where the head superintendent had a tiny office. She knew the guard would be watching on his monitors, so she hurried along, head down, clutching her overstuffed messenger bag.

The basement was a warren of dark offices, storage rooms, and utility closets. The smell of mold, mildew, and diesel fumes nearly choked her. Who could work down here? She roved around a bit, knowing she'd look exactly like a new employee seeking her boss's office. In reality, she knew every step of the way, even though she'd never been in the building before that evening. Building plans were easily available at City Hall, along with a friendly guided tour of the facility available for your viewing pleasure on the ProfitMax website.

*"See our beautiful premises where we do important work. Our drugs save lives. Here's our lab. Look at the brilliant scientists busy at their jobs. Here's our boardroom. Look at the corporate overlords deciding your future. Don't they look fat and happy?"*

Okay, the voiceover had said more about health and medical advances, but Agatha could read between the lines.

There was always the danger the building had deviated from the architect's plans with interior renovations implemented over the years, so she sighed with relief when the ladies' room was exactly where the blueprints said it would be. Rerouting plumbing was costly, after all.

Although CCTV cameras were illegal in bathrooms, she checked anyway. She flipped the light switch off, then made a careful sweep of the room with her phone's camera. Most video equipment featured infrared lights for night vision, which would appear like tiny, bright dots on a camera screen. She made a second sweep with an app she'd downloaded using a false account. Nothing. She was good to go.

Turning the lights back on, she touched the mirror in various places. Thankfully, a thick pane of glass separated her finger from its reflection. If it were two-way glass, there would be no gap—her fingertip would meet its mirrored twin directly.

Next, she entered the cubicle designed to accommodate a wheelchair. Latching the door, she spat the snaggletooth prosthetic into her palm, wiping it on her thin cotton apron before stashing it in her bra. She'd fashioned it from dental acrylic so it wouldn't show up on a metal scan. After that, the wig, apron, and baggy cardigan went into the messenger bag, revealing a business-casual outfit of black trousers and white blouse. Each item was stretchy enough to accommodate unexpected athletics, such as hiding in a credenza or wiggling out a tiny vent. Once she'd spent a long weekend hiding in the walls of an old bank building. Agatha was lean and lithe and, despite being in her forties, could wriggle through an air duct if necessary.

With the right outfit and makeup, she could easily impersonate a middle-aged cleaning lady—or a self-important junior lab rat. To complete the latter ensemble, she extracted a thrifted, well-worn lab coat and pulled it on over her clothes.

From a small compartment on the outside of the bag, she pulled out a pair of heavy-framed glasses that didn't suit her thin face and kept sliding down her nose. Besides being memorable, she'd glazed the lenses with a special chemical which reflected light—the opposite of the anti-glare coatings most eyeglasses were treated with. When they checked the surveillance footage later—and they would—they'd see a slim woman in a lab coat with huge glowing eyes, a cross between an owl and an alien.

The final accessories were a couple of "chopsticks" which she used to construct a messy bun in her dyed blonde hair. One hid a screwdriver designed to be uncapped at different points, revealing a selection of heads: flat, Robertson, Phillips, hex. The other "chopstick" was a sharp, pointed pick. It could shatter glass, break through a simple lock, or serve as a weapon. She'd never harmed anyone and wasn't sure she could, but she liked to keep her options open.

Knowing it would be a while before she got another chance, she made use of the facilities before slinging the messenger bag over her shoulder.

She left the bathroom, low heels padding softly on the coffee-stained carpet. If anyone remembered her, they'd recall a blonde lab employee with big glasses and nothing more.

Once in the hallway, she sidled along the wall until she stood directly beneath the security camera where it couldn't capture her image. Standing on tiptoe, she slid a pair of pantyhose over the lens. It wouldn't black out the camera, but it would render it so blurry as to be useless. To the security guard, it would just look like a malfunction. He'd tell his partner to check it on his next round, which would be—Agatha checked her watch— in about ten minutes. She'd be well hidden by then.

Or she'd better be.

Dashing down the hall, she tried door after door, until she found an unlocked one. A supply closet. She cursed under her breath. That wouldn't work because the cleaning staff could access it at any time. She tried two more doors. She was almost at the end of her rope—literally. Finally, she found a copier room with a tiny office at the back. Perfect. She slipped inside, and just before closing the hallway door all the way, she tugged at the dental floss, reeling it in hand-over-hand until she gently pulled the pantyhose back off the camera and yanked them, flopping like a two-legged octopus, down the hall. Once they were in her hands, she slowly closed the copier room door the rest of the way and returned stockings and floss to the messenger bag. Now the security guard would write off the disturbance as a temporary glitch.

She checked her watch: 6:45. She had five hours and fifteen minutes to kill. Crawling under the desk in the tiny back office, she pulled a novel up on her Kindle app, set it to dark mode, and began to read, chewing on an entire package of breath mints to mask the garlicky fish breath she'd used on the security guard. You never knew when you might need feminine wiles.

But Patterson's latest thriller couldn't hold her attention. Her mind kept drifting to the events that had led her to this moment. A month ago, ProfitMax was just another faceless pharmaceutical company—a name she'd heard, maybe even seen on a prescription bottle. It wasn't until she'd encountered a crying child, desperately handing out "Missing" flyers, that ProfitMax came onto Agatha's radar.

The child's tearful explanation hit her harder than expected. Agatha had always lived by her "Robin Hood" style code of ethics— protecting people from criminals—criminals worse than her, that is. So, despite her desire to stay uninvolved, in her effort to console little Gracie MacDonald, she'd made promises she had no business making, but which she felt morally bound to keep.

What started as a simple vow led to late-night research sessions and subtle inquiries through her underworld connections. It didn't take long for ProfitMax's secrets to surface. Their research methods and the ways they tested new products made them Agatha's next target.

At midnight, her phone vibrated, shocking her thoughts back to the dark office where she hunkered under some low-level clerk's ancient desk.

It was time.

After listening carefully, she stuck her head out of the copier room. The hallways were now darkened, lit only by the emergency lights and the exit signs. Her research had shown what she was looking for was on the fourth floor. Following the bright red exit lights, she headed to the stairwell. Her calves would ache tomorrow.

The fourth floor featured state-of-the-art security. But Agatha had state-of-the-art tools. State-of-the-art *homemade* tools. While she would buy items off the dark web or from local "craftsmen" if necessary, the more independent she was, the better. There was no honor among thieves, and they wouldn't hesitate to blackmail you out of your hard-won booty. In her case, since she tended to rob the robbers, extort the extortionists, and trick the tricksters, returning stolen money and goods to the victims, a threat to turn her in to the cops wasn't the worst-case scenario. It was enough that her client knew what she was up to.

A week ago, she'd shadowed Doctor Reggie Porter, ProfitMax's most junior scientist. When he'd gone into a bar after work, she'd followed, wearing a slinky dress and skillfully applied makeup, her chestnut hair curling seductively around her face. She'd let Reggie buy her drinks, slipping a mild sedative into his beer when he wasn't looking. Once sure that he was under the influence, she pressed his hand into her cleavage, getting a clear imprint of his thumb on some fast-dry modeling clay.

Then, she'd held up her phone, gushing, "Let's get a selfie." Framing herself out of the shot, she zoomed in on his face. When she'd reached behind and goosed him, he'd opened his eyes wide in shock. Later, she'd printed his face life-size on quality photo-paper, carefully cutting out the eyeball, and gluing it onto a marble she'd affixed to a popsicle stick.

Next, she'd used his imprint as a mold, fashioning a reverse impression out of pliable silicone, then affixed Reggie's thumbprint to a plastic magician's thumb she'd ordered from Amazon. Now she could wear it over her own thumb without arousing suspicion, whether caught on camera or, if she was unlucky, in person.

Because she was wearing the thin plastic device over her own thumb, the heat would transfer and fool the scanner, which registered body heat, as well as loops, arches, and whorls. With a click, the scanner beeped her through the first barrier.

Next came the true test of her abilities. She raised her hi-res eyeball-on-a-stick up to the retinal scanner, feeling like a seventeenth-century partygoer holding a masquerade mask to their face.

*"Hold still, please,"* a mechanical voice droned. Agatha tried to still her shaking, taking one deep breath after another. She wasn't usually nervous, but then she rarely had a brokenhearted child depending on her. After a few interminable seconds, the lab door whooshed open.

Shoving the fake thumb and eyeball into her pocket, she entered the lab. Thanks to the website video, it looked exactly as expected. What she didn't expect was a disheveled scientist, staring at her from behind a computer monitor, a handful of popcorn frozen halfway to his mouth. He tried to swallow, choke, and speak, all at the same time, accomplishing none of them very successfully.

She took a moment to be grateful it wasn't Reggie, the junior scientist she'd scammed the eyeball shot from. Even the most basic scanner would have registered he'd come in twice without leaving in between and sounded an alarm.

Finally, the choking lab tech took a swig of diet cola and managed, "Um, hi?" He looked at some papers on his desk. "I didn't think my relief was until morning."

Taking another deep breath, she smiled, showing her real straight, white teeth and strode purposely over to him. "I thought if I came in early, I could log some overtime. I'm Sam." She patted her badge, careful to obscure the fact that it was a visitor issue.

"Herman," he replied, holding out his hand, then realizing it was full of popcorn. He dumped the handful back into the bag with an embarrassed giggle.

Before the conversation became any more awkward, she added. "I have insomnia. If I have to be awake, I might as well get paid for it, right?" She added a giggle of her own, hoping that would put him at ease.

"Well, okay. I was just about to take the dogs out. Do you want to join me?"

*Take the dogs out?* She'd brought a heavy-duty harness and webbing contraption to exit out a window or, worst case, down the elevator shaft. But to just walk out the front door? This was an unexpected bonus.

"That'd be great. I'm new, so you can show me the ropes. Then you can take off for the night." She peered up at him through her lashes. "I mean, if you don't mind, Herman."

"Absolutely," the lab tech said, gathering his phone, keys, and the half-empty bag of popcorn. "I'm thrilled to be getting out of here a bit early. Come to the back. I'll show you where we keep the leashes."

Herman led her to a back area with about a dozen cages. All but three were empty. Agatha loved dogs and expected them to be barking madly when they entered. Instead, they sat quietly in their kennels, looking hopeful.

Herman removed three leashes from a row of pegs on the wall, handing one to her. "You can take the beagle. She's friendly. Actually, they're all friendly."

He opened the cage, clipping a lead on a small dog that looked like a schnauzer-poodle cross. The little guy licked his hand and hopped around a bit. Agatha followed Herman's example, opening the beagle's cage and clipping the leash to her collar. The last dog was a medium-sized lab cross. "This guy pulls," he explained, fastening the leash onto a cruel-looking choke collar.

Agatha hadn't counted on three dogs. She was only interested in one, but if she could save three, then she would. The beagle stood obediently by her side, the schnoodle sniffed her shoes, and the lab-cross took a few steps toward the door.

"These dogs are so friendly. It's almost like they're pets."

Herman pushed the door open, the lab trying to drag him along, before being brought up short by the collar. "Well," he said, "it's illegal to use former pets for most kinds of testing and experiments."

Something about his tone caught Agatha's attention. She followed with the well-behaved beagle at her side, figuring Herman had more to say. People, especially nervous people, tended to babble. Particularly when trying to impress a new colleague. With the glasses, he probably couldn't tell she was at least a decade older than him.

And sure enough, he kept talking, calling back over his shoulder, "I'm not supposed to know, but we get our test subjects from a shady organization. I wouldn't be surprised if some of these animals were dognapped." He peered around as if one of the dogs might report him for spilling corporate secrets.

"Oh, Herman," Agatha cried. "That's awful. But at least it's just these three."

"As if. There are a hundred or more out at the manufacturing facility. We only keep a few at this location for beta purposes."

One of the other advantages of the heavy black glasses was the recording function built into the thick frames, which she'd switched on when entering the lab. Now Agatha was very glad she had. It uploaded to the cloud as it recorded, so no matter what happened, a record of ProfitMax's inhumane and illegal activities could be accessed from anywhere.

Unsure of the exit protocol or if her visitor's pass still worked—it might be programmed to reset at midnight—she "accidentally" crowded up next to Herman in the exit turnstile, pretending the dog had pulled on the leash. "Oops," she said. He blushed and swiped his pass in the elevator. The five of them, two humans and three dogs, descended to the main floor.

Once again Herman filled the silence, providing Agatha with the name of the company who supplied the lab with animals of questionable origin. "Some come in with fancy collars. Most are microchipped. The company claims the dogs were surrendered because they've bitten someone, but I've never found a single dog to be vicious." Leaning down, he patted the lab cross, baby-talking, "Who's a big vicious biter? It's not you, is it, cutie-pie?"

The elevator door pinged their arrival on the ground floor. As they exited security, Herman waved at the sleepy-looking guard, calling a cheery goodnight. The guard barely looked up.

Once outside, they walked the dogs together as if it was some sort of late-night date. Like a true gentleman, Herman did the stooping and scooping. When they reached his car on the return trip, he thanked her again for arriving early for her shift so he could head out. Agatha felt a teensy bit guilty about how much trouble Herman would be in when the actual day-shift tech showed up and found the place empty. When he finally climbed in his Mini Cooper and drove away, Agatha herded the dogs to her vehicle, straining to help the lab cross into the backseat while the beagle and schnoodle jumped in after him.

It was nearly two a.m., but she had to drop the dogs off somewhere. She couldn't show up at her apartment with three dogs in tow without attracting unwanted attention from at least one nosy neighbor. She drove to the client's house and rang the doorbell. They were grumpy at being awakened until they recognized their beloved Murphy, the lab cross. The kids shrieked and danced around, vying for a chance to hug and pet their beloved pup.

"Thank you! Thank you! Thank you!" Gracie chanted, hugging Agatha so hard her bones creaked.

Agatha declined to come in and refused a reward. Instead, she insisted Gracie's mom take the other two dogs and try to find their owners. Then she headed off into the night, her driving punctuated by jaw-cracking yawns. Despite her exhaustion, when she arrived back at her rental, she opened her laptop and composed a letter to the *Tribune Times'* chief investigative reporter, detailing the dognapping ring Herman had revealed and ProfitMax's involvement in conducting illegal tests on stolen pets.

She attached the video along with a threatened deadline—*get this article on the front page by Friday or the footage gets posted all over social media and your exclusive is history.*

Her phone pinged just as she was shutting off the lights. She opened the email with half-closed eyes. It read, "Thank you!" with an attached picture of the MacDonald family camped out on their living room floor along with three happy dogs.

Agatha's heart swelled. She'd helped people. Good people. That was what life was all about. And if she had also grabbed the formula for ProfitMax's newest drug on her way out with a plan to sell it to the highest bidder, well, a gal's gotta eat, right?

# Michael Penncavage

A Derringer Award-winning author, a quarter finalist in the 2012 PAGE Awards Screenwriting Contest, and a finalist for the prestigious PAGE Award, **Michael Penncavage's** fiction can be found in more than 100 magazines and anthologies from seven different countries. His horror short story, *The Converts*, was filmed as a short movie of the same name in 2008, while another, *The Landlord* was adapted into a play. His debut novel, *Person Unknown*, a thriller adapted from his screenplay, was released by All Due Respect Press.

Michael has been an Associate Editor for *Space and Time Magazine*, as well as the Editor of the horror/suspense anthology, *Tales From a Darker State*. He is a member of the Short Mystery Fiction Society.

Find him at www.facebook.com/michael.penncavage.

# Try Hard

## Michael Penncavage

Cliff was almost giddy with excitement. He'd been dreaming of having the entire evening to himself. More importantly, he had the entire *house* to himself. On the way home from work he stopped at Liquor King and picked up two sixes of Modelo. Not long after he arrived home, Victor's Pizza dropped off a large pie, two dozen buffalo wings, and an order of garlic knots.

Cliff looked lovingly at the spread that was on the coffee table in front of him.

He was ready.

Yes, he was ready.

From across the room the ninety-inch *4K UHD OLED TV* television stared back at him like the monolith from Kubrick's *2001*. He cued up the platform service that was streaming the movie. He had gone the entire year without watching it. He'd been tempted to in the summer, but it just hadn't felt right. It wasn't December. Christmas movies were meant to be watched during the *Christmas* season. No exceptions. No *Christmas in July* nonsense. Especially for the quintessential Christmas movie.

*Die Hard.*

His wife Barbara had argued endlessly with Cliff that *Die Hard* was by no means a Christmas movie. Cliff decided to get a third party's opinion on the matter, had gone over to his smart speaker, and had asked for the computer's opinion. The woman's voice at the other end confirmed that *Die Hard* was indeed considered a Christmas movie. *Who was Barbara to argue with AI?*

The opening credits were flashing when he felt his phone vibrate in his pocket. Cliff pressed Pause. The screen flashed a phone number from Billings, Montana. He sighed and let it go to voicemail. He was about to press Play when the phone lit up again with the same number. "Telemarketers," he grumbled, but answered the call.

"I don't want what you're selling," he said, not bothering with hello. "I'm on the do-not-call list."

"Is this Clifford Krugler?" a man's voice asked.

"Yeah. I still don't want any."

"We have your wife."

Cliff was taken aback. "What are you talking about, buddy?"

"We have your wife. If you want to see her again you will do exactly what I ask."

Cliff felt his heart skip a beat as panic set in. Then, processing what he had just heard, a moment of clarity fell over him. The voice on the other end of the phone. It sounded familiar. "Is that you, Ted?"

"Excuse me?"

"I can tell that it's you. What are you scheming, Ted?"

"This...this isn't...I'm not Ted."

"Sure you are. I can tell by how congested you sound. You were sneezing all throughout lunch. I even mentioned how I finally have the house to myself tonight. It's the only time until Christmas that I'll be able to watch *Die Hard* in peace and quiet."

"My name is Simon. Not Ted."

"I invited you over, Ted. You're the one who said no. Victors just dropped off a large pepperoni and onions. I got wings and knots. I've got two six-packs in the fridge. But no hard feelings, I'll keep the movie paused if you promise to leave your house *right now.*

"You don't understand. We abducted your wife in the parking lot of the shopping mall."

"All right. *Fine.*" Cliff rubbed his brow. "I'll play along for a minute. You got her at the mall. Which store was she walking into?"

"Excuse me?"

"What store was she walking towards? It's a simple question."

"She was..." His voice became muffled for a moment. "She was walking into a Value Universe—"

Cliff cut him off. "*Value Universe?* Now I know you are full of it, Ted. There is no way that Barbara would be caught dead in a VU. Sure, our bank account would appreciate it. Now, if you had said Nordstrom or Saks, that would have been a little more believable." He shifted in his recliner to get more comfortable. "Listen, I'm going to keep watching my movie. If you show up in the next fifteen minutes I promise to restart it from the beginning."

Cliff disconnected the line before he got a reply.

*Hans Grueber, the leader of the robbers had just announced themselves to the employees who were remaining in the building where he was in charge. Meanwhile, John McClane had killed one the bad guys and had sent him back down the elevator...*

Cliff's phone began to vibrate again. He let out a long groan as he looked at it and then answered the phone. "I thought you were coming over."

"I am dismayed that you don't believe we have your wife."

"*Dismayed?*" Cliff repeated. "What type of kidnapper talks like that?" He cleared his throat. "I'm going to remember this the next time you want to watch the Giants at my house, Ted. I'm going to heckle everyone on the coaching staff the entire game."

The phone pinged softly. Someone had sent him a text.

"I just sent you a photo of your wife."

Cliff put the phone on speaker and opened his message app. There was a photo of Barbara standing in a dark room. She was holding a newspaper in her hands. He stared at it for a moment before he shook his head in annoyance. "You could have used a better photo, Ted."

"Excuse me?"

"How many bars and restaurants have we gone to with our wives? This looks like the place over on Sullivan Avenue."

"This...this wasn't taken at a *bar*. You can clearly see that the newspaper in her hands is today's edition."

Cliff zoomed in on the photo. "Nah. That's fake news. I've never even heard of that paper."

"*The Sentinel* is your county newspaper."

"Is that right? I haven't read one in over ten years." Cliff looked at the picture more closely. Looks like it's been photoshopped, Ted. You should have used something timelier. Like photoshopping Barbara holding a tablet that had BBC on the screen."

There was a long pause at the other end, then, "I'd like to discuss the ransom."

"Ransom? Let me guess. $640 million in bearer bonds."

"What?"

"That's what Hans Gruber is trying to steal from the Nakatomi Plaza. You would know that if you were over here watching the movie with me instead of wasting my time with your hairbrained jokes or schemes or whatever it is that you are trying to do here."

"No. One million. In twenty-dollar bills."

"Only one million? How modest of you."

Cliff disconnected the line.

*Hans Gruber was toying with John McClane over the walkie talkie as he tried to determine who the foil was in his plans...*

Cliff's phone began to vibrate and his frustration set in. "This is getting old, buddy."

"Have you gathered the money?"

"You know, at some point over the next few months I'm going to get even. Come up with a pretty good prank."

A soft ping sounded on Cliff's phone. "Let me guess. Another photo?"

"Video, actually."

"Is it a clip from *Die Hard?*"

"Why don't you take a look?"

Cliff opened the message. Sure enough, a video had been attached. He hit play. It was a clip of Barbara. She was staring directly into the camera. "What do you want me to say?"

"Start by stating your name," an offscreen voice replied.

"My name is Barbara," she said, and turned her head. "What else?"

Cliff paused the video. "Okay. I watched some of it."

"You didn't watch it all?"

"No, Ted. It looks like a classic deepfake to me."

"A...what?"

"I saw a special about deepfakes on 60 *Minutes*. That's when you digitally alter footage to make it appear as if someone said or did something that they really didn't. To make it seem as if they're flying in a spaceship. Maybe it's something more sensational, like shooting someone when they really didn't. None of it is real, Ted."

"Please stop calling me Ted. Are you saying that the video is *fake?*"

"Fake. And a bad fake. Barbara is on Atkins. She's lost some weight recently but that video...well, she didn't lose *that* much."

Cliff heard yelling on the other end of the phone that he couldn't quite make out.

"I think we should discuss payment again—"

Cliff disconnected the line.

*Hans Gruber begins to relay his demands to the police in an effort to keep them busy and confuse them while he continues to execute the robbery...*

Cliff's phone begins to vibrate.

"What a surprise," he said, putting the phone on speaker. "I was beginning to think you forgot about me, Ted."

"I'm...never mind. There is someone who would like to speak with you."

Cliff glanced at the clock. At this rate he was never going to finish the movie. He lowered the volume and turned on the subtitles.

"Hello...Cliff?" A woman's voice.

"Is this supposed to be Barbara?"

"It *is* me, Cliff. Me. Barbara. Your wife."

"Really? I thought you were supposed to be kidnapped. Or is the right term *abducted*? Is it only called kidnapping when it happens to a kid?"

"Can you please just pay the man so he will let me go?"

"You sound very calm, Barbara-not-Barbara."

"I'm trying to keep my composure, Cliff. It's been a long day."

"You're damn right it has. And what I'm trying to do is enjoy my one evening alone watching my favorite Christmas movie before the holidays arrive. Instead, I have Ted prank-calling me."

"What are you watching?"

"How could you *not* know what I'm watching?"

"I don't know, Cliff. Like I said it's been a long day."

"It's *Die Hard*, Barbara. I'm watching *Die Hard*. I only told you about ten times over the course of the week."

"Tell you what. Pay the man and I'll come home and watch it with you."

"*You're* going to watch *Die Hard* with me? Now I *really* know that I'm not speaking with my wife."

There was silence on the other end followed by muffled arguing. More time passed before the man got back on the line. "Barbara is very upset."

"Not half as upset as I am, Ted," Cliff shouted at the phone. "Especially now that your wife is playing this ridiculous game along with you."

Cliff disconnected the line.

*Han's team of criminals were just about to break into the vault containing the bearer bonds. They had tricked the FBI into cutting the power to the building, which would assist them in getting into the vault...*

It was no surprise that his phone began buzzing again.

"Hello?"

"You blocked my phone number."

"Can you blame me, Ted? I'm just annoyed that it took so many calls for me to do it. Rest assured, once I hang up I'll block this one as well."

"Wait a moment. *Please.* Your wife. I brought her back to the shopping mall."

"Is that right? She's back at the stores?

"Yes."

"No more ransom?"

"No. No more ransom. I just wanted to let you know she was delivered safely. But she is quite upset."

"I guess being kidnapped will do that to a person," Cliff replied in as much of a snarky voice that he could muster. "You've got a lot of explaining to do tomorrow, Ted. I'm not sure how long it's going to take me to forgive you."

This time it wasn't Cliff who disconnected the line.

The credits began to roll as movement by the family room window caught his attention. Small white flakes fluttered by the glass. He smiled as he ate the last garlic knot and drank his last beer. It was beginning to look a lot like Christmas.

A minute later he heard the front door open and then slam shut. Feet began stomping across the hardwood floor. A moment later Barbara appeared in the doorway, fists clenched, eyes full of rage. Her makeup was smeared, her hair unkempt.

"Crazy day at the mall, honey?" Cliff asked, placing the empty bottle onto the coffee table. The credits ended as the Michael Kamen score came to a close. Cliff turned off the television. He could hear Barbara breathing hard behind him, as if she had just run a marathon.

"I warned you it was a bad idea to go shopping on a Friday right before the holidays."

Cliff opened the last Modelo and took a long drink.

# C.W. Blackwell

**C.W. Blackwell** is an American author from the Central Coast of California. He is a two-time Derringer Award winner and four-time nominee. C.W. is a member of International Thriller Writers and the Short Mystery Fiction Society. His recently released short story collection, *Whatever Kills the Pain*, is available from Rock and Hard Place Press.

Find him on Instagram at @cw_blackwell_writer.

# Making Up for Lost Time
## C.W. Blackwell

It wasn't the first time someone told me I looked like Tag Sandoval, the famed Silicon Valley tech CEO, but it carried an unbearable irony now that I was living in a downtown shelter with two dozen men whose luck had run completely dry.

"Maybe not twins," Jerry said. He was a new social worker on shift, a guy who had a ready comment for everything. He studied my ears as if they had something to do with the resemblance, but I'd always thought it was my nose and jaw that were most similar. "But you could be his older brother. Cousins for sure."

"Maybe I'll ask Sandoval for a bridge loan," I said. "Since everyone thinks we're long-lost brothers."

"Ask him for me, too. I'm this close to getting a cot here myself."

There'd been a recent analysis of the most expensive rental markets in the country, and Santa Cruz topped out at number one. Basic supply and demand, they said. Everyone wanted to live in a coastal town surrounded by redwood forests, where fog cooled the hot summer days, and the winters never dropped below freezing. But I knew there was more to it than that. Silicon Valley had produced a new class of billionaires so incomprehensibly wealthy they could buy homes no matter the price. You could shake their couches and million-dollar bungalows would drop out. Rich men like Tag Sandoval bought vacation homes they never used. Homes for their children. Homes for their secret mistresses. Homes for their personal dieticians and their numerology consultants.

Meanwhile, the tent cities grew.

I was strolling past one of the latest tent cities to pop up on River Street when my ex-wife called. I had counted at least a dozen tents, all different colors. There was a woman with long gray hair setting up a new one in the back, close to the levee. It had started to drizzle, and her hair looked wet and stringy as she fumbled with the tent poles.

I answered just before the call went to voicemail.

"Where are you—are you okay?" Jennifer asked. She was trying to sound concerned and sympathetic, but I knew what she wanted. I'd been stalling on signing the custody agreement for our five-year-old daughter, Alex. A part of me was holding out for a miracle, a stroke of luck big enough to even the scales. "You didn't return my call this morning."

"I've been busy. You know, looking for work."

"Where'd you sleep last night?"

I lied and told her I'd slept on a friend's sofa. I wasn't too proud to sleep in a shelter if I needed to, but I didn't want her to know about it right then. Just another point in her column, more proof that she'd been right that I wasn't husband material after all—or father material, for that matter.

"I need those papers signed," she said. "I'll give you another day to keep job hunting, but if you don't sign by Monday, my lawyer will take things in a different direction."

I didn't know exactly what that meant, but knowing Jennifer, she wasn't bluffing.

"How's Alex?" I asked. "Can I talk to her?"

"She's napping," she said, a little too quickly. I heard a door shut as if she'd entered a private space where no one could hear her side of the conversation. "She's comfortable here. She has her own room, and we're using my dad's old Toyota to get her to school. She misses you, but it's the best place for her. You have to know I'm right about that."

I got off the phone. It hurt so damn much.

The guitar shop had just opened when I passed by, and the morning drizzle had let up. You could see a few patches of blue in the cloud cover between the downtown buildings. It was Saturday, and Pacific Avenue had begun to swell with tourists. Mostly daytrippers from the South Bay and beyond. They scuttled through the bookstores and antique shops like hermit crabs at low tide. I slicked my hair and went to the guitar shop counter where I found Ronnie Spatz. We'd played in a rock band together centuries ago and hadn't really kept in touch, but he was the closest thing I had to a friend.

"Hey Ronnie," I said, with a manufactured grin. "What's shakin'?"

He shook his hands in the air as if I were a celebrity.

"Damn, brother. With your hair slicked back you look like—"

"I know. Don't say it."

I told him I was looking for work, and a little about my family falling apart. I don't like sharing those kinds of personal details, but working the sympathy angle was the only play I had left.

"Man, I'm sorry," he said, and it sounded genuine. "We can barely afford the crew we have. We're fighting each other for shifts. But hey, I can give you fifty bucks if you want it. Don't worry about paying me back."

"I wouldn't take your money," I said. "But if you loaned me a guitar, I could busk to get through the weekend. A metal slide, too—if you can spare it."

"What happened to all your gear?"

"I was between bands and behind on rent. Most of it went straight to pawn shop heaven. When the baby's hungry, you do what you have to do." I turned my palms up to show nothing could be done about it. "Maybe if you gave me until the end of the day?"

I could tell the idea made Ronnie uncomfortable. It seemed like the kind of thing he could get fired over. Still, he agreed. The guitar he loaned me was a mid-grade six-string Yamaha. Nothing fancy, but it didn't need to be. As long as it stayed in tune I could set myself up on a busy corner and see what fell into the case.

"You know, it's funny," Ronnie said. I didn't want to know what he thought was funny, given how humiliated I felt at the moment, but I didn't want to be rude, either.

"What's funny?"

"My cousin Beemo is working on Tag Sandoval's new vacation house up on West Cliff. Big expensive remodel. It's right next to that house we gigged at all those years ago. Bet you could show up with your hair slicked back and start bossing them around and nobody would know the difference." He gave a demented chuckle. "Ah man, that would be hilarious."

"Yeah," I said, trying to smile. "Hilarious."

I found a busy spot by the bookstore and dove into an old Son House tune I'd learned when I was a teenager. Something about pulling the slide to the twelfth fret always captivated folks, and once they stood longer than a few seconds, most felt obligated to tip. The worst part about busking—other than sitting on cold cement for hours at a time— is that many folks tip change, and what the hell can you buy for change anymore? That was exactly how it went outside the bookstore —a few dimes, a few quarters. A dollar bill here and there. All I needed was a portal to the 1950s and I'd eat like a king.

After an hour, a city cop walked up with his hands on his duty belt, watching me with a cat-like intensity. He had some kind of tiger tattoo on his neck, peeking over his starched blue collar, and his belt creaked when he shifted his weight.

"You got a permit?" he said, when I'd finished the song.

"A permit?"

"You need a permit to perform on Pacific. If you don't have one, you can submit an application with Parks and Rec. But you can't play here without it."

"I never needed one before. How long does it take?"

I felt myself heating up, and the cop noticed it too. He took a step back and rested a thumb on the bright yellow taser holstered into his belt.

"Well, they're closed on the weekends. You'd have to catch up with them on Monday. They say it takes about three days to process."

I scooped all the change out of the guitar case and poured it into my pockets. The weight of it threatened to pull my pants down. I didn't say a word to the cop as I packed up and sulked across the street to the guitar shop. I ditched the Yamaha behind the counter and didn't speak to anyone as I ran jangling out the door.

I'd hiked a few blocks to the municipal wharf and was counting all the change on the counter of a greasy seafood diner when my phone rang again. A local number. I didn't recognize it, but I answered anyway.

"Hey man, it's Ronnie."

"I didn't scratch the guitar, did I?"

"No, nothing like that. Hey, listen, I hope you don't mind, but I talked to my cousin Beemo and he said they could use a scrapper tomorrow at the Sandoval job if you're interested. He says they're almost done with the remodel. I guess there's a big dumpster in the driveway and all you gotta do is clean up after them."

"Just a one-time gig?"

The waitress came around and refilled my coffee. I'd stacked about fourteen dollars in quarters, dimes, and nickels in a big half-moon around the ceramic mug and she paused to study it with mild interest before shuffling off.

"Yeah, that's what he told me," Ronnie said. "But who knows, it could lead somewhere. It's better than nothing, right?"

I glanced out the window where a trio of sailboats drifted slowly over the gray-blue water. Up on the cliffs, you could see the row of West Cliff mansions lit up in all that hard afternoon light. I'd never be a billionaire, but I supposed I wouldn't mind cleaning up a billionaire's scraps for some quick under-the-table food money.

At least I wouldn't need a permit.

"Thanks, man," I said. "Tell him to count me in."

I returned to the shelter that night but couldn't sleep with all the noise. Even with a ten p.m. "light's out" policy, you still have to hear all the moaning and crying in the dark. I wondered what it would be like in a tent by the river, wrapped up in a soft down sleeping bag, a little lantern at my side. But I knew that wasn't a picnic either. With all the Fentanyl on the street, they'd been pulling at least two ODs out of the tent cities per week. I kept telling myself I was lucky to have a shelter bed, with a community bathroom and a shower stall. But the more I kept telling myself, the sadder I felt, and before long, I was just another voice moaning in the dark.

I left the shelter at daybreak and walked the mile or so up West Cliff Drive to Sandoval's vacation home. The morning fog hung heavily in the cypress trees, and you could barely see all the surfers lining up in the water below. A jogger passed me on the sidewalk like an airplane popping out of a cloud and quickly disappeared again. I almost couldn't tell which block I was on, as heavy as the fog was, so when I stumbled past the rusty blue dumpster sitting coldly in Sandoval's driveway, it took me a moment to realize where I was. The house was a three-story Spanish-style adobe with terracotta tiles and a prominent sea-facing balcony fit for a military dictator. Construction trash lay over the fresh sod, bits of stucco and drywall scraps everywhere.

I looked around for Ronnie's cousin Beemo but couldn't find him. They hadn't finished building the fence around the property, so I wandered into the backyard, looking for anyone I could find. It looked like they'd just poured a foundation for a king-sized jacuzzi, with another adobe hut beside it. Maybe it would be a bar or a pool house. I called out, but no one answered. A pair of ornate French doors hung at the back of the house with brass door handles, but the cylinders were all missing from the locks. I pulled the doors open and called again.

The interior looked mostly finished, though still dusty and peppered with construction debris. A few loose tools lay scattered on the stone kitchen counters. It looked like the house had been abandoned in a hurry with little regard to security. I knew I wasn't supposed to, but I shuffled up the wrought-iron staircase to the second floor. A part of me was curious how the house had been built, and I had a good excuse if I got caught. But when I saw the California king bed and the bathroom full of expensive-looking glass bricks and granite counters, luxuriously soft towels in the linen closets, I started to get other ideas. Had Sandoval been living here? Would he return? I found shampoo and soap in the shower, two waterfall showerheads cut from the granite like a Roman fountain. It felt like every square inch of the bathroom had cost a million dollars or more. I scrubbed my face in the sink, studied the bags under my sleep-starved eyes. I wet my hair and slicked it back with a stainless-steel comb.

*Goddamn*, I thought. *I look beat.*

I woke in the king bed two hours later, after a hot shower and a change of clothes. I'd shaved my shaggy beard and gave myself a spritz of some Italian-looking cologne I'd found in the medicine cabinet. I even trimmed my squirrely eyebrows.

The clatter of construction outside the window had woken me, mostly hammering and drilling and the crass banter of workmen. I was coming down the stairs in Sandoval's signature red sweater and white tennis shoes when I found a middle-aged man with a 49ers ball cap and a leather toolbelt standing in the living room, watching me.

"Mr. Sandoval," the man said. "We didn't know you were home." He dipped his head the way you'd regard royalty, and I remember thinking how pathetic and small he'd made himself appear. This man didn't respect Sandoval—*he feared him.* Ronnie Spatz thought it would be funny if I bossed the workers around as a prank, but that's not what I had in mind.

"I'm going to need this place for a few days," I said. "Please clean everything up the best you can and take the week off."

He didn't answer right away, just stood there with his palms upturned. He seemed to be choosing his words carefully.

"I hear you, but we're behind as it is, sir. And these workers—"

"Consider it a paid vacation," I said. "I don't care that you're behind. Quality work takes time. Didn't you hear about my new crypto venture on the news? I think I can afford it. Oh, and everyone gets a one-thousand-dollar bonus if you clean this place spotless in two hours. Write up a work order and I'll sign it."

He clasped his hands together and gave another obsequious bow.

"Yes, sir. You're a very generous man."

By noon, I had the villa to myself.

I thought the luxurious room I'd napped in had been the main bedroom, but what I found on the third floor was even more astounding. Everything up there had been adorned in Old World artisan tiles and wrought iron, as if Sandoval had looted a Spanish cathedral. I wandered slack-jawed beneath those large improbable archways and marble columns. The afternoon light fell softly on the walls in the tile hallway as if different physics were at work on this floor. Up here, it was always golden hour. I found a pair of vintage acoustic guitars hanging on the walls and I took one down and strummed it on the balcony, watching as the fog dissolved in the cypress trees and retreated slowly into the bay.

My phone rang. Jennifer again.

I set the guitar down and answered.

"How's job hunting going?" she asked, with that same hint of an ulterior motive. When Jennifer wanted something, she couldn't help but push it as far as it would go. "Did you try all those new restaurants they're opening downtown?"

"I'm a musician, Jennifer."

"Musicians can't flip burgers? And please don't snap at me."

I apologized, and told her it wasn't going well, but that I'd talked to some old friends and had a few good leads. I could hear Alex chatting in the background, asking questions the way five-year-olds do, like there was somehow an answer to each one, like everyone lived perfectly rational lives.

"I'm staying at one of those big villas on West Cliff Drive," I said. "A friend's house. He's renovating, but the top floors are already finished. You should see this view. It's unbelievable."

"Wow. Sounds amazing. But I really—"

"I'll sign tomorrow, okay? You don't have to keep calling every day."

"Tomorrow?" She sounded surprised, as if I'd had a lawyer in my back pocket the whole time and was waiting for a chance to catch her off guard. "Oh, that would be perfect."

"I was hoping since I have this place, maybe you could drop Alex off tomorrow and I can do cake and ice cream for her, since I missed her birthday? You know, just some father-daughter time. I don't want to lose touch with her completely."

"Of course you won't lose touch. You know I never meant it that way."

Still, she didn't answer my request.

"Just for a few hours," I said, before she could say no. "We'll eat cake, then walk to the wharf so she can laugh at the silly sea lions. You're not afraid I'm going to kidnap her, are you? I hope you don't think that."

"No, of course not. I have a few things I can do on that side of town. And it really would be great to get those papers—"

"So, six o'clock, then?"

"Yes," she said. "I think we can make that work."

Next day, I sold one of Sandoval's guitars at the guitar shop for eight-hundred dollars and treated myself to breakfast. A big plate of Eggs Benedict with bacon and potatoes. I noticed curious looks as I sat eating, and again at the grocery store while I shopped for cake mix and strawberry ice cream. Locals took covert selfies with me in the background, making number threes with their fingers to represent Sandoval's popular Zed-Three crypto trading platform. The constant attention worried me, so I bought one of those big floppy gardening hats from a downtown thrift store. The hat, together with a cheap pair of aviator sunglasses gave me the cover I needed to hike back to the villa unnoticed.

It took me a few minutes to figure out Sandoval's oven. Eventually, I hit a voice command button on the front panel and told it to bake the cake, which it promptly agreed to do. I remember feeling disappointed that I couldn't enter the times and temperatures to bake my daughter's birthday cake. It all felt so impersonal and artificial, though the sweet aroma that soon filled the villa felt right.

With the cake in the oven, and Dave Brubeck piping over the built-in speakers throughout the dark corners of the house, I pored over the custody papers and signed every line. I'd found a wine cellar beneath the kitchen hallway with a half-dozen bottles, and I sat drinking a glass, trying not to berate myself. No matter what happened tomorrow, next week, or next year, I figured I'd still be good for one nice birthday for my Alex.

"You weren't kidding about the view," Jennifer said, as the three of us stood on the top-floor balcony watching little white triangles sailing away in the distance. The sardines had come in, and the air carried a strong, briny tang. The arrival of fish excited the pelicans and sea lions, and we stood pointing them out as they hunted in the cold bay waters. "How long are you staying here?"

"Just till the end of the week," I said. "Maybe longer, if I can swing it."

"You look good," she said. "Well rested." She ran her hand along the wrought iron railing, tracing the twisted bars with her fingertips. "Who's your hotshot friend? He must be crazy rich."

Something about the way she said it felt barbed, like I couldn't possibly have made any wealthy friends on my own. Maybe I felt insulted because her instincts were right. So, I lied to her. I told her the owner of the house was a guitar enthusiast, and that he'd hired me to play a private party a few months back. I gestured at the remaining guitar on the wall, alluding to some sort of brotherhood among musicians, as if that's all it took to trust someone with a zillion-dollar vacation home.

When Jennifer left, Alex and I walked the half mile to the municipal wharf where we peeked in at the colony of sea lions and giggled at the way they bobbed in the water and barked like dogs. Some were leaping onto the wooden crossbeams below the wharf with bright silver fish in their mouths, bullying others for a spot to digest their catch in the low autumn sun.

Later, as we ate the lemon cake with buttercream frosting and strawberry ice cream, she said she liked the coast better than her grandparent's neighborhood. She said it was boring there, and everyone had to whisper so grandpa wouldn't wake from his nap.

"And there's no sea lions in the mountains," she said. "Just lots of squirrels."

"But there's lots of deer, too," I said. "You like deer, don't you?"

"I saw a dead one, that's all."

She stabbed at her cake with a heavy pout. The three of us had talked about the divorce when it became official, but Jennifer had done most of the talking. I wasn't sure what to say now that I'd signed the custody papers. I was just a little older than Alex when my parents split up, and I remembered how painful it was, all the anger and worry. But most of all, I remembered how the heartbreak never really ended, how it became a burden I could never set down. If there was a way to console a child facing that kind of heartbreak, I didn't know it.

"The sea lions won't ever go away," I said. "There are too many fish for them to leave. I bet when you visit next, they'll be twice as fat. They'll look like giant basketballs with flippers. We can visit them whenever you want."

"Will your friend let you live here forever?"

"We can dream, can't we?"

"Maybe you can move to the wharf and live there?"

"They don't have houses on the wharf, honey." I wondered how much Jennifer had told her about my living situation. If she'd told her I was unhoused, I'd be crushed. "But some people live in boats. Wouldn't that be fun?"

"I guess. But what if a tidal wave comes?"

I laughed. "Then I'd ride it all the way to the mountains and bake you another cake."

"Are you crying, daddy?"

"No. I just bit my tongue on this delicious cake is all."

She was making a crayon drawing of sea lions on a paper grocery bag when Tag Sandoval came through the back door. He wasn't wearing his signature red sweater, but his hair was slicked, and his white shoes were so bright they looked like he stood on a pair of phosphorescent light bulbs. He didn't notice us right away, just strolled through the kitchen and into the front room as if joining us for cake. He had a stack of mail in one hand and his phone in the other.

When he saw us, he stumbled and dropped the mail on the floor.

"Who the hell are you?" he asked, pedaling back a step to the kitchen. "Where is the work crew?"

Alex stopped coloring and looked up. "Who is that, daddy?"

I rose from the floor and walked toward him.

"I'm not with the work crew," I said. "I can explain, just not in front of the girl. Can we talk about this outside?"

"Absolutely not." He threw open one of the kitchen drawers and found a ten-inch chef's knife and held it like a microphone as if he were speaking into it. I wondered if a part of him saw the resemblance, if he was smart enough to piece together what I'd been up to. But the way his eyes flared and the kitchen knife shook in his billion-dollar fingers told me it didn't matter. "You just made a huge mistake, pal. I'm calling the police. Get out now and take the brat with you."

I spoke to him calmly and gave the friendliest smile I could muster.

"No need for that. I can explain."

"You can explain it to the police." He was shouting now. Maybe the uncanniness had dawned on him, like he'd wandered into a bizarre dream. "Get the hell out of my damn house," he said, thumbing at his phone.

I told Alex to go hide in the bathroom and lock the door. She ran crying, the tension too great. When I heard the lock engage, I closed in on him with my palms showing, trying to explain the situation the best I could. I told him the police weren't needed, that if he was a reasonable man, he'd just hear me out.

Instead, he jabbed the knife at me—not as a warning, but like he was really trying to stab me. I pulled my hands back in a hurry.

He was dialing now, making little grunting sounds as he jammed his thumb against the screen. He looked so terrified and nothing I said was working. But I couldn't let him call the police. Not with Jennifer due back any minute. Not with Alex cowering in the locked bathroom.

The next time he glanced at his phone, I slapped it out of his hands. It fell screen down and shattered on the black tile floor. I don't think he'd managed to complete the call, as manic as he was. And I don't know why he didn't run out the back door, but he'd managed to back himself against the refrigerator, jabbing the knife at me and mewling like a lost child. I tried to explain again, even though he wasn't listening. I tried to tell him how it happened so gradually and naturally, how I'd been down on my luck and things got carried away. But the more I explained, the crazier I sounded—even to myself.

Then we were fighting over the knife.

I took him by the wrist and tried to shake it out of his hands.

He bit me in the shoulder, and I stifled a scream. I couldn't let Alex know I was hurt. So, when he started screaming for help, I took him by the throat to quiet him down. We stood that way, locked in a grim tango, my left hand holding back the knife and my right hand squeezing his windpipe. Sure, we looked alike, but I had twenty pounds of muscle and three inches of height over Tag Sandoval. I didn't want to kill him—I remember thinking that whatever happened, I absolutely could not kill him. But every time I let up, he tried to scream, and when I gave an inch on his wrist, the knife came that much closer.

We stood that way for two minutes before he finally sank to the floor, though it felt like thirty years. Later on, thirty years would prove to be a significant number.

It took a while to convince Alex that it had all been a misunderstanding. I told her the man she'd seen had been confused, and that he'd wandered into the wrong house by mistake. He was fine of course, and he'd even apologized and taken a slice of birthday cake with him. I told her everyone made mistakes, and it was important to forgive people when they do. She came out slowly, peeking into the kitchen. She still had a red crayon clutched in her tiny hand.

"You look scared, daddy."

"No, not scared. I'm just going to miss you when you go."

"Is mommy almost back?"

I could hear the sea lions barking down on the wharf. Maybe the winds had shifted, but they sounded louder than before, more urgent. You could see the night fog rolling in again, the cypress softening in the gloom.

"Yes, sweetheart. She'll be back any minute now."

"You promise?"

"Yeah, angel. Have another piece of cake."

The workmen found Tag Sandoval's body in the wine cellar a few days later. By then I was long gone. I'd taken his vintage Martin six-string and busked my way up the coast to San Francisco. Then Portland and Seattle. I slept in tents, shelters, wherever. I followed the murder investigation in the newspapers with mild interest, as if it had little to do with me. I didn't care that I'd killed Sandoval. As rich as he was, he'd already lived ten lifetimes by the time I choked him out and hurled his limp body down those cellar stairs. But I felt devastated knowing that I'd never see my Alex again. At least not until she was a mid-career professional, her first gray hairs coming in, maybe even with children of her own. I pictured her in a few years, studying the case, learning what happened that day. No doubt there would be books written about it, true crime documentaries. I wondered if she'd be able to eat a lemon birthday cake with strawberry ice cream again.

I'd crossed into British Columbia when they finally caught up to me.

By then, my photo was plastered all over the television.

A city cop had stopped to hear me play as I sat on a bench by the waterfront. I could hear the sea lions barking in the harbor, the sad bellow of a foghorn calling out from the fogbank. Together with my strumming, it made for a strangely haunted kind of music.

"You know who you look like?" he said. "I mean, you could be twins."

When he put it together, his grin faded fast. I tried to resist, but after months on the road, I didn't have any fight left. The guitar went clattering over the concrete, and the city cop pinned me to the cold, dirty ground.

"Did you really think nobody would recognize you up here?" he asked.

He was right, that's precisely what I thought. I figured the more distance I put between me and that big mansion on West Cliff Drive, the better my chances would be. But with his knee on my back, and the sound of sirens gathering in the distance, I wasn't about to give him the satisfaction.

"I just thought I had one of those faces."

# Judy Penz Sheluk

The Past Chair of Crime Writers of Canada (CWC) and a former journalist and magazine editor, **Judy Penz Sheluk** (author/editor) is the multiple award-winning author of seven bestselling mystery novels, two books on publishing, and several short stories. She is also the editor/publisher of five Superior Shores Anthologies, including the 2025 Derringer-nominated *Larceny & Last Chances*. In addition to CWC, Judy is a member of International Thriller Writers and the Short Mystery Fiction Society.

Find her at www.judypenzsheluk.com.

# A Foolproof Plan
## Judy Penz Sheluk

I watch Mark's black SUV turn out of our long, narrow driveway and feel the tightness in my chest loosen, knowing my husband will be gone for the next two days. Another unavoidable q trip, an emergency in a town just far enough away that he'll have to spend the night.

As if.

Not that I care. I stopped caring about Mark's infidelity a dozen business trips ago, mostly because I've stopped caring about Mark. I used to be obsessed with him, with his streaked blond hair and ripped abs, warm brown eyes tinged with just a hint of hazel, the perfect blend of Chad Michael Murray and Matt Czuchry. Now, my only obsession is scouring the internet looking for someplace where I can reinvent myself. Bye-bye, Amanda Porter. Hello, Ingeborg Anton.

Ingeborg, Inge for short, was my German next-door neighbor when I was a kid. She was a nice woman who made great oatmeal raisin cookies and told terrible knock-knock jokes. Her husband, a quiet guy who wore blue coveralls and did something in construction, went by Tony, which, Ingeborg told me, was short for Anton. I think Ingeborg Anton has a nice ring to it, don't you?

There's just one teeny, tiny problem. Mark will never agree to a divorce. He'll kill me with his bare hands before giving up half of *his* hard-earned assets. I know his temper, and what he's capable of when provoked.

It's a dilemma, no question about it. What I need is a foolproof plan.

Midnight. There's a knock at the front door. I apply some lipstick, fluff up my hair, and trot downstairs. Mark's twin brother, Carter, often drops by when Mark is on one of his many bogus business trips.

Okay, fine, I've been waiting for him. We've been having an affair for just about as long as Mark's been cheating on me. Maybe longer. All right, definitely longer. Did I mention they were identical twins? Which means Carter also has that whole Murray/Czuchry vibe going for him.

Hey, I never said I was perfect.

It's Lisa, not Carter, at the front door. Lisa's been my best friend since kindergarten, my prom "date" when neither of us had one. My maid of honor on the day I foolishly said, "I do."

Mark despises her, because Lisa is the one person who knows me better than he does. And unlike me, Lisa has seen through him from the beginning. She dated him for a while, though who dumped whom was up for debate. Either way, Lisa remains bitter.

"You're finally ready to leave him?" She leans against the bedroom door, arms folded, surveying the suitcase lying on the bed, the clothes strewn haphazardly around the bedroom.

I point to a pile of running gear. "I've signed up for the Toronto Marathon. It's on Sunday." That part is true.

I should have stopped there. Didn't.

"I'm going to stay with Jody for a few days."

Lisa sighs, a wounded look on her face. "You and I both know that you aren't running a marathon and you aren't going to Jody's. You're leaving. Good. I could never understand why you stayed. Or why you married Mark in the first place."

I've often wondered that myself, but then I'd remember the way Mark swooped into my life, gentle and loving—attentive to my every need. A real catch, my friends told me. All except for Lisa. "He's got a jealous streak a mile wide and just as long," she'd warned. "Before long, it will feel like you're sleeping with a boa constrictor. Trust me, I've been there, done that."

I should have listened to her, but hindsight is twenty-twenty and I was flattered in the beginning. I loved that he was protective, but I should have paid closer attention to the rude comments he made about any man who dared look at me, let alone talk to me. Barista at Starbucks, cashier at the supermarket, the Amazon delivery guy, no man was above suspicion, and it's gotten worse over time. If he ever learns that I've been seeing Carter... but that won't happen. I haven't even told Lisa about us, though I suspect she knows. Or at least guessed.

Not that I don't trust her. But Lisa and Carter also have a history, and despite her repeated assurances that he dumped her and good riddance, I'm not convinced she's over him. Lisa isn't big on forgiveness.

"I'm just going away for a few days," I repeat. "To run the Toronto Marathon. To visit Jody."

Lisa shakes her head. "You know Mark won't rest until he finds you. And when he does, he'll drag you back here and never let you out of his sight again."

I flop down onto the king-size bed and pound my fists into the mattress, forcing back tears, knowing Lisa is right. I get up and start unpacking.

"Not so fast," Lisa says, handing me a small vial. "There are four pills in here. Two of them will knock Mark out for at least eight hours, more if you're lucky, long enough to give you a decent head start." She leans over to hug me goodbye and whispers, "I'll miss you," into my ear.

*Four pills, not two,* I think, after she leaves. I sink back onto the bed and permit myself the smallest of smiles. Lisa knows me well, knows I will want to do a trial run.

It isn't a foolproof plan—yet—but it will be.

The salon is inside a strip mall that has seen better days, the sort of place where the flagship store is a Chinese takeout, stylists are called hairdressers, and cash is still king. In less time than it took me to drive there, I am transformed from long-haired blonde to buzz-cut brunette, and I think I look a bit like Demi Moore in *G.I. Jane*. I snap a selfie and text it to Lisa. Caption it "Going, going, almost gone." She'll get a kick out of that.

On the way home, I buy a turban to cover my head, a flamboyant pattern that I can explain away as a fashion statement if Mark asks (doubtful), and a pair of colored contact lenses. I'll need those when I land in a new town with a new name.

My next stop is an ATM, where I withdraw the maximum daily limit. It won't last more than a couple of weeks—a month at best—but I've been siphoning and saving money from my weekly grocery allowance for the better part of a year. Besides, I'm not above working in the gig economy until I'm safe and settled.

Finally, a trip to the grocery store. Tomorrow night, when Mark returns, I'll make his favorite meal—pot roast with honey-glazed carrots and garlic mashed potatoes. It's the least I can do. After all, it will be the second last supper I'll ever make for him.

As usual, Mark eats his dinner in front of the TV without so much as a grunt of thanks, not that I expect one. I clear the table and put the plates, pots, and glasses in the dishwasher and stifle a laugh. Does Mark know how to empty a dishwasher? Well, he'll have to learn to make his own meals and wash his own dirty laundry. It's high time, too. He's forty-two, not fourteen.

And then I hear him snore. The pills I've crushed into the garlic mashed potatoes are doing the trick. I glance at my watch. My moment has arrived and there's no need for a dress rehearsal. If I don't do this now, I know I never will.

It isn't until I've finished loading the car that I allow myself the faintest sigh of relief.

But what if Lisa's calculations are off? Mark has the constitution of an ox. I tiptoe into the living room to make sure he's still asleep.

Something is wrong. His breathing is shallow, his face a mottled blue. I've watched enough episodes of *Grey's Anatomy* to recognize the color of approaching death.

I should call 911.

But do I really want to save him? What would I tell the paramedics?

Should I flush the other two pills and leave? How long will it take for someone to find him? Monday when he doesn't show up for work? Should I go to Jody's and run the marathon? Would that be a good alibi? Do I even need an alibi? Will the paramedics call the police?

I touch my buzz-cut brown hair. Will the drastic change seem suspicious? *Think*, Amanda, *think*.

I can say I'm getting even with Mark for cheating on me, how much he loves my long blonde hair. A childish gesture, nothing more.

Except if the police suspect anything, they'll find out about yesterday's withdrawal. Learn that I haven't used an ATM in the past five years.

What if they talk to Lisa? What if she shows them the text with the selfie and the message "going, going, almost gone."

That's when I realize what Lisa has done. Why she's given me four pills instead of two, and it has nothing to do with a trial run. She's often joked that the best way to "get rid of Mark" is to "get rid of Mark."

Except she hadn't been joking, and part of me has always known it. I just never expected to be part of the plan.

I take the remaining two pills out of my pocket. I can leave them on the bathroom counter and hope the police will think they are Mark's and he'd OD'd while I was gone. But there is still the problem with Lisa.

I can swallow the two pills and join Mark in eternal slumber. Leave a suicide note implicating Lisa. It's comforting to think she'll have to shoulder the blame, but I'll still be dead. Seems like a hollow victory.

And I'm not ready to die. Not yet, anyway. This is my chance to reinvent myself. I can gain or lose weight, be an athlete or a couch potato, wear any clothes I like, keep my hair short or grow it back out. Dye it any color I want.

Because I will be free.

I put the pills back into my pocket, a way out if I ever need one. Or perhaps, once enough time and distance has passed, I'll reach out to Lisa, invite her for dinner. She's always loved my pot roast and garlic mashed potatoes.

I walk out of the house, lock the door behind me, and make my way to the car, Mark already in my rearview mirror. Destination: anywhere but Toronto.

Maybe Ingeborg Anton will make it. Maybe she won't.

It isn't foolproof.

But it *is* a plan.

# The Lineup

Pam Barnsley: www.pambarnsley.com
Linda Bennett: https://finelineeditservices.com
Clark Boyd: www.linkedin.com/in/clarkboyd
C.W. Blackwell: www.instagram.com/cw_blackwell_writer/
Amanda Capper: www.amandacapper.com
Susan Daly: www.susandaly.com/
James Patrick Focarile: www.JamesPatrickFocarile.com
Rand Gaynor: www.amazon.ca/stores/author/B07Z7984L5
Gina X. Grant: www.ginaxgrant.com
Julie Hastrup: https://hastrup.com/
Beth Irish: https://amazon.com/author/beth_irish
Charlie Kondek: www.CharlieKondekWrites.com
Edward Lodi: www.amazon.com/stores/author/B0BH4VZ6MB/
Bethany Maines: www.BethanyMaines.com
Jim McDonald: www.jimmcdonald.ca
donalee Moulton: www.donaleemoulton.com
Michael Penncavage: www.facebook.com/michael.penncavage
Judy Penz Sheluk: www.judypenzsheluk.com
KM Rockwood: www.kmrockwood.com
Peggy Rothschild: https://peggyrothschildauthor.com
Debra Bliss Saenger: www.dblisssaenger.com
Joseph S. Walker: www.jswalkerauthor.com/

# Repeat Offenders

Many thanks to the following authors for trusting me with their stories on more than one occasion:

Clark Boyd: *Moonlight & Misadventure*

C.W. Blackwell: *Moonlight & Misadventure*

Susan Daly: *The Best Laid Plans, Heartbreaks & Half-truths, Moonlight & Misadventure, Larceny & Last Chances*

Gina X. Grant: *Larceny & Last Chances*

Julie Hastrup: *Larceny & Last Chances*

Charlie Kondek: *Larceny & Last Chances*

Edward Lodi: *The Best Laid Plans, Heartbreaks & Half-truths, Larceny & Last Chances*

Bethany Maines: *Moonlight & Misadventure, Larceny & Last Chances*

KM Rockwood: *The Best Laid Plans, Heartbreaks & Half-truths, Moonlight & Misadventure, Larceny & Last Chances*

Peggy Rothschild: *The Best Laid Plans, Heartbreaks & Half-truths*

Joseph S. Walker: *Heartbreaks & Half-truths, Moonlight & Misadventure*

# Publisher's Note

The Superior Shores Anthologies are largely a labor of love, a way of giving back to the short story community and the format that served as validation (and encouragement) for my early writing efforts.

They are also a way of shining a light on the work of many talented authors. If you've enjoyed this collection, or any of the other titles in the Superior Shores Anthology collection, please consider leaving a review on the social media or retail platform of your choice.

Thank you.

Judy Penz Sheluk, Author/Editor/Publisher

# More Superior Shores Anthologies

**BEST LAID PLANS: 21 STORIES OF MYSTERY & SUSPENSE**

books2read.com/SSA-Plans

Whether it's a subway station in Norway, ski resort in Vermont, McMansion in the suburbs, or trendy art gallery in Toronto, the 21 authors represented in this superb collection of mystery and suspense interpret the overarching theme of the best-laid plans in their own inimitable style. And like many best-laid plans, they come with no guarantees.

**HEARTBREAKS & HALF-TRUTHS: 22 STORIES OF MYSTERY & SUSPENSE**

books2read.com/SSA-Heartbreaks

Whether it's 1950s Hollywood, a scientific experiment, or a yard sale in suburbia, the 22 authors represented in this collection of mystery and suspense interpret the overarching theme of "heartbreaks and half-truths" in their own inimitable style, where only one thing is certain: Behind every broken heart lies a half-truth. And behind every half-truth lies a secret.

**MOONLIGHT & MISADVENTURE: 21 STORIES OF MYSTERY & SUSPENSE**

books2read.com/SSA-Moonlight

Whether it's vintage Hollywood, the Florida everglades, the Atlantic City boardwalk, or a farmhouse in Western Canada, only one thing is assured: waxing, waning, gibbous, or full, the moon is always there, illuminating things better left in the dark.

**LARCENY & LAST CHANCES: 22 STORIES OF MYSTERY & SUSPENSE**

books2read.com/larceny

Sometimes it's about doing the right thing. Sometimes it's about getting even. Sometimes it's about taking what you think you deserve. And sometimes, it's your last, best, chance. Nominated for the 2025 Derringer Award for Best Anthology.